# Anne García-Romero

## Collected Plays

*NoPassport Press*

**NoPassport Press**
**Dreaming the Americas Series**

<u>Series Editors:</u> Caridad Svich, Jorge Huerta, Otis Ramsey-Zoe
<u>Advisory Board</u>: Daniel Banks, Maria M. Delgado, Amparo Garcia-Crow, Randy Gener, Elana Greenfield, Oliver Mayer, Saviana Stanescu, Sarah Cameron Sunde, Tamara Underiner.

Other texts in this series:
<u>Lorca: Major Plays Volume I:</u> (Blood Wedding, Yerma, The House of Bernarda Alba)
<u>Lorca: Major Plays Volume II:</u> (The Shoemaker's Prodigious Wife, The Public, Doña Rosita)

*NoPassport Press is a division of NoPassport an unincorporated international theatre alliance founded in 2001 by Caridad Svich devoted to diversity, difference and freedom of expression in theatre arts. For more information about NoPassport and/or this print series contact* <u>*NoPassportPress@aol.com*</u>

ISBN: 978-0-6151-8888-1
$19.95 paperback.

Dedicated to la familia García-Romero and the Clarke family
who inspire me to explore the rich terrain
of my cultural heritage.

# Contents

## Acknowledgments

The author would like to thank the following people and organizations for their support and encouragement: Caridad Svich, Susan Gurman, Leah C. Gardiner, José Cruz Gonzalez, Andy Garcia, Juliette Carrillo, Naomi Iizuka, Octavio Solis, David Emmes, Martin Benson and South Coast Repertory, Shelby Jiggetts-Tivony, Shirley Fishman, George C. Wolfe and the cast and company of the Public Theater/NYSF, Erica Christ and the cast and company of Cheap Theatre, Luis Alfaro, Diane Rodriguez and the Mark Taper Forum's Latino Theatre Initiative, Elaine Romero and Arizona Theatre Company, Arielle Tepper and the cast and company of SPF, Barclay Goldsmith and the cast and company of Borderlands Theater, Eva Zorilla Tessler, Camillia Sanes, Jonathan Del Arco, Mercedes Herrero, Todd London, Emily Morse, John Steber, New Dramatists, The MacDowell Colony, The Playwrights' Center in Minneapolis, The Jerome Foundation, Yael Prizant, Gina Gold, Vince Garcia, Elizabeth and Dan Anderson, Ellen Clarke, Barbara, Alicia, Toño and Mercedes García-Romero, Paul Fariello and to the spirit of José Antonio García-Romero, whose singular artistic passion prepared the way.

## Foreword

### Words with Wings

I first met García-Romero in 1998 when she contacted me at South Coast Repertory where I was the director of the Hispanic Playwrights Project. She had recently graduated from Yale School of Drama and was eager to find her community in Southern California. I folded her right into the "HPP Familia" and she jumped in with great enthusiasm. She took on the role of dramaturg for a couple of projects, a role we had traditionally given to playwrights, and was fantastic at it. Playwrights loved her insights and the abundance of research she brought to the table. When SCR signed off on a site-specific project I was pursuing, I immediately thought of her as a playwright. We created *California Scenarios*, a series of short plays to be performed in an outdoor sculpture garden designed by Isamu Noguchi entitled, inspirationally, "California Scenario." The garden had different areas that were influenced by the landscapes of California. Each playwright took a different area, and with a very talented ensemble of Latino actors, we developed a unique theatre-going experience about Latinos in California, past and present. García-Romero had chosen to work in the desert area, a cactus filled, beautifully rounded mound perfectly situated in the white-walled surrounds. She wrote "Desert Longing/Las Aventureras," a historically-driven comedy about Tiburcio Vásquez and his many love-and-adventure craving women. The entire evening was a success, but García-Romero's was a favorite for many.

García-Romero's love for language is apparent in all her work. Like many of today's Latino writers, she is highly influenced by the Greats--- Borges, García Lorca, García Márquez, Neruda---but she makes the work entirely her own. She has created her own language, a language influenced by her relationship to her Spanish heritage as well as her American upbringing. It is the language of a contemporary American woman, a Latina, inspired by her struggles in defining herself as a woman and as an artist. It is clearly a voice that loves words, using them to catapult characters into deep and complex emotional journeys.

Although I had read *Earthquake Chica,* my first real theatrical experience with it was during the Summer Play Festival in New York. At first glance, the play is a simple two-hander about a pair of misfit lovers.

But what struck me about the play in performance were the risks García-Romero took with language. It is a remarkably stylized play even though it is set in a contemporary realistic setting with two contemporary realistic characters. Language becomes a character in itself. It juts, pokes and jumps out, earthquake-like:

> SAM (as Esmeralda begins to kiss his neck...arms):
> And it's like...wow...madre mia...it's like I've been on this iceberg-glacier thing floating in the Arctic Ocean...and now there's this...ay, ay, ay...this beam of light...so bright above me ...descending...and like my down parka which I bought especially to keep the tundra-like freeze away is...is getting very...hot and heavy ...um...yeah... okay...uh...and I desperately want to remove it but my feet are kinda stuck in ice and my hands are ...wow...still...cold.

García-Romero uses the unusual rhythms in speech and sharp transitions to mimic a kind of an emotional earthquake, the kind experienced when lovers meet and jump head first into the unknown territory of a new relationship. Uncomfortable and unsure, the lovers leap between states of repression and utmost freedom, from risk-taking to search for safety. García-Romero captures these movements in language by twisting and turning our expectations of where we think a sentence is going to go and then doubling back unexpectedly. Sentences represent a birthing of sorts---characters go from their own inner sanctuary to an exterior world by using words to liberate themselves.

Language also plays a large role in her comedy *Santa Concepción*, one of her earliest plays. García-Romero explores images of chastity and religious devotion juxtaposing them with images of sexuality and fertility and does so using potent, often very sensual language:

> CONNIE (holding up a papaya seed): Black currant seeds awaiting to be born into smooth, yellow- orange, fruity flesh. (holding up the papaya). A fantastical physical model of the female reproductive system...to give myself perspective and hope.

Two sisters, one fertile and sexually liberated and the other a religiously dedicated virgin, switch life views throughout the course of the play only to find that their original paths are closest to their heart's desire.

García-Romero is able to walk a very fine line here. The characters use larger than life poetic speech, not unlike a Lorca play, to comment upon themselves and their situation. But the lyrical style she chooses is far from distancing. They are thinking, feeling, desiring human beings:

> CONNIE: Five weeks pass…and I've stopped talking to Dios. I sit here alone day after day. And I lie in bed motionless night after night. And I feel dry like the grass in the field burned brown by the sun's scorching heat.

Images of emotional and sexual containment abound with images of freedom and release throughout the work. Characters struggle with restraining moral values and physical boundaries to then find liberation.

In her play *Mary Peabody in Cuba*, her protagonist, Amy, excavates her life to find her free will, independent of parental figures. Again, we see the theme of longing for liberty and an ultimate release. She goes to Cuba to follow the path of an ancestor and along the way comes to a greater understanding not only of her own personal restrictions but those of her distant family. Even the political oppression of Cuba becomes a symbol of personal repression:

> AMY: I desperately want a collection of his poems. Where could I find one?
>
> MIGUEL: My library. Mi biblioteca ilegal.
>
> *LIGHTS SHIFT. LIGHTS RISE ON AMY AND MIGUEL IN HIS LIBRARY HOUSED IN A WALK-IN CLOSET. BOOKSHELVES OVERFLOW. STACKS OF BOOKS ON THE FLOOR. AN INNER SANCTUM OF SORTS.*
>
> AMY: An illegal library?
>
> MIGUEL: The closet itself? No. What's inside this closet? Yes.

The subjugation of literature in Cuba is a reflection of her own inner workings. Where does her passion lie? What is her path? Who is she if she is not the person everyone thinks she should be? Her insights into the country and her personal history provide the key for which she has been searching. In revealing her ancestor's ardor for the poetry of Cuba, she finds her own.

Although in *Mary Peabody in Cuba*, García-Romero ventures away from heightened language to a more naturalistic speech, she does not ignore her great love for poetry. She weaves the contemporary world with 1800's formal period speech effortlessly. Amy and her potential flame, Miguel, come together in the sharing of a poet's great work, while in the parallel story, Juan and Mary Peabody fervently discuss poetry of their day. In a discovery that parallel's Amy's personal revelations, Mary realizes her own zeal for translating poetry from Spanish to English:

*MARY PICKS UP THE THESAURUS*

MARY: Pair...twain...couple...yoke...twain...twain...yes

Always searching its twain
As doing would be fain
For another beauteous soul the gain

Yes...yes...yes

The heart meanders all the while
Twixt the majestic palm
O'er the magnificent isle.
Always searching its twain
As doing would be fain
For another beauteous soul the gain

O...sí...sí...Sí!

In discovering her ability to disentangle images and words, she finds great exaltation. Emotional currents of the character are represented through their relationship to words. Words become healers, opening pathways to joy and expression. Mary speaks to her sister about their journey to Cuba:

MARY: We will return with the knowledge of the luxuriance and ills of this island...and we will share this knowledge with our community in need of such awareness. I dare say this island has provided healing for more than just one sister.

SOPHIA: But what has ailed you?

MARY: At times an impenetrable reserve which lacks an exposure to the depths of passionate expression. This exposure gained in large part by the literary cultivation on this island will ultimately strengthen our private as well as public education.

García-Romero's insight into emotional life and her beautifully crafted expression of those insights is a delight to experience. Directing her work, particularly my experience with "Desert Longing/Las Aventureras" was one of being inside a joyful spirited world, with characters filled with deep desires and quirky instincts. Comic gags abounded, much fun for actors and director alike. But ultimately, the depths of the plays come to the surface with great ease. These plays are not by any means superficial, they are meant to touch her audiences. And they do.

Her gifts of understanding the depths of a character and expressing it in a purely theatrical form are rare and distinct. I look forward to reading her future work.

Juliette Carrillo

*Freelance director;*
*ensemble member, Cornerstone Theater Company*

September 2007

## SANTA CONCEPCIÓN
For José Antonio

SANTA CONCEPCIÓN was first produced on April 9, 1998 as part of the First Stages series at the Joseph Papp Public Theater/New York Shakespeare Festival, (George C. Wolfe, producer.) with the following cast:

Connie................................................................Zabryna Guevara
Aurora................................................................Maricela Ochoa
Dolores................................................................Divina Cook
Reynaldo................................................................Al Espinosa
Griselda................................................................Maria Cellario
Father Pena................................................................Mateo Gomez

The Production was directed by Susana Tubert. Set and Costume Design by Clint E. B. Ramos, Lighting Design by David Higham, Sound Design by Don Dinicola .

SANTA CONCEPCIÓN received its world premiere on March 16, 2000 at Cheap Theatre, Minneapolis, MN, (Erica Christ, Artistic Director) with the following cast:

Connie................................................................Teresa Lopez
Aurora................................................................Julie Estrada
Dolores................................................................Liliana Espondaburu
Reynaldo................................................................Daniel Rangel
Griselda................................................................Delta Rae Giordano
Father Pena................................................................Steven Young

The Production was co-directed by Erica Christ and the author. Set and Lighting Design by Erik Paulson; Costume Design by Alicia Vegell, Sound Design by Aaron Biren.

## CHARACTERS

CONNIE, early 20's
AURORA, mid-20's, Connie's sister
DOLORES, early 50's, mother of Connie and Aurora
REYNALDO, early 30's, a suitor
GRISELDA, early 50's, mother of Reynaldo
FATHER PENA, 30's, local Catholic priest

## SETTING

Present. The countryside of a Spanglish-speaking land.

# SANTA CONCEPCIÓN

## ACT ONE

## SCENE ONE

*LIGHTS RISE ON CONNIE KNEELING DOWNSTAGE OF A SMALL, MAKESHIFT ALTAR. WHITE, LIGHTED CANDLES, OF ALL SHAPES AND SIZES, SURROUND HER. SHE HOLDS A SMALL STATUE OF THE VIRGIN MARY IN ONE HAND.*

CONNIE: (praying) Oh, I know my life will transform, mi Dios. (beat) Formed without fertile flesh. To be redeemed by your hand. (beat) I believe in your milagros. And I'm not afraid. Just like La Santa Madre María, I will be siempre virgen...as a sign of my faithfulness to you. (beat) Aurora...says I am loca...crazy...nuts...because I haven't done...IT...yet. But I tell her I am waiting for you to create a little one inside of me. (beat) I desire it to be right this momento that your miracle begins...but I'll try to be patient...and wait for your timing. (beat) But por favor, perform your milagro any day now? (beat) Muchíssimas gracias. Amen.

*LIGHTS SHIFT.*

*LIGHTS RISE ON AURORA LYING IN A GARDEN OF CRIMSON TULIPS. A MAN'S LEGS PROTRUDE FROM BEHIND A PATCH OF TULIPS.*

AURORA: Your ebony hair slides through my fingers. Your perfectly rounded earlobes slither off my tongue. Your pectoral muscles surrounded by tufts of ebony wool press against me...flattening my tender breasts. My shiny calves wrap themselves around your tender hips. O sí! I don't need to know your name. Two forces of nature. Your pair of lips...so supple and soft attach themselves...to the nape of my neck...to my two salivating lips... O sí!...a connection...a union...lying on the moist soil...among the blossoming, crimson tulips. O sí! Sí! SÍ! GRACIAS A DIOS!

*LIGHTS SHIFT.*

*LIGHTS RISE ON DOLORES SITTING UP IN BED, LEANING AGAINST THE WROUGHT IRON HEADBOARD.*

DOLORES: (happy, calling, sing-song) Concepción! Aurora! Vengan aqui! Now come talk to your Mami who prays for you, hijas mias. Come be with your Mamita who loves you, queridas. (SILENCE) Hijas? (praying, pleading) Ay Dios, please protect mis hijas. I worry about them. How are they going to find husbands if they continue to behave like this? Ay...la Concepción with no sexo y la Aurora with all the time sexo. How did my daughters turn out to be like this? I want to see them with esposos...married and joyful so I can die in peace. Ayudame. Help me please! (beat) (calling, sing-song) Concepción! Aurora! Your Mami cannot come walk to you...el artritis...colitis...flebitis...ya lo saben. Hijas. Vengan aqui. (SILENCE) (angry) VAYANSE A LA MIERDA. GO TO HELL.

**SCENE TWO**

*LIGHTS RISE ON CONNIE SITTING IN THE FIELD UNDER A PAPAYA TREE HOLDING AN OPEN PAPAYA IN ONE HAND AND A PILE OF MOIST PAPAYA SEEDS IN THE OTHER. REYNALDO OBSERVES CONNIE UNBEKNOWNST TO HER.*

CONNIE: (counting seeds) Five hundred and forty one.

*CONNIE HOLDS UP A SEED.*

CONNIE: Blessed is the fruit of thy womb.

*CONNIE KISSES THE SEED AND TOSSES IT OVER HER SHOULDER.*

CONNIE: (counting) Five hundred and forty two. Forty three. Forty four...five.

*REYNALDO APPROACHES HER.*

CONNIE: Five hundred and...forty six.

REYNALDO: Ripe fruta.

*CONNIE LOOKS UP, STARTLED.*

CONNIE: Rotten.

REYNALDO: And you want to eat it?

CONNIE: (holding up a seed) Black currant seeds awaiting to be born into smooth, yellow-orange, fruity flesh. (holding up the papaya) A fantastical physical model of the female reproductive system...to give myself perspective and hope.

REYNALDO: You will have many children with long, flowing dark hair and piercing chestnut eyes.

CONNIE: I will have one holy and precious child.

REYNALDO: One...only? (beat) And does your...boyfriend agree?

CONNIE: Don't make rude assumptions. Besides, I wouldn't tell a stranger what my boyfriend thinks about my conceiving...even if I had a boyfriend.

REYNALDO: Seeing you, I sense a deep connection...that we already know each other.

CONNIE: Rude and persistent.

REYNALDO: Concepción.

CONNIE: (stunned) Did Dios tell you my name?

REYNALDO: Your Mamá did. She offered me a place to stay tonight on my way to the city. I'm the son of her childhood friend, Griselda.

CONNIE: Call me Connie.

REYNALDO: Call me Rey, short for Reynaldo.

CONNIE: I like Reynaldo better.

REYNALDO: I like Concepción better.

CONNIE: Reynaldo.

REYNALDO: Concepción.

CONNIE: I don't like the city. Too much commotion...noise. I lose my serenity there. I prefer the country. Where I can be close to the sapphire sky and the papaya trees and the cleansing river and to mi Dios.

REYNALDO: Religiosa.

CONNIE: Don't you believe in Dios?

REYNALDO: (trying to impress) Well...uh...yes...claro...of course.

CONNIE: Out here...surrounded by all this majesty...how couldn't you?

REYNALDO: You will have to show me around then...so I can fully appreciate this majesty and have a...religious experience.

CONNIE: You won't experience Dios like this in the city.

REYNALDO: That's why you must show me his wonders here in the country side. My meeting at the steel mill will wait.

CONNIE: Mi Dios is so poderoso.

REYNALDO: You are una santa. La Santa Concepción.

*CONNIE SMILES.*

**SCENE THREE**

*LIGHTS RISE ON DOLORES' BEDROOM. DOLORES SITS UP IN BED. AURORA LIES ACROSS THE BED.*

AURORA: I desire him.

DOLORES: Ay, no, Aurora. He's staying here para one night only. Let him be.

AURORA: One night. Rapid pleasure. Perfect.

DOLORES: Ay, Aurora, can't you stop?

AURORA: I am hungry, Mami. I have a deep, dark appetite.

DOLORES: Why, Dios mio? Why did I get one hija who will not start? And one hija who will not stop? Ay, it's not normal.

AURORA: He looks delicious.

DOLORES: Why can't you go out and get a job?

*AURORA GETS UP OFF THE BED.*

AURORA: I get too distracted. I work in a store. A man walks in. I want him. I can't do my job. I get fired. My last job at the bakery lasted five hours. I sold five loaves of bread to a dark haired man with an exquisite smile. I counted out his change. (coyly) I smiled at him. (seductively) He smiled at me and raised his eyebrow. I took off my white baker's apron and walked out the door. Then, we ran to my garden to frolic for hours in wild abandon. I'm not meant to live a life in the world of public commerce.

DOLORES: Ay, pobrecita, what am I going to do with you?

AURORA: I don't take up too much space. I cook delicious concoctions full of light and love for you and Connie. I bathe you. I serve meals to you. I keep you company when I'm not busy. And I like sleeping out in my tulip garden. The moist green grass is my mattress. The tall green stems are my curtains of privacy. The ruby and crimson blossoms are my stimuli. The sun by day is my comforter. And the stars by night are my canopy. There I can have men to my heart's desire without bothering you or Connie.

DOLORES: But, you do bother me. It isn't right. El sexo is beautiful but not para todo el tiempo...not for all day and night. Y it's not safe for you either. Hay peligros. Diseases. Pestilence. Death. Podrias morir. But you never listen to your Mami...you do what you want and you don't care about me. No puedo. I cannot stop you.

AURORA: I am a force of nature. My urges come from Mother Earth...Madre de la Tierra. I am a ravenous creature. I have a gift. I must share this gift with as many men as possible.

DOLORES: Ay y you never get pregnant. Maybe if I had nietos I wouldn't mind so much...but all this sexo y no hijos? Never will I have tiny grandchildren for mi casa?

AURORA: I don't need or want a child. That's my gift...endless hours of pleasure...no consequence.

DOLORES: Ay m'ijita...he is the son of my friend, Griselda. He is looking for a nice honorable girl. He wants Concepción. Griselda and I are trying to arrange it.

AURORA: He won't even be able to kiss her. Didn't you tell Griselda about me?

DOLORES: The whole countryside knows all about you. Your scent flies through the wind to the noses of all concerned madres and they know where not to send their sons.

AURORA: You are just jealous because you don't have any more libidinous drive left inside of you.

DOLORES: No, m'ija. I am not jealous. I am tired. And protective. But not jealous.

AURORA: Connie won't let him touch her. She thinks she's waiting to receive the second Virginal Conception!

DOLORES: You will not tell him. Reynaldo is a nice...attractive boy. I keep praying and asking mi Dios to change Concepción's mind.

AURORA: Why...when there is already a woman who wants him?

DOLORES: He is not for you to have. He is too good for you. Besides...I also have lustful feelings for him...ay, he looks just like your Papi when I first met him...but I am too old and shriveled down there for that. We must restrain ourselves for the good of Concepción. This is her one chance.

AURORA: Why always Concepción? (beat) She can never bear him any children. I, on the other hand, can reverse my gift at will if I want to be with one man...and then I can choose to bear as many offspring as he and I desire.

DOLORES: You will not say anything. Connie cannot give him niños but she will make a wonderful esposa in all other ways.

AURORA: My sister is happy with her prayers and her candles and her craziness. Why waste him on her?

DOLORES: Do you know how hard it will be to find her a husband? You will find one easily. But if she doesn't...when I am gone, who will take care of her? NADIE!

AURORA: You are obsessed with death. You will live a long life, Mami. Connie does not want to be married...she wants to be una santa.

DOLORES: Of course, she wants to be married. She just doesn't realize it yet. Concepción is scared. She hides in la religión. Pero, she won't be una virgen for much longer.

**SCENE FOUR**

*LIGHTS RISE ON DOLORES' BEDROOM. REYNALDO, CONNIE, DOLORES AND AURORA ARE HAVING DINNER AROUND DOLORES' BED. THEY SIT AT THE BED AS IF IT WERE A TABLE. THERE IS A TABLE CLOTH ACROSS THE BED AND PLATES AND TABLE SETTINGS.*

REYNALDO: Thank you, Señora, for the wonderful meal.

DOLORES: Thank m'ijita, Aurora. Since I cannot get out of bed, she does all the cooking for us.

AURORA: A delicious meal can be such an aphrodisiac.

REYNALDO: (looking at Connie, speaking to Dolores) Such a lovely house, Señora...tranquil rooms to rest in...peaceful porch to enjoy the cool evening breeze...luscious gardens right outside the back door...and all of this surrounded by the splendors of nature.

DOLORES: My husband Joaquin, may he rest in peace, built it for us right after our wedding. He went out into the jungle, cut down fifty trees, brought them back here and with a couple of the other men in the village built us this house. Ay, mi esposo.

REYNALDO: A strong and gifted arquitecto.

DOLORES: He was like a tree. His arms were strong como las giant palmeras in the jungle. His legs were like las tree trunks. And his hands...ay madre mia...what hands he had. Yes, mis hijitas, your Papi was a strong man.

CONNIE: But he knew Dios, Mami, just before he died, right? Tell Reynaldo.

DOLORES: Mira...right before my husband went to be in La Gloria, he saw the sky open up and he saw the hand of his Maker reaching down to touch him. And he cried out, "I see the Hand of Dios coming down to grab me. I see His knuckles...they are huge and bulging and hairy and calling out to me." And then he went to be in La Gloria.

AURORA: He was delusional...hallucinating. He thought the fist of the Almighty was going to punch him and punish him for all his sins.

CONNIE: You are lying.

AURORA: Face it. He abandoned his wife and children. He lived a crazed, passion-filled life in the wilds of the jungle. Got sick. The cholera ravaged him. Constant loss of bodily fluids...muscles cramps...

DOLORES: Aurora! Our stomachs! La digestión! Acabamos de comer.

AURORA: Leading to severe dehydration and sudden death. End of story.

CONNIE: Mi Dios forgave him. He tried but he just couldn't control himself just like you can't control your earthly desires. He provided for his family. He loved us in his own way.

AURORA: You are wrong.

CONNIE: You would know if you hadn't been out at all hours running around the pueblo square trying to find any man available...

AURORA: Pues...and you lying in the field with that ridiculous grin on your face all day long...

CONNIE: Seeking a holy connection not an earthly, soiled one...

AURORA: Blood never flowing through you...never knowing the monthly aches in the lower regions...never knowing passion...

CONNIE: Free to concentrate on the wonders of mi Dios...

AURORA: Being religiosa and hiding from desires...

CONNIE: Reveling in la tierra and hiding from Dios...

DOLORES: Basta ya! Reynaldo...perdoneme...mis hijitas are not accustomed to having a guest at the dinner bed are they?

CONNIE: Perdoneme, Mami.

AURORA: More plaaaaatanosssss Reynaldo?

REYNALDO: No gracias.

AURORA: They are soaked in oil and fried to the perfect consistency so they are still all soft and supple inside.

REYNALDO: I'm full, gracias.

AURORA: So what will you do in the big...sssspraaawwwling...city, Reynaldo?

REYNALDO: A friend from mi pueblo has arranged an interview for me...at the steel mill. They offer good pay and hire men with no previous experience. The money from my carpentry isn't enough to support myself and a familia when I have one.

DOLORES: Ay, Reynaldo wants una familia.

REYNALDO: I do, Señora. I want to marry, have una familia...living a life of excitement in the city...not a quiet, country existence.

AURORA: Such ssstrong biceps you have to carry all those hhheeavy materials.

REYNALDO: I prefer carpentry. Carve fine furnishings, doors, chairs, tables, window frames, cabinets...working with my hands to create and craft, but...I'll start in the mill and then maybe carve and whittle a little on the side.

CONNIE: María's husband was a carpenter.

REYNALDO: María?

CONNIE: La Santa Madre.

AURORA: She idolizes La Virgen María. Can you believe how crazy...

DOLORES: (interrupting) Reynaldo, por favor stay here one more day and get your rest before you set out to the big city. You've traveled half a day to get here and you need your strength for all that hard...muscular...work.

REYNALDO: Well, if you don't mind...(looking at Connie) I do find so much beauty in the landscape here.

DOLORES: The views are breath taking, aren't they? (beat) Concepción, why don't you show our guest the river in the field behind the house. He will like that.

REYNALDO: Yes, I would.

CONNIE: Come on, Reynaldo.

AURORA: I'm coming too.

DOLORES: I need you here, Aurora. (to Connie) Hasta luego, m'ijita.

*CONNIE AND REYNALDO EXIT.*

AURORA: Oh but he is so good. Why can't I have him?

DOLORES: He is not for you.

AURORA: Forget it, Mami. Connie has her heart set on being up there with La Santa Madre María. Concepción will not even caress Reynaldo.

He'll be frustrated with no release for his mounting desire. Then...he comes to me.

DOLORES: Que no!

**SCENE FIVE**

*LIGHTS RISE ON CONNIE AND REYNALDO AT THE RIVER.*

CONNIE:
(singing)
Agua del río
Pleno de brío
Traeme el Espíritu Santo
Llenando el vientre mío

Agua del río
Cuna del crío
Traeme el nacimiento
Reluciendo al Señor Mío

Agua del río
Dulce y frío
Traeme corrientes frescas
Bautizando al niño mío

REYNALDO: Tan dulce...sweet sounds...tender lips.

CONNIE: (speaking, as she places her hand in the water) Water in the wild...sweet and so mild...carry me cool currents...baptizing my holy child.

*REYNALDO SPLASHES IN THE WATER.*

REYNALDO: The liquid against my skin so soothing.

CONNIE: When they baptize you, you go under like you are going to die. That symbolizes death en el infierno. Then you come back up out of the water. La Resurección. New life.

REYNALDO: You love la religión.

CONNIE: Religión no. It's diferente with mi Dios. In la religión, people make life so formal and heavy and boring. With mi Dios, simplicity. He is. I am. Beings. Together. Not todos los men in white robes swinging el incense making everybody cough and choke.

REYNALDO: So this river is your church.

CONNIE: This river. The field. The house. My bedroom. All of it. Everywhere.

REYNALDO: Dios frightens me.

CONNIE: Just listen for his voice and follow it. He speaks so softly so you have to listen very quietly. Your hearing gets better each day the more you recognize the sound of his voice.

REYNALDO: For you es natural. For me, no.

CONNIE: As natural as this river, these trees, this sky.

REYNALDO: You've probably always talked to him.

CONNIE: When I was little, I saw my Mami talking outloud alone in her bed and I said, "Who are you talking to?" And she said, "Mi Dios." And so I just started talking to him too...each day serenity growing deeper inside me.

REYNALDO: You're embraced by beauty...this makes talking to him easier. The house of my youth wasn't surrounded by such splendor. Outside my window I saw desert and rock formations and carrion birds pecking at the carcasses of coyotes.

CONNIE: I pray inside. And outside. In the warmth of my room and in the expanse of the field and river. It's the same. Both places. Everywhere. Anywhere.

REYNALDO: What's your...bedroom...like?

CONNIE: There's a small altar I built myself out of bricks and wood with a white linen cloth...a small statue of the la Santa Madre and a crucifix I found in the river here. White candles of all shapes and sizes...tall ones...round ones...small votive ones...skinny tapered ones. My worn out leather bound Biblia. And...a mattress on the floor.

REYNALDO: A peaceful place. Could I...see it sometime?

CONNIE: Seduction will not work, Reynaldo. It's better if we stay friends.

REYNALDO: Concepción. Deep inside my heart, I know I am meant to be with you. Your lips are pastel rose petals. Your eyes are burnished onyx jewels. Your arms are like the careening neck of a swan so graceful. Your breasts are small, ripe papayas hanging delicately from a lovely tree.

CONNIE: I've read la Biblia, Rey. I know the Song of Solomon. King Solomon writes love letters to his beloved and gets all sexy..."Your breasts are like two fawns...that feed among the lilies." It's seducing for some people but not for me.

REYNALDO: (suddenly) Concepción. I want to marry you.

CONNIE: Lo siento. But I can't. I have other plans.

REYNALDO: Who is he?

CONNIE: Mi Dios has other plans for me. You'll find another.

*REYNALDO PUTS HIS HAND IN THE WATER.*

REYNALDO: My soul wells up with desire. The waters are churning. When I set out on this journey to the city deep inside I knew my life would be transformed. I have been lonely inside... longing for the marital union between a husband and wife. The women back in my pueblo...none of them compare to your radiance. Mi mamá told me about your beauty but I ignored her words until I approached you sitting under the papaya tree and knew. I am sure of this...you will be my wife.

CONNIE: No.

REYNALDO: Concepción...

CONNIE: Reynaldo...it's impossible.

REYNALDO: Doesn't la Biblia say "With Dios, nothing is imposible?"

CONNIE: Sí. El angel Gabriel said that to la Virgen Maria. Pero in this case, that saying doesn't work.

**SCENE SIX**

*LIGHTS RISE ON DOLORES' BEDROOM. DOLORES SITS UP IN BED. REYNALDO SITS AT THE FOOT OF HER BED.*

REYNALDO: Her face glows when she speaks. She has an innocence radiating from her eyes as her lips move. Ay madre mia, from the pit of my stomach, my body cries out, "Mi esposa...mi esposa...wife...come to me."

DOLORES: Patience, m'ijo. Concepción is not accustomed to being with los hombres. Her Papi died when she was still una niñita...and since then she has stayed home with me and Aurora. She has lived a simple life with her naturaleza...el river...las trees...y el field y her Dios. Courting her will take a little while. Stay here a few days. Spend time with her. She will soon be under your spell.

REYNALDO: What do I do, Dolores?

DOLORES: Show her who you truly are on the inside...el hombre verdadero...not the man who pretends to be brave but is scared...el miedoso...who pretends to be el macho and hides his vulnerability. Show her your sensitivity...your femininity...your spirituality.

*REYNALDO GRABS DOLORES' HAND. HE KISSES IT. DOLORES SWOONS.*

REYNALDO: Muchisimas gracias, Señora. I will stay. I will do all of this. I will win her acceptance and love.

*REYNALDO EXITS. DOLORES FANS HERSELF.*

DOLORES: (praying) Ay Dios. Help me control myself. He looks so much like mi esposo...mi Joaquin. Those eyes...so brown and full of life...those sparkling teeth...that wavy black hair...Ay madre mia...it is too much for a bed ridden woman.

*CONNIE ENTERS AND LIES ON THE BED.*

CONNIE: My time to hear from heaven approaches. I feel the vibrations in the air. My blood weighs heavy inside me. Faint whisperings in my ears...warmth beginning in my palms. With each step I take, I walk through a thick fog. I know I'm going to get a message. I know I am.

DOLORES: Concepción. Reynaldo is simpático y so handsome. I think he likes you.

CONNIE: I like him...but as a friend only.

DOLORES: Pero he really likes you, m'ija. (beat) Maybe Dios will tell you that you are not going to be like la Santa Madre...no Virginal Concepción. Maybe this Reynaldo is for you.

CONNIE: Mami, what man will want to marry a woman who cannot bear him hijos?

DOLORES: (suddenly panicked) Did you tell him?

CONNIE: No.

DOLORES: (relieved) Not all men want hijos. Many men want the love and companionship of a wonderful woman like you.

*CONNIE GETS UP OFF DOLORES' BED.*

CONNIE: Mami...women were created so we could bear niños in this vida..."And He blessed them and said, 'Be fruitful and multiply.'" But Dios has blessed me and made me diferente than other women. I am going to be just like la Virgen Maria. My whole life has been leading me in this direction. (rhetorical) Why did He create me without fertile flesh? So carnal pleasures won't distract me...so I can bear his holy niño.

DOLORES: Do you think Dios will repeat himself after what happened the first time? A son murdered and hung on una cruz like un criminál?

CONNIE: With la Santa Madre, He wanted full cooperation from his chosen one. And I am ready to fully cooperate with his plan.

DOLORES: Ay, Concepción. You were created diferente, sí.

CONNIE: El angel Gabriel saluted her...

DOLORES: You cannot bear niños of your own so you are afraid of los hombres.

CONNIE: (getting caught up in her own world) "Maria! Llena de gracia! Do not be afraid!"

DOLORES: You are shy. Pero es normal.

CONNIE: "Blessed are you among las mujeres"

DOLORES: You will learn the ways of the flesh.

CONNIE: "You will conceive in your womb a son"

DOLORES: I never had little boys for you to play with...so you do not know about los hombres.

CONNIE: "And El Espiritu Santo will come upon you in a haze of brilliance"

DOLORES: Only mis hijitas preciosas.

CONNIE: "And your child will be born holy."

DOLORES: Ay, don't be imposible.

CONNIE: "With Dios, nothing is impossible."

DOLORES: You are not la Virgen María.

CONNIE: No, of course not, I will be La Santa Concepción. So...marvelous...miraculous...stupendous...fantástica.

DOLORES: Pero, m'ija...Reynaldo is such a nice, hermoso boy.

CONNIE: Let Aurora have him. They can run off together and have hijos and hijas to their hearts desire.

DOLORES: Concepción, if you don't get a husband, who will take care of you when I die?

CONNIE: Mami, por favor...my path in life is unique. Aurora's path is to revel in the carnal pleasures. But...I am on a journey...holy and mysterious.

DOLORES: Just because you can't have hijos doesn't mean you can't be with un hombre. Dios likes el sexo. Some of Jesucristo's best friends were las prostitutas.

CONNIE: For some it's fine. But not for me.

*CONNIE EXITS.*

DOLORES: (praying, pleading) Ay, please tell her it can't be so. Por favor.

**SCENE SEVEN**

*LIGHTS RISE ON CONNIE IN HER BEDROOM SURROUNDED BY WHITE, LIGHTED CANDLES, OF ALL SHAPES AND SIZES. REYNALDO SITS NEXT TO HER.*

CONNIE: My message arrives soon...whisperings increasing in my ears...heat pulsating through the center of my palms...

REYNALDO: I'm scared about my future.

CONNIE: You'll go to the city...start your job...meet some wonderful woman...get married...have children...you will live a joyful life.

REYNALDO: What if I am so miserable that I cannot get out of bed in the morning? What if each day is a dark night of the soul and my blood becomes a sluggish fluid that weighs me down and transforms my face into a blank slate?

CONNIE: Trust.

REYNALDO: Will you hold my hand?

*CONNIE TAKES HIS HAND.*

REYNALDO: Will you pray to your Dios for me?

CONNIE: A quick prayer only.

REYNALDO: Go ahead.

CONNIE: (praying, impatient) Dios mio, be with Reynaldo. Calm his fears. Grant him peace. Amen.

*REYNALDO GETS UP AND KISSES CONNIE ON BOTH CHEEKS.*

REYNALDO: Gracias, Concepción. I'm going out to the river now. I am going to ponder my life and sit by the water and weep.

CONNIE: Bye, Rey.

*REYNALDO EXITS. CONNIE CLOSES HER EYES.*

CONNIE: Okay, Dios mio.

*CONNIE HOLDS OUT HER HANDS AND RAISES HER ARMS. A STRANGE LIGHT AND MUSIC FILL THE ROOM. CONNIE LEVITATES. SHE SPEAKS PROPHETICALLY.*

CONNIE: Concepción. Reynaldo. The two shall join together in holy matrimony. So says your Dios.

*CONNIE DESCENDS BACK TO THE FLOOR AND COLLAPSES INTO A HEAP OF SORROW.*

CONNIE: What did I do wrong?

**SCENE EIGHT**

*LIGHTS RISE ON DOLORES' BEDROOM. DOLORES SITS UP IN BED. AURORA PACES.*

AURORA: She won't come out of her room. She won't accept any food. She won't say anything to me except, "Go away." My sister is a religious nut but I'm worried about her this time, Mami.

DOLORES: I feel it in my bones. Dios has spoken to her. She will come out into the world when she is ready.

AURORA: It's just not right for a twenty year old woman to want to have el niño de Dios and remain una virgen for the rest of her life. Loca. Crazy. Nuts.

DOLORES: (forceful) Santificada!

AURORA: Desire is a force of nature that should be in her and is not.

DOLORES: When los doctores told us she would never bear niños, I was tristíssima, sí. Why doesn't Dios give los ovarios...fertile flesh...to every female child? No lo sabemos. Los misterios. Pero...she has other creative forces inside of her. She is como una rosa that reaches to the sky and will only bloom in her earthly pleasures when she is older. (beat) You on the other hand m'ijita want el sexo and only that. Ever since you were thirteen, you have been consumed by passion and what does this bring you? A ravenous appetite and a bed in a tulip garden. (beat) This is not normal either.

AURORA: At least I am closer to normal than she is.

DOLORES: Ay Dios mio, maybe I am loca to think Concepción will accept Reynaldo.

AURORA: So...I can have him then?

DOLORES: Vete ya. Your hermana suffers y look how you behave...begging for the one man who will bring her happiness in esta vida. Fuera de aqui. Take your two eyes...your two hands...your two lips...and go back to your garden of tulips....to your flowering and deflowering.(beat) Dejame. Leave me in peace!

*AURORA EXITS. CONNIE ENTERS LOOKING PALE AND WITHDRAWN.*

DOLORES: Ay m'ijita. Come to Mami.

*CONNIE APPROACHES DOLORES BLANKLY AND RESTS HER HEAD ON DOLORES' CHEST.*

CONNIE: I had my heart set on sainthood but Dios changed His mind.

DOLORES: Calmate ya.

CONNIE: To be like La Santissima Madre. He blessed her more than any other persona.

DOLORES: Shhhh...Calmate hija.

CONNIE: To conceive and bear el baby de Dios. I really wanted to, Mami. To have un niño of my own...formed in my flesh...witnessing my belly protrude month after month...feeling my holy hijo's tender feet kicking the palm of my hand.

DOLORES: Stay with Mami.

CONNIE: But I know it was Dios talking to me...I recognized His voice.

DOLORES: Of course you did, m'ijita.

CONNIE: And...he wants me to get...married.

*DOLORES' FACE BRIGHTENS CONSIDERABLY.*

DOLORES: He does?!

*CONNIE PULLS AWAY FROM HER MOTHER.*

CONNIE: He wants me to marry Reynaldo.

DOLORES: Un esposo para mi niña?!

CONNIE: I don't know anything about men, Mami. I've spent my whole life preparing for sainthood and now I have to throw all that away and experience carnal pleasures?

DOLORES: Reynaldo is a gentle man, m'ijita. He will show you.

CONNIE: So much confusion.

DOLORES: Los misterios, m'ija. Accept this mystery in life. And celebrate because you will be starting una nueva aventura. With a husband. Tu esposo. Ay Dios is so poderoso.

CONNIE: But la Santa Madre was una virgen her whole life. No distraction. Complete connection to Dios and her son. I'm afraid if I am no longer una virgen then I will lose my ability to communicate with mi Dios in a way that is santificada.

DOLORES: You will be una santa with your esposo.

CONNIE: But I will never deliver el baby de Dios.

DOLORES: Quieta.

CONNIE: Teach me, Mami. You must teach me how to be a woman in this world.

*DOLORES EMBRACES CONNIE. CONNIE AGAIN RESTS HER HEAD AGAINST HER MOTHER'S CHEST.*

CONNIE: I want to go back to being a little thirteen year old girl. I don't want to be a grown up woman. I want to stay small where I am safe and I trust everything. I am afraid to enter that huge world where I have no control and I am unknown.

DOLORES: Trust, m'ijita. The knowledge is inside of you. You will know what to do. Dios will show you. Reynaldo will help you.

CONNIE: Ay Mami.

DOLORES: AND CONNIE:(singing)
Los dolores aparecen con
Días de armonía
Vienen por buena razón
Enseñándonos de la vida

Los dolores de la vida son
Misterios que Dios nos da

Para alentarnos con
Paz, Gozo y Alegría

## SCENE NINE

*LIGHTS RISE ON AURORA IN THE KITCHEN. SHE STIRS A POT OF
SOUP AND ADDS SPICES.*

AURORA: Rosemary...romance. Thyme for tempo. Oregano...orgiastic
activities.

*REYNALDO ENTERS SLOWLY, IN A MELLOW STATE.*

AURORA: Que pasó, Reynaldo? You need some nourishment for your
luscious body.

REYNALDO: I sat by the water and wept. For thee Concepción. I sat by
the water and wept for my life. Mi vida will be so empty without her.

AURORA: La segunda. La Aurora. (seductively) Ooowww...(animal-like)
Rrooaarr...(serenely) Ahhhh. The dawning of a new day. You just sit here,
mi hermoso...handsome hunk of flesh. You sit here and Aurorita will fix
you a delightful meal that will caress your tongue, activate your salivary
glands, slide down your throat, down your esophagus, into your stomach
and radiate throughout your intestines sending shafts of lifting light
coursing through every inch of your entire body.

REYNALDO: Bueno...

AURORA: Pollo asado. Patatas. Frijoles. Y a soup that will ignite your
senses!

REYNALDO: I don't like chicken.

AURORA: But that's what I've prepared for you, querido mio.

REYNALDO: I'm allergic to potatoes and beans create long episodes of
flatulence.

AURORA: What in the world do you eat anyway?!

REYNALDO: I like fruta. Apples. Peaches. Pears. Mangos. Papayas. Paraguayas. Cherries. Grapes. Bananas. Oranges.

AURORA: Alright...alright. What else?

REYNALDO: I like vegetales. Tomatoes. Lettuce. Spinach. Collard Greens. Arugula. Watercress.

AURORA: All you eat are fruits and vegetables?

REYNALDO: And nuts. Pine nuts. Hazel nuts. Almonds. Brazil nuts. Walnuts.

AURORA: Okay. Okay. But how do you get your iron...fortitude... strength?

REYNALDO: Mi Dios.

AURORA: What has Connie done to you?

REYNALDO: Concepción is my destiny.

AURORA: Did she put a spell on you with one of her prayers? This is not the Reynaldo who walked through that door yesterday...all manly energy pouring out of each pore.

REYNALDO: Concepción wants a sensitive, emotional, spiritual man.

AURORA: Loca. Crazy. Nuts.

REYNALDO: She wants a man who can show his true self.

AURORA: This is not your true self.

REYNALDO: A man who can display who he genuinely is on the inside.

AURORA: You need some aphrodisiac soup and quick.

*AURORA POURS HIM SOME SOUP.*

AURORA: Drink this, Reynaldo el loco.

REYNALDO: I'm not crazy. What's in this?

AURORA: Fruits and vegetables and nuts.

REYNALDO: Bueno...

*REYNALDO DRINKS THE BOWL OF SOUP IN ONE GULP.*

REYNALDO: Concepción!

AURORA: Reynaldo!

**SCENE TEN**

*LIGHTS RISE ON CONNIE, EXPRESSIONLESS, SITTING IN THE FIELD ON A TREE STUMP STARING OFF INTO THE DISTANCE. REYNALDO COMES RUNNING TOWARD HER FOLLOWED BY AURORA. CONNIE DOES NOT RELINQUISH HER GAZE. CONNIE DOES NOT LOOK AT HIM. AURORA RUNS AFTER REYNALDO AND GRABS ONTO HIM.*

REYNALDO: Concepción mia...my Connie...my beloved one.

*CONNIE REMAINS SILENT.*

AURORA: Reynaldo. Focus your eyes on me. That soup is supposed to work para mi.

*REYNALDO PULLS AURORA'S HANDS OFF OF HIM AND STARES AT CONNIE.*

REYNALDO: Connie...your radiant eyes glisten through the silence.

*AURORA LIES ON THE GROUND AND TRIES TO PULL REYNALDO DOWN ONTO THE GROUND WITH HER.*

REYNALDO: Concepción...I can hear your thoughts. And your pensamientos tell me that even though you are silent now...you desire me here by your side.

AURORA: By <u>my</u> side!

*AURORA PULLS REYNALDO DOWN TO THE GROUND BUT HE QUICKLY GETS BACK UP.*

REYNALDO: Concepción mia.

*CONNIE DOES NOT LOOK AT HIM AND SHE REMAINS MOTIONLESS.*

AURORA: Reynaldo...

REYNALDO: Aurora...basta ya! Enough with your lascivious exploits. I DO NOT WANT YOU. I WANT CONCEPCIÓN. GET THAT THROUGH YOUR HEAD AND HEART.

*AURORA STANDS UP AND DUSTS THE DIRT OFF OF HER.*

AURORA: I will not be humiliated any longer. Just know, Reynaldo, that you are in for a horrible surprise and I was only trying to guarantee you the physical pleasure you so obviously desire and deserve (pointing to Connie) but will never receive there.

REYNALDO: BE GONE.

AURORA: Unfortunate hunk of flesh.

*AURORA EXITS. REYNALDO GETS DOWN ON ONE KNEE.*

REYNALDO: Concepción. I have prayed to Dios for you. I have wept for you until I fell asleep exhausted on the river bank. I tossed and turned through turbulent dreams of tunnels and turrets waking up in a cold sweat for you. You sit on this remnant of a tree in the middle of this barren field and you are a stunning creation. Even the very blades of grass cry out, "Concepción. Concepción."

*CONNIE'S FACE REMAINS EXPRESSIONLESS. REYNALDO TAKES CONNIE'S HAND.*

REYNALDO: Concepción. Will you be my wife?

*CONNIE LOOKS STRAIGHT AHEAD AND REMAINS MOTIONLESS.*

CONNIE: I will.

*REYNALDO JUMPS UP AND DOWN.*

REYNALDO: Yes, mi Dios. She will be mine. She will be mine!

*CONNIE STARES OUT INTO THE DISTANCE AND REMAINS MOTIONLESS.*

**SCENE ELEVEN**

*ONE DAY LATER. LIGHTS RISE ON DOLORES' BEDROOM. FATHER PENA SITS NEXT TO DOLORES' BED AND WRITES IN A SMALL NOTEBOOK, WHILE TAKING FURTIVE GLANCES AT CONNIE.*

DOLORES: We want a small ceremony, Padre. But so magnífica. Just the immediate familia. But such a holy familia we are, Padre. (to Connie) Concepción, how lucky we are to have Padre Pena to perform the ceremony.

CONNIE: (expressionless) Sí.

DOLORES: Just arrived to our pueblecito last week and the first marriage he performs is yours, Concepción. Ay que suerte. Muchissimas gracias, Padre, for agreeing to marry m'ijita.

FATHER PENA: (nervous, staring at Connie) My matrimonial...I mean...(snapping back to attention with Dolores) the matrimonial covenant by which a man and a woman establish between themselves a partnership for the whole of life is by its nature ordered toward the good of the spouses and the...pro...cre...ation and (gazing longingly at Connie) ven...er...ation... (snapping back to attention with Dolores) I mean...education of...offspring and is a holy sacrament in which...I...am called to...assist.

DOLORES: Ay, nietos. Oh this house with grandchildren will be so full of joy, Padre.

*CONNIE RUNS OUT OF THE ROOM.*

DOLORES: (calling, angry) CONCEPCIÓN! (beat, sweetly) Perdoneme, Padre.

FATHER PENA: Did I frighten her?

DOLORES: El matrimonio is so new to m'ijita...she accepted the proposal just yesterday...she's only a little nervous.

FATHER PENA: Of course. (writing in his notebook) Concepción...will... marry...Reynaldo.

DOLORES: Such a precious couple.(beat) Young lovers. Oh Padre, m'ijita Aurora and I desired Reynaldo, he is so delicious, but we restrained ourselves, we practiced self sacrifice and now we are giving the gift of...la vida...to mi hijita Concepción. (beat) Mi esposo Joaquin, may he rest in peace, would have loved to see his hijita getting married.

*AURORA COMES BURSTING INTO THE ROOM.*

AURORA: Mami, NO!

DOLORES: Si, m'ijita. Your sister will become una señora before you.

AURORA: The best male specimen ever to walk into our house and La fria...the frigid one...truly gets him?!

DOLORES: Do not insult your sister. She is not fria. She is just diferente than you. She needs time to adjust to her new life. But she will make a wonderful esposa.

AURORA: My blood surges and boils inside my body. At night, I lie in my tulip garden and dream of his gorgeous face...his teeth ...pushing my tongue against each pearly one.

DOLORES: M'ija. We have a guest. Padre Pena this is my other hijita, Aurora.

FATHER PENA: En...can...tado.

AURORA: He can handle this, Mami. He hears confessions every day.

FATHER PENA: (nervous) Yes...yes...I do. Um...that's...correct.

AURORA: I dream of his soft neck...pressing my lips into it...his muscular chest...grasping handfuls of ebony hair through my fingers...his rosy nipples...sucking each one until it hardens into a little acorn top under my lips.

DOLORES: Basta ya!

AURORA: Then my nocturnal mind travels to his loins and my heart pumps faster and faster and blood gravitates toward my garden of delight...I caress my budding button...I stroke his orchestral organ and I feel his instrument crescendo and crescendo and CRESCENDO!

DOLORES: (embarrassed) Aurora...

AURORA: I DESIRE REYNALDO, MAMI. I MUST HAVE HIM!

*AURORA RUNS OUT OF THE ROOM.*

DOLORES (forceful) AURORA!

*FATHER PENA MOPS HIS BROW.*

DOLORES: Pray for her, Padre. Please pray for her. I do not know what she will do.

FATHER PENA: I'll be...content to pray for...for both your daughters, Señora. (praying) Dios te salve, María...llena eres de gracia, el Señor es contigo, bendita tu eres entre todas las mujeres...

**SCENE TWELVE**

*LIGHTS RISE ON CONNIE AND REYNALDO SITTING UNDER THE PAPAYA TREE IN THE FIELD. CONNIE REMAINS LISTLESS AND STARES OFF INTO THE DISTANCE.*

REYNALDO: Concepción mia, yours are the lips I will caress every day until I die. Yours are the eyes I will see transposed onto the faces of my children. I yearn to create niños of my own flesh and blood with my fantástica esposa. I feel this deep down to the soles of my feet...an electric energy telling me this. (beat) La vida juntos...we'll marry, consummate our joy and in a few short months, si Dios quiere, we'll have our own niñitos running around our home. I'll build a little workshop behind this house and I'll carve and create beautiful objects with my hands surrounded by a view of majestic nature. Everyday at the noon day meal, Little Connie and Little Rey Jr. will run out to the workshop into my arms and we'll bound into the house together and sit at the table for a delicious, spectacular meal. Oh la vida casada will be everything I hoped it could be. I don't need to go the city. I will live in the holy countryside with you y la familia in joy y felicidad.

*CONNIE, LISTLESS, STARES OFF INTO THE DISTANCE AS REYNALDO BEAMS BRIGHTLY.*

**SCENE THIRTEEN**

*ONE WEEK LATER. LIGHTS RISE ON DOLORES' BEDROOM. GRISELDA SITS ON A CHAIR NEXT TO DOLORES' BED. THEY BOTH WEAR FANCY WEDDING OUTFITS AND PRIMP HOLDING HAND MIRRORS.*

DOLORES: Your son will be so extático con his new esposa.

GRISELDA: He is so eager to jump into the wedding bed with his wife-to-be.

DOLORES: He knows she is una virgen?

GRISELDA: Ya lo sabe. Is she prepared?

DOLORES: She is so scared. I was scared on my wedding night too. Ay, mi esposo was so sexy.

GRISELDA: Once I was pregnant with Reynaldo, my husband Manuel ran off with la puta, the baker's wife.

DOLORES: He was loco not to want children. Los niñitos continue our happiness to the next generation. La inmortalidad.

GRISELDA: He said, "Griselda, I want to be free. No children. You have niños, I leave." And so...se fue.

DOLORES: You are a good woman, Griselda. Dios will bless you for your years of hard work con tu hijo. He is so maravilloso. Ay...so handsome. He even tempted me...an old woman.

GRISELDA: Dolores, por favor.

DOLORES: It's true. Verdad.

GRISELDA: And your Concepción is so gorgeous...tan guapíssima. (beat) Now, I will remain close to m'ijito, my only joy in this vida. I will not lose him to the crazy city life. They will have many hijos and hijas and the babies will grow into beautiful children and I will be a grandmother and never be alone.

DOLORES: He will take care of mi niña and I can die in peace knowing m'ijita is safe y secure.

GRISELDA: Our plan worked, mi amiga.

DOLORES: Pues all these months of arranging their meeting...and finally the proposal...and then a week of preparations...and finally the day arrives por fin.

GRISELDA: Our children will unite and we'll be rewarded after so many years of suffering.

DOLORES: Life is blessing us, Griselda.

GRISELDA: Eso es...amiga...eso es.

**SCENE FOURTEEN**

*LIGHTS RISE ON FATHER PENA STANDING IN THE FIELD, IN FRONT OF REYNALDO, WHO WEARS A SUIT, AND CONNIE, WHO WEARS A BRIDAL OUTFIT. DOLORES SITS IN HER BED, NEAR CONNIE. AURORA STANDS NEXT TO DOLORES' BED. GRISELDA STANDS NEXT TO REYNALDO. CONNIE STILL REMAINS EXPRESSIONLESS, BORDERING ON CATATONIC.*

FATHER PENA: Reynaldo, will you...have this woman to be your wife; to live...together in the matrimonial covenant? Will you love her, comfort her, honor and keep her, in sickness and in health, and, forsaking all others, be faithful to her as long as you both shall live?

REYNALDO: I will.

*REYNALDO SMILES.*

FATHER PENA: Concepción, will you have...this man to be your husband; to live together in the matrimonial covenant? Will you...love him, comfort him, honor and keep him, in sickness and in health, and, forsaking all others (beat) be faithful to him as long as you both shall live?

*CONNIE STAMMERS.*

CONNIE: I...think...I....well....I....oh...I...

*FATHER PENA CLEARS HIS THROAT.*

FATHER PENA: ...as long as you both shall live?

*CONNIE STAMMERS AGAIN.*

CONNIE: Well...I....oh....I...if...I...

DOLORES: She will.

CONNIE: I...will.

*REYNALDO SMILES. CONNIE REMAINS EXPRESSIONLESS.*

FATHER PENA: The rings por favor.

*DOLORES TAKES THE RINGS OUT OF HER PILLOW AND WAVES THEM HIGH IN THE AIR.*

DOLORES: Pure gold. Only the best for mis niños.

*DOLORES GIVES THE RINGS TO AURORA WHO SHOVES THEM INTO THE HAND OF FATHER PENA. HE GIVES ONE TO REYNALDO.*

FATHER PENA: (to Reynaldo) Repeat after me. Concepción...

REYNALDO: Concepción.

FATHER PENA: With this ring...

REYNALDO: With this ring...

FATHER PENA: I thee wed.

REYNALDO: I thee wed.

*REYNALDO SLIPS THE RING ONTO CONNIE'S FINGER AND KISSES HER FINGER.*

FATHER PENA: Ah, ah, ah. Not...yet.

*FATHER PENA GIVES CONNIE THE RING.*

FATHER PENA: (To Connie) Repeat after me. Reynaldo.

CONNIE: Reynaldo.

FATHER PENA: With this ring...

CONNIE: Can't we sing?

FATHER PENA: With this ring...

CONNIE: With...this...ring...

FATHER PENA: I thee wed.

CONNIE: Not in bed.

FATHER PENA: I thee wed.

CONNIE: I...thee...wed.

*CONNIE PUTS THE RING ON REYNALDO'S FINGER.*

FATHER PENA: Now, if there is anyone who feels these two should not...

DOLORES: No...no...Padre...

FATHER PENA: Should not be joined in holy matrimony...

DOLORES: (interrupting, sing-song) La, la, la, la, la, la, la.

FATHER PENA: Speak now...

DOLORES: (interrupting, sing-song) Ay, ay, ay, ay.

FATHER PENA: OR FOREVER HOLD YOUR PEACE!

AURORA: That's me. My turn. I don't think that Reynaldo should marry Concepción because she is una virgen and is afraid of men and will... probably...never bear him any children.

DOLORES: (aghast) Aurora...

AURORA: I believe he should marry me because I can satisfy all his cravings.

DOLORES: (sharply) Por favor...

AURORA: As you may not know Padre, my gift has been that I can enjoy endless hours of sensual pleasure without danger of conception. However, the gift is reversible by an act of my will and so when I decide to remain with one man, I can choose to conceive and bear him as many offspring as our hearts desire.

DOLORES: Basta ya!

AURORA: I inherited this gift, Padre, from my Papi's side of the familia. They lived deep in the jungle and practiced dark and magical rituals. I embody a supernatural gift not to be treated lightly.

GRISELDA: Puta! Calla!

AURORA: And now to show Reynaldo what he truly deserves...what he is lacking...I will perform a little dance that I created in the wilds of my tulip garden.

*AURORA STARTS TO HUM AND BUMP AND GRIND, GYRATING HER HIPS IN FRONT OF REYNALDO. SHE DANCES A SEDUCTIVE DANCE.*

DOLORES: AURORA! (pointing away) FUERA DE AQUI!

AURORA: (frantic) FATHER PENA UNDERSTANDS MY PAIN, MAMI. (rhetorically, suddenly calm) Don't you, Padre?

FATHER PENA: LET...HER...DANCE...HER...PEACE!

*FATHER PENA MOPS HIS BROW.*

GRISELDA: Desgraciada.

*AURORA FINISHES HER DANCE. SILENCE. THEY ALL STARE AT REYNALDO.*

FATHER PENA: Ah...Reynaldo?

*REYNALDO LOOKS LOVINGLY AT CONNIE WHO STILL REMAINS EXPRESSIONLESS.*

REYNALDO: I...love...Concepción.

*AURORA SCREAMS A PRIMAL SCREAM TEARING AT HER CLOTHING AS SHE EXITS, RUNNING.*

FATHER PENA: Bueno...therefore those whom Dios has joined together, (looking at Connie) let a man...I mean...(looking out) let no man put asunder. I now pronounce you husband and wife. En el nombre del Padre, del Hijo y del Espíritu Santo. Amen. (beat) (looking at Connie) You may not...I mean...(looking at Reynaldo) you may now kiss the bride.

*REYNALDO IS OVERWHELMED WITH JOY. HE MOVES TO KISS CONNIE AND SHE SLAPS HIM. HE STOPS, SMILES AND RUBS HIS CHEEK.*

FATHER PENA: Perhaps you shouldn't kiss the bride.

DOLORES: (to Reynaldo) Dulce. (to Father Pena) Padre, she is just scared. (to Reynaldo) Be gentle. Suave. (to Connie) M'ija. Kiss your new esposo. He loves you.

GRISELDA: (forceful) Kiss your new husband.

REYNALDO: I am gentle. I will not hurt you. I love you. I love Dios. We will be so increible together.

GRISELDA: (incensed) Increible.

DOLORES: Her first kiss. She's frightened. Por favor. Show some compasión.

REYNALDO: We'll try again...slowly.

CONNIE: But...I...don't...know...how.

*REYNALDO CHUCKLES TENDERLY AND CARESSES HER FACE.*

REYNALDO: (tenderly) I'll show you, querida. Do not worry.

CONNIE: Do...not...laugh...at...me. ANY OF YOU!

FATHER PENA: (tentatively) I...would never laugh at you.

DOLORES AND GRISELDA: We will not laugh.

CONNIE: (to Father Pena) Say it again.

FATHER PENA: I...would never laugh...oh...right...you mean...

*FATHER PENA CLEARS HIS THROAT.*

FATHER PENA: Once again...I pronounce you husband and wife. En el nombre del Padre, del Hijo y del Espíritu Santo. Amen. You may now kiss the bride.

*REYNALDO LURCHES FORWARD. CONNIE PUTS UP HER HAND AND FEELS HIS LIPS.*

CONNIE: Suave.

REYNALDO: For you, querida.

*CONNIE CLOSES HER EYES AND PURSES HER LIPS. REYNALDO CARESSES HER HEAD AND TRIES TO GIVE HER ONE PASSIONATE KISS. CONNIE, RESISTANT, NEVER RELEASES HER PUCKER AND BREAKS AWAY AFTER A FEW MOMENTS, COVERING HER FACE WITH HER HANDS, EMBARASSED. REYNALDO SHRUGS AND SMILES. DOLORES AND GRISELDA BREAK OUT IN LAUGHTER AND APPLAUSE. FATHER PENA MOPS HIS BROW.*

FATHER PENA: Damas y caballero...ladies and gentleman...that's me...I now present to you...husband and wife.

*REYNALDO BEAMS FROM EAR TO EAR. CONNIE SMILES NERVOUSLY. DOLORES, GRISELDA AND FATHER PENA SING.*

DOLORES:, GRISELDA: AND FATHER PENA:
(singing)
Los niños se casaron
Con tanta alegría
¡Sí! ya empezaron
La vida fantástica

*GRISELDA TAKES FATHER PENA'S ARM AND FORCES HIM TO DANCE A LITTLE JIG NEXT TO DOLORES' BED. DOLORES SNAPS HER FINGERS AND SWAYS BACK AND FORTH. REYNALDO LOOKS AT CONNIE LOVINGLY AND SHE LOOKS AT HIM TENTATIVELY AS THEY DANCE TOGETHER SLOWLY.*

DOLORES, GRISELDA AND FATHER PENA:
(singing)
Los niños se besaron
Con tanta armonía
¡Sí! ya llegaron
A la fecundidad

Los niños se juntaron
¡Ay que maravilla!
¡Sí! ya comenzaron
La nueva familia

*AURORA ENTERS RUNNING, HER CLOTHES ARE IN TATTERS. HER HAIR IS WILD. SHE HAS A CRAZED LOOK ABOUT HER. THEY ALL STOP THEIR MERRIMENT AND STARE AT HER IN SHOCK.*

AURORA: (ominously) The sky blackens. The trees rips their limbs out from their trunks. The grass transmogrifies into charcoal. The tulips disintegrate into ashes. Molten lava erupts forth from the burning soil. Heat consumes and devours the earth. Two days. Two days. Two days. So says mi Diooos!

**SCENE FOURTEEN**

*TWO DAYS LATER. LIGHTS RISE ON DOLORES' BEDROOM. DOLORES SITS UP IN BED. GRISELDA PACES.*

DOLORES: Paciencia.

GRISELDA: Two days is plenty of patience for a newly married man.

DOLORES: She is scared.

GRISELDA: And sick.

DOLORES: She is young.

GRISELDA: And disturbed.

DOLORES: Ay por favor, ten compasión.

GRISELDA: Your daughter put my son under a spell and he could not think for himself before he married her. He lost his mind at the altar.

DOLORES: To lie with a husband is frightening for las virgenes.

GRISELDA: Pero dos dias, amiga, is not normal. A few hours. One day maybe. But not two days!

DOLORES: Tonight will be the night.

GRISELDA: Maybe yesterday when you said that, I could have believed you. But now...I cannot.

DOLORES: I was wrong yesterday. Tonight, Griselda. Esta nochecita.

GRISELDA: My son and I will go to Father Pena for an annulment. The church has rules about this.

DOLORES: No...no...por favor...one more night.

GRISELDA: Dolores...we've been friends since our youth. You have always been a good person. You pray every day. You are kind to your loved ones. But your luck has been terible. A husband who dies at an early age. And you lying in bed, unable to get up, living with two locas...locas daughters for children. Ay...I do not know why this happens to you.

DOLORES: Suffering teaches us about life.

GRISELDA: Bueno...pues your mother named you after suffering. Dolor.

DOLORES: Sí amiga.

GRISELDA: Pero, there are limites. A family can take only so much pain. Reynaldo is a good boy, Dolores. He only asks for what is rightfully his now.

DOLORES: He must be just a little more patient.

GRISELDA: He kisses her and she runs out of the room saying, "I will disappoint you."? Then, he sits on his bed pulling at his hair and crying out her name in agony and frustration. His patience has vanished.

*A FEW BEATS.*

DOLORES: (meekly) Por favor, Griselda?

GRISELDA: Bueno...(beat) I will leave you alone and give this marriage one very last opportunity. I expect cheerful news tomorrow morning or

Reynaldo and I will go straight to Father Pena for the annulment. After todo eso, I am not going to end up alone with no son y no grandchildren. I will go and find m'ijo another esposa. I will receive the reward I deserve in life after so many years of agony.

DOLORES: You will have wonderful news.

GRISELDA: Espero que sí!

DOLORES: Gracias...adios, querida amiga.

GRISELDA: Hasta mañana.

*GRISELDA EXITS.*

**SCENE FIFTEEN**

*LIGHTS RISE ON CONNIE KNEELING BY THE RIVER.*

CONNIE: (praying) Dios, Reynaldo desires hijos of his own flesh and blood. Even you wanted one. I've tried to follow your will. But I cannot continue. The road is too steep and my feet are getting cut on all the shards of glass and stone that mark the way. (beat)  You sent el angel to Joseph in his dreams...you opened his eyes and ears to the truth about his beloved virgen fiancee Maria giving birth. (beat) I can't tell Reynaldo. If he knows he won't have any children of his own then he'll become angry and abandon me...and no other man will desire me...and I will be truly desolate... more barren than before. I will die an early death because of my looming grief and suffering. (beat)  It was so much easier when it was just me and you.(beat) If Reynaldo's going to stay with me, you must show him. A sign. A message. Something? Por favor? Now?! Amen.

**SCENE SIXTEEN**

*LIGHTS RISE ON DOLORES IN BED.*

DOLORES: (praying, frantic) Please Dios. Please Dios. Concepción and Reynaldo. Por favor. Mira, now that m'ija is married, I'll come to you soon, mi Dios.

*CONNIE, WEARING A NIGHTGOWN, ENTERS RUNNING AND JUMPS ONTO DOLORES' BED.*

CONNIE: Mami, no puedo.

DOLORES: Ven aqui.

*CONNIE RESTS HER HEAD ON HER MOTHER'S CHEST.*

DOLORES: Try, m'ija. Try. No te preocupes tanto.

CONNIE: Mami, but I can't.

*REYNALDO ENTERS RUNNING.*

REYNALDO: Ay pero Dolores. This is outrageous, ridiculous, preposterous, increible!

*CONNIE HIDES HERSELF IN HER MOTHER'S CHEST.*

REYNALDO: Tell your daughter I am a gentle, emotional, spiritual man and I will not hurt her!

DOLORES: Listen to your esposo, m'ija.

*CONNIE NODS AND BEGINS TO WEEP.*

REYNALDO: Bueno, Concepción, come with me to bed.

CONNIE: Reynaldo...it's...impossible for you to have what you desire.

*AURORA ENTERS THE ROOM. SHE IS IN A TRANCE-LIKE STATE. SHE WEARS THE SAME TATTERED CLOTHES AS BEFORE.*

AURORA: (to Connie and Reynaldo) Your inner cores prepare to boil. Gaseous fumes will mount on dragon fly wings soaring high into the stratosphere. Swirling particles will magnetize forming electric currents which will consume each body. The sky will coagulate and burst forth a message. A message will arrive on wings of chirping pajaritos...tiny doves floating gently above the squalor.

*DOLORES, SMILING, MUMBLES PRAYERS UNDER HER BREATH.*
*AURORA PACES BACK AND FORTH MUMBLING TO HERSELF.*
*CONNIE CLOSES HER EYES AND BEGINS TO PRAY SILENTLY.*
*REYNALDO BEGINS TO GRAB HIS HAIR IN UTTER FRUSTRATION.*
*THE LOW SOUNDS RISE IN INTENSITY AND BURST FORTH WITH*
*REYNALDO'S CRY.*

REYNALDO: Ayyyyyyyyy es que no puedo. I cannot suffer any longer.
My manhood demands restitution. The wedding union of body and soul.
Our bodies together. "And they became one flesh." That's what Dios says.
That's what Dios wants!

*THE ROOM FILLS WITH A STRANGE LIGHT AND SOUND. ALL STOP*
*AND LOOK UP AS CONNIE BEGINS TO LEVITATE IN FRONT OF*
*THEM.*

DOLORES: Ay, Dios. Ay, Dios. Eres tu!

AURORA: THE MESSAGE ARRIVES!

*CONNIE SPEAKS PROPHETICALLY AS SHE RISES ABOVE THE BED.*

CONNIE: Concepción. Reynaldo. The two shall be as one. They shall not
bear children of their own. They shall take in niños. Theirs shall be a house
filled with infant faces from all over the earth. They shall be blessed. They
shall nurture the lost and unwanted souls, and create for them a home. So
says your Dios.

AURORA: Dios has spoken. It is him.  He has come on a shining cloud.

DOLORES: (praying) Eres tu! Eres tu! Mi salvación!

AURORA: I no longer revel in la tierra. I now soar in el espíritu.

DOLORES: Ya vengo. Here I come.

AURORA: (praying) I release my ways to you. I release them.

| AURORA: | DOLORES: |
|---|---|
| (simultaneous) | (simultaneous) |
| Take me. Take me. | Here I come. I am coming |
| Take me. TAKE ME!!!! | to you, mi Dios. |

*AURORA COLLAPSES IN A HEAP ON THE FLOOR. DOLORES GETS UP OUT OF HER BED. SHE STANDS AND RAISES HER ARMS TO THE SKY. SHE CLOSES HER EYES AND SMILES. SHE THEN SLUMPS DOWN ONTO THE FLOOR NEXT TO THE BED AND DIES.*

*CONNIE DESCENDS BACK ONTO THE BED.*

REYNALDO: (ecstatic) Una profeta. I married una profeta. Like in La Biblia.

CONNIE: Reynaldo...we will have niños...but...

REYNALDO: (awed) Concepción. You are precious. (beat) We will take in children. I don't need niños of my own flesh and blood. (beat) I have you. You are holy. (beat) You are my wife.

CONNIE: Oh Rey...

*REYNALDO AND CONNIE: FALL ON TOP OF EACH OTHER ON DOLORES' BED. BLACK OUT.*

**END OF ACT ONE**

**ACT TWO**

**SCENE ONE**

*ONE DAY LATER. LIGHTS RISE ON CONNIE AND REYNALDO DANCING IN THE KITCHEN AROUND THE TABLE. (THE DANCE SHOULD BE PLAYFUL, THEN SEXY, THEN JUBILANT).*

REYNALDO: (playful) Argentina, Bolivia, Brasil...

CONNIE: (playful) Chile, Colombia, Costa Rica, Cuba...

REYNALDO: (sexy) Eeecuaaadooor, El Sssalllvaaadooor, Essspaaaañaaa

CONNIE: (sexy) Guatemaaalaaaa, Honduuuraaaas, Méeejicooo

REYNALDO: (sexy) Nicaraaaguaaaa, Paaanaaamáaaa

CONNIE: (sexy) Paaaraaaguaaayyy

REYNALDO: (jubilant) Perú! Puerto Rico! República Dominicana!

CONNIE: (jubilant) Uruguay! Venezuela!

REYNALDO AND CONNIE: (exultant) From all over the earth!

REYNALDO: De todos partes we will take in children. We will be like los pied pipers...con todos los niños. "Theirs shall be a house filled with infant faces from all over the earth...."

REYNALDO AND CONNIE: "They shall be blessed. They shall nurture the lost and unwanted souls, and create for them a home.."

CONNIE: Our home. Nuestro hogar.

REYNALDO: Two.

CONNIE: Four.

REYNALDO: Eight!

CONNIE: Ten!

REYNALDO: (rhetorically) And how do we find enough food to feed them all?!

REYNALDO AND CONNIE: Dios!

REYNALDO: What did he whisper to you today?

CONNIE: We didn't talk.

REYNALDO: Because you were too busy with your nuevo esposo.

CONNIE: I mean I talked and He listened. Then I sat silently while a warmth consumed my hands and slowly traveled up my arms enveloping my chest in tranquility and peace. (beat) You could talk to him too.

REYNALDO: (emphatic) No...no no...one profeta is enough for this house. (beat) I will ask you and you will ask him for me y es todo. (beat) Before I saw you, I was so afraid my life would become desolate. Toiling in the city at the steel mill. Sweating and pounding surrounded by steaming machinery. Traveling home a deserted road. Eating stale bread and rotting meat. Falling asleep on an old, stained mattress in the middle of a barren room and repeating the same thing over and over again each day...week...month...year. But now...with you, querida, my life will never be dismal...not even for one minuto.

CONNIE: Never, querido.

REYNALDO: We are walking a spiritual path...living a prophecy...como en la Biblia.

CONNIE: Una vida santificada. A holy and mysterious plan. Full of pleasure and peace...our bodies and souls now one.

*THEY KISS.*

**SCENE TWO**

*LIGHTS RISE ON FATHER PENA STANDING IN THE FIELD IN FRONT OF DOLORES' GRAVE. GRISELDA HOLDS A HANDKERCHIEF AND DABS HER EYES. CONNIE AND REYNALDO HOLD HANDS AND SMILE AT EACH OTHER, STILL EXPERIENCING THEIR NUPTIAL BLISS. EACH HOLDS A FLOWER.*

FATHER PENA:
(singing a capella)
Cordero de Dios
Ayúdanos

FATHER PENA, GRISELDA, CONNIE AND REYNALDO:
(singing a capella)
En nuestro dolor
Cordero de Dios

Ayúdanos
Danos paz

Cordero de Dios
Ayúdanos
Danos paz

*REYNALDO AND CONNIE KISS.*

FATHER PENA: Lamb de Dios help us in our pain. (entranced by the kiss, to himself) Ay Dios...(catching himself...then to the others) Lamb de Dios help us. Grant us peace.

GRISELDA: Reynaldo!

FATHER PENA: (to Griselda) Dios...is granting them peace.

GRISELDA: She cannot grieve for her poor Mami if her husband is kissing her. My son made a mistake marrying into this familia. Ay y that Aurora...I don't care if she lives in a convento now. Aren't the nuns holy enough to allow her to come to her own Mami's funeral?

FATHER PENA: Aurora is communing with the holy mysteries. She is with us in spirit.

GRISELDA: I never liked the church. Too many rules y complications. What is important is la familia. Eat. Drink. Sleep. Y la Familia.

FATHER PENA: Bueno...Dios hears you.

GRISELDA: You priests are the crazy ones. No familia and running around in a dress. Locos todos!

FATHER PENA: En el nombre del Padre, del hijo y del Espíritu Santo. Amen.

*ONE BY ONE, EACH TOSSES A FLOWER ONTO DOLORES' GRAVE.*

GRISELDA: Ay pobrecita, y she was so young.

FATHER PENA: She died in la gloria.

GRISELDA: She died because of that loca daughter of hers. Too much excitement. Levitation? Ridículo! She died after years of anguish over her crazy children. She was a good woman.

FATHER PENA: Spiritual mysteries.

GRISELDA: No mystery. People do not levitate. Estupido. That girl is loca and now my son is married to her. Look at him! He is under her spell. Why Padre, why?

FATHER PENA: You must have faith, señora.

GRISELDA: And end up like Dolores? Dead? In la tierra? Y no grandchildren? No gracias, Padre. (beat) Reynaldo, show respect for the dead.

*REYNALDO AND CONNIE STILL CANNOT TAKE THEIR EYES OFF EACH OTHER.*

REYNALDO: Happiness. Peace. Contentment. Joy. This is what Dolores wanted for us.

CONNIE: Gifts of the spirit.

GRISELDA: Your mother's dead body lies in front of you y look how you behave...

CONNIE: Mami's soul is dancing in heaven.

GRISELDA: Standing there staring at each other with loco eyes.

REYNALDO: My life submitted to my glorious wife...mi vida sometida a mi esposa gloooriosaaaa.

GRISELDA: Now he is loco too.

REYNALDO: You just don't understand, Mami...in time you might...if you open yourself up to the possibilities.

GRISELDA: What have they done to you, m'ijo? I should be mourning the death of my son here today, Padre, because I do not recognize this young man.

FATHER PENA: He is experiencing a spiritual transformation.

GRISELDA: He has been put under a spell by these curanderas. TODAS SON BRUJAS. BRUJAS DEL DEMONIO. My son possessed by witches from the devil. Ya me voy. LOCOS TODOS. CRAZY. CRAZY. CRAZY.

*GRISELDA EXITS SCREAMING AND CRYING. FATHER PENA LOOKS ADMIRINGLY AT CONNIE. REYNALDO AND CONNIE HAVE NOT MOVED FROM THEIR PASSIONATE GAZE.*

FATHER PENA: Bueno...III'm going for...ahhh...a little swim in the river. All this...ahhh...paaassionate...mourning...makes e...sssweaty...and… hh...parched. (beat, awkward silence) Aanyone...cccare to join me?

*REYNALDO PICKS CONNIE UP IN HIS ARMS.*

REYNALDO: No gracias, Padre.

CONNIE: Adios, Padre

*REYNALDO AND CONNIE KISS AS THEY EXIT. FATHER PENA KNEELS.*

FATHER PENA: (praying) Ayúdame. Please. I know I shouldn't be entertaining these sentiments but I am. Her eyes like shimmering pools, her neck like a glistening tower, and her...breasts like two fawns that feed among the lilies. Ay Padre Nuestro, help me. Por favor. Amen.

**SCENE THREE**

*ONE WEEK LATER. LIGHTS RISE ON REYNALDO STANDING IN THE BEDROOM, PACKING CLOTHING INTO A LEATHER SATCHEL AND LOOKING AT CONNIE. HE WEARS A SUIT. CONNIE SITS ON THE BED NEXT TO HIM. SHE WEARS A NIGHTGOWN AND HOLDS A BIBLE, GLANCING DOWN AND THEN LOOKING UP AT REYNALDO.*

CONNIE: See how Dios likes el sexo? Solomon's bride writes to her husband,"My beloved is all radiant and ruddy. His cheeks are like beds of spices yielding fragrance. His lips are lilies, distilling liquid myrrh." Bueno, it's been six hours, don't you think it's time...again?

*SHE TRIES TO PULL HIM DOWN ONTO THE BED.*

REYNALDO: Querida, I have to travel to the city...for <u>us</u>.

CONNIE: Pero La Concepción is so sexy.

REYNALDO: The mill could only give me a late afternoon interview. They're hiring hombres with no previous experience...

CONNIE: After six glorious days, don't you want to continue to lie for hours and hours and frolic in la cama with your esposita? You know, on the seventh day Dios rested...but we don't have to...

*CONNIE TRIES TO PULL HIM ONTO THE BED AGAIN. REYNALDO FALLS ONTO THE BED, THEN PULLS HIMSELF AWAY.*

REYNALDO: Querida, believe me, I would love to, I would...but after we spend all day and night en la cama, we have to eat...and the money from my carpentry isn't be enough to support you and myself and una familia.

CONNIE: Pero, when los niños arrive, Dios will provide for us...

REYNALDO: How? How do you know? He told you the details of his plan?

CONNIE: Well not exactly. But I know he will.

REYNALDO: Bueno until he does, I need to be sure we have enough food to feed us all.

CONNIE: So let me travel with you, we'll be like María and Joseph...passing through the big city gates...riding on a donkey...well, okay so we don't have un burro, but that's okay, Dios would understand...

REYNALDO: I'll be gone one day only.

CONNIE: No entiendo, just a few days ago you believed in the prophecy...in our vida together with los niños...

REYNALDO: I still do...but would Dios want us lying around waiting for miracles to fall out of the sky when concrete oportunidades materialize right in front of us?

CONNIE: I think we just have to be patient...for his timing.

REYNALDO: Connie, te quiero muchíssimo but I've been having alarming visions in my sleep. In my nocturnal mind, I'm a ravenous canine, in the front yard, digging my sharp incisors and salivating tongue into la tierra, attempting to devour large mouthfuls of soil and grass because I have no food for our table.

CONNIE: And where are los babies in your dream?

REYNALDO: I can't see them...

CONNIE: Because they haven't been placed on our doorstep yet...

REYNALDO: Yet.

CONNIE: But they will. You know they will.

REYNALDO: Of course, they will, cariño.

CONNIE: Bueno, if you have to leave, come back so soon to your sexy esposita.

REYNALDO: As soon as I humanly can.

*HE KISSES HER.*

AURORA: (offstage) Connie? Reynaldo?

*AURORA ENTERS WEARING A BROWN NUN'S TUNIC WITH VEIL, HOOD AND BELT.*

CONNIE: Aurora...

AURORA: Postulant Aurora...

CONNIE: Una monja.

REYNALDO: Aurora...you look so...so...calm.

AURORA: La serenidad. The hermanas say your body transforms internally when you encounter Dios.

CONNIE AND REYNALDO: Religiosa.

AURORA: I now revel in the sanctity of sisterly life...opening my arms to the Almighty...fixing my eyes on the aisle I will walk down as I become a holy wife of Jesucristo. (beat) The hermanas gave me leave for a short visit to say...adios to mi familia and my earthly existence before I take my vows of poverty, chastity and obedience.

CONNIE AND REYNALDO: Increible.

AURORA: And I've also decided to take the vow of isolation...to be sequestered from the world...so that I no longer encourage any temptation.

CONNIE: We can't even visit you?

AURORA: You can only see me singing and praying with the other hermanas behind the grill work on the other side of the altar during mass.

REYNALDO: La vida santificada agrees with you then.

AURORA: I feel pure as una virgen.

CONNIE AND REYNALDO: Ay Dios is powerful.

CONNIE: Do you have to say farewell to all your earthly existence?

AURORA: It's what Dios wants.

REYNALDO: Then, I'll let you say farewell to Concepción...alone.

*REYNALDO KISSES CONNIE.*

REYNALDO: (to Connie) I'll be back en la mañana. (to Aurora) May you continue to find happiness...Que Dios te bendiga, Postulant Aurora.

*REYNALDO PUTS ON A HAT AND EXITS.*

CONNIE: I have a new, hermoso husband, Aurora.

AURORA: And soon I will marry Jesucristo, the holiest hombre of all.

CONNIE: Oh the earthly delights...ay Aurora, his bare body holds me so close en la cama...

AURORA: I will walk down the aisle and take his holy hand...

CONNIE: His fantástico frame lies tangled in mine...

AURORA: And we will join together

CONNIE: I never imagined I'd do IT...

AURORA: In saintly spiritual bliss...

CONNIE: Again and again and again...

| AURORA: | CONNIE: |
|---|---|
| (simultaneous) | (simultaneous) |
| Singing A-lle-lu-ia... | Hermana, ay, ay, ay |

CONNIE: Such satisfaction, more than I could imagine. Mami was right when she said Rey would teach me. I'm learning a lot.

AURORA: He's a...talented teacher?

CONNIE: At first I was..shaking and shivering all over...but his gentleness guided me...slowly at first, some pain, then pleasure, then pain, then pleasure and then pleasure, more pleasure, more pleasure, and then hermana, ay what joy y felicidad!

AURORA: (boastful) I myself no longer need the carnal pleasures...they could pull me away from my new calling. I now pray every hour, in my cell or in the chapel. (beat) Do you still pray every hour, in the field and in your room?

CONNIE: I've been too busy lately.

AURORA: All day and night?

CONNIE: Being una esposa in bed takes up a lot of time.

AURORA: (boastful) I no longer even think of my former days. The novice mistress, Hermana Angelica, says I am the most promising postulant to enter el convento in years... (alternately spiritual then sensual) In my cell...I pray on my mat and soon I begin to picture my holy esposo to be...his curvaceous loins barely covered by a tiny cotton cloth...as he hangs on una cruz...yet so gentle...caressing me...with his hands...pulling me...to his chest...fulfilling me in every way.

CONNIE: What lives we now lead with new husbands, hermana.

| AURORA: | CONNIE: |
|---|---|
| (simultaneous) | (simultaneous) |
| (melancholy) So joyful. | (ecstatic) So joyful. |

AURORA: And the promise, prophecy? When are you starting your wonderful familia with your maravilloso, handsome husband?

CONNIE: We're still waiting for them to arrive on our doorstep. My desire to be una madre grows inside me each day.

AURORA: You will be una maravillosa madre with your esposo.

CONNIE: Oh, I want to visit you to receive the guidance I so desperately need.

AURORA: You seem to be doing just fine, hermana.

CONNIE: But like how do I keep him contento in our bed...hour after hour...so he doesn't run to the city, like he just did?

AURORA: Ay hermana, the carnal pleasures no longer concern me.

CONNIE: Not even one little piece of advice...ahorita?

AURORA: Bueno...(beat) The hips. Touch them. Know them. Move them. Side to side. Back and forth. Up and down. Yours. And his.

CONNIE: Así?

*CONNIE PLACES HER HANDS ON HER HIPS AND MOVES THEM BACK AND FORTH AWKWARDLY.*

AURORA: Sí. Dios gave them to you for a reason...maybe not to bear niños in this vida but to bring pleasure to you and your husband.

CONNIE: Keep praying for me, hermana.

AURORA: I will pray every hour for you...and your husband. Adios, hermana.

*AURORA AND CONNIE EMBRACE.*

**SCENE FOUR**

*LIGHTS RISE ON AURORA BY THE GARDEN. SHE PICKS THE SOLE REMAINING TULIP FROM THE GROUND.*

AURORA: The cool crimson petals against my palm...so distant now. The jade stems against my fingertips...the only remaining evidence of my earthly decadence.

*AURORA DROPS THE TULIP AND EXITS.*

**SCENE FIVE**

*FIVE WEEKS LATER. LIGHTS RISE ON CONNIE IN THE KITCHEN. SHE STIRS A POT AND HOLD SPICES IN HER HANDS. SHE AWKWARDLY TRIES TO SWAY HER HIPS BACK AND FORTH AS SHE STIRS.*

CONNIE: Rosemary, roguish glance. No. Uh...Rosemary, rolling dance?

REYNALDO: (offstage) Where are my black socks?

CONNIE: In the dresser drawer. (beat) Thyme, tip-toe. No. Thyme, tango?

REYNALDO: (offstage) And my white linen shirt?

CONNIE: In the closet behind the grey jacket (beat)  Oregano, organismic festivities? Ay no puedo.

*CONNIE THROWS A BUNCH OF SPICES IN THE POT AND BEGINS TO STIR FURIOUSLY. REYNALDO ENTERS.*

CONNIE: Soup, Reynaldo?

REYNALDO: I'm dining with the men from the mill tonight.

CONNIE: Again? Ay pero, Reynaldo...this is my special soup for mi esposo...to help you feel so sensual and...

*SHE KISSES HIM LIGHTLY. HE DOES NOT RESPOND.*

REYNALDO: Not now, querida. I must protect mi apetito.

CONNIE: But I made it especially for you. My first time trying Aurora's recipes...I remembered how much you liked her soup...it tastes just like hers...I hope.

REYNALDO: Gracias, mi amor, pero this time the big honchos have invited me to a huge meal...pollo asado, arroz, platanos, vino and a feast of the ripest fruta. They like my work at the mill and want to discuss "my future in molten steel."

CONNIE: Not even a little soup...to whet your apetito?

REYNALDO: Not tonight, querida. (beat) Connie. Mira.

*CONNIE SLAMS THE WOODEN SPOON DOWN ONTO THE TABLE.*

CONNIE: (desperate, suddenly) Five weeks pass...and I've stopped talking to Dios. I sit here alone day after day. And I lie in bed motionless night after night. And I feel dry like the grass in the field burned brown by the sun's scorching heat.

REYNALDO: Without my job at the mill we would be begging in the streets for our food, living a life of pestilence and squalor.

CONNIE: And now not even one child. Ni uno, Reynaldo.

REYNALDO: Who ever heard of a newlywed couple with no money adopting children?

CONNIE: First you stopped creating objects out of pine, spruce, maple...

REYNALDO: And even if we did adopt the child of another man's loins... the baby grows up and feels diferente than your kind...

CONNIE: Then you wanted loud machines not silent, patient peace...

REYNALDO: And rebels...

CONNIE: Slowly you stopped trusting the promise and followed the ways of the metallic noise...

REYNALDO: And then it's la vida en el infierno.

CONNIE: You listened to all those men at the mill...and hardened inside...and stopped trusting Dios.

REYNALDO: I never really knew Dios.

CONNIE: You didn't give Him enough time.

REYNALDO: I was listening to my hormones and I thought I was having a religious experience. Sexuality and spirituality kissed each other on the lips.

CONNIE: You stopped trusting and now my body grows cold, no fire for the earthly pleasures, and my ears grow deaf, my eyes blind, no fuel for the spiritual urgings.

REYNALDO: Only niños of one's own flesh and blood. (beat) If I can't have that then I don't want any.

CONNIE: But I want niños...to live my life in the countryside with mis hijos, mi esposo y mi Dios.

REYNALDO: All I desire is my wife. I come home from the mill. I'm with her and that's enough.

*REYNALDO PLACES HIS HAND ON HER ARM AND KISSES CONNIE WHO RECEIVES HIS KISS COLDLY.*

REYNALDO: Don't be ungrateful for all I'm doing for you.

CONNIE: My arms frozen.

REYNALDO: Don't release our connection.

CONNIE: My lips numb.

REYNALDO: At night, when I try to caress you underneath the covers in the darkness, I no longer recognize the woman who lies there motionless.

CONNIE: Emptiness fills my body.

REYNALDO: I'll be back late.

CONNIE: Couldn't this be a farewell dinner, and you'll say adios to the mill and stay with me in the countryside?

REYNALDO: No.

CONNIE: Oh. (beat) I won't wait up for you.

REYNALDO: Connie. Concepción. Mira. (beat) The power of molten steel...a raw...sheer force. You can't comprehend the beauty of it. Only three weeks of training and I started working with this spectacular, gargantuan substance and making good money for us...such power and profit. Tons of red hot steel...it will burn you to death if it touches you, the steel will burrow inside your skin looking for carbon until you are a heap of smoking flesh. We corral death every day...we play god...supernatural power in our own hands.

CONNIE: Supernatural power.

REYNALDO: Sí. Exacto. (beat) Through my glasses, I watch the sparks fly and I feel my bones quiver and my throat vibrates and the furnace pops and my whole chest spasms. And then the arc light heat grows and expands until the burning substance is almost twice as hot as the surface of the sun. These are ancient rituals, querida. Men have been melting metal since before the days of your Virgen María and Jesucristo.

CONNIE: María. Ave María. Gone.

REYNALDO: And a golden light fills the melt shop as the furnace gives birth to a shining, new heat of steel.

CONNIE: Gives birth.

REYNALDO: They're going to promote me to melt shop manager. They see I have ease and confidence with this work. You can't even begin to comprehend the force of what I deal with daily. (beat) This is my power, querida. (beat) You have your spiritual Mass. I have my molten mass. Es así. (beat) No more worrying about money. We live a tranquil life. You are tired but you will regain your strength.(beat) I'll see you in the morning.

*REYNALDO EXITS. CONNIE TASTES THE SOUP AND QUICKLY SPITS IT BACK INTO THE POT.*

**SCENE SIX**

*ONE DAY LATER. LIGHTS RISE ON GRISELDA AND CONNIE SITTING AT THE KITCHEN TABLE. THEY PACK BABY CLOTHES INTO A BOX.*

GRISELDA: Nietos. I always wanted them. Your mami did too. But Reynaldo told me,"No Mamá, I will not do it." y I cried...tristíssima.

CONNIE: He'll never change his mind.

GRISELDA: Why did your mother lie to me? Why didn't you tell Reynaldo you could never bear him niños of your own? Why?

CONNIE: (sharply) I couldn't, Griselda.

GRISELDA: Oh...you couldn't. Do you know how long I have waited for grandchildren? When Manuel left once I was pregnant with Reynaldo, I swore I would never be alone again...that one day I would be surrounded by mi niño, his esposa y mis nietos. But soon I will die with no one to love.

CONNIE: I did not want it this way.

GRISELDA: If you had told m'ijo, he could have left in time, I could have found him another esposa and you could have gone off to el convento like your sister.

CONNIE: You have no nietos, Griselda. But at least you have one hijo. And I will have neither.

GRISELDA: But now I am losing the only hijo I have...leaving just like his padre...head like a piece of burning granite...will like a furnace of molten steel.

CONNIE: Carnal pleasures have dismayed me. Oh...I want to hide my face in your breast again, Mami, and lie on your bed in safety.

GRISELDA: That's where you should have stayed...in her bed and not with m'ijo.

CONNIE: Magnets pull me down into the ground. Ay Mami.

GRISELDA: Ay Reynaldo.

CONNIE:
(singing)
Los dolores de la vida son
Misterios que Dios nos da
Para alentarnos con
Paz, Gozo y Alegría

CONNIE: In our life the suffering...Mysteries from his Holiness...For our very strengthening...Peace, Joy and Happiness. (beat) I don't understand.

## SCENE SEVEN

*ONE DAY LATER. LIGHTS RISE ON CONNIE SITTING AT THE KITCHEN TABLE. REYNALDO ENTERS WEARING A SHINY, NEW SUIT. SHE POURS HIM A CUP OF COFFEE.*

REYNALDO: REYNALDO'S...MOLTEN...MASS...PRODUCTION. I'll wear a new tie to work every day. I'll receive a brand new pair of furnace greens and I will supervise all phases of liquid steel. (beat) And I'll be earning three times my old salary, querida. We'll be able to buy a huge house in the city. I'll buy you elegant silk dresses and shining metal tables and chairs and a whole new existence. I will continue to rise up in factory management...melt shop manager...floor foreman...mill supervisor...and then one day..mill owner. (beat) They like me and trust me, querida. And I am working so hard for them. (beat) Come give your esposo a kiss.

*REYNALDO KISSES HER AND SHE RESPONDS COLDLY.*

REYNALDO: I'm going to gather some ripe vegetales from our garden...so we can savor the fruta of la tierra as we prepare to say adios to our country existence.

*REYNALDO EXITS. FATHER PENA ENTERS.*

FATHER PENA: Pardon me Concepción...

CONNIE: Father Pena...

FATHER PENA: But on my way back to the chapel, I needed to visit...

CONNIE: (motioning for him to sit down) Café?

FATHER PENA: No gracias. (beat) Oh...Connie...your eyes are radiant...

CONNIE: My eyes...arid pebbles housed in tired sockets...

FATHER PENA: You maintain such an air of faithfulness about you.

CONNIE: No remnant of faith remains, Padre.

FATHER PENA: Oh...to be connected to you...to live just one day under the same roof...

CONNIE: You pray, Padre...

FATHER PENA: All the time...for you...uh...I mean....for two...for two...three... four...ten...people a day...my daily office.

CONNIE: but I can't anymore.

FATHER PENA: Perhaps I could say a quick prayer for you?

CONNIE: I no longer hear the heavenly whisperings...your words will descend on deafness...but if you want to...bueno...

FATHER PENA: (praying) Padre nuestro...be with your servant Concepción.... please let her know how much I...ay Dios...how much you care for her. En el nombre del Padre, del Hijo, del Espíritu santo. Amen. (beat) Oh...Concepción...how can you continue to exude such saintliness without flying up to heaven in a moment?

CONNIE: Sainthood...no longer even a possibility...a thought...an action.

FATHER PENA: On the contrary...so close...mind you, the veneration, beatification and canonization process is a long and arduous one...but I can see the evidence radiating in front of me...if I could only have just one ounce...just a droplet of that...

CONNIE: I can't bear this desert any longer, Padre.

FATHER PENA: Oh...neither can I...

CONNIE: I long for cool currents to carry me.

FATHER PENA: Such cool currents...

CONNIE: For whispering in my ear again...

FATHER PENA: So tenderly...

CONNIE: For the warm embrace, Padre...

FATHER PENA: Oh sí...

CONNIE: of mi Dios...

FATHER PENA: Ay Dios!

*REYNALDO ENTERS HOLDING A TOMATO. FATHER PENA IS STARTLED.*

FATHER PENA: Reynaldo...I was just...ah...saying hello to your lovely...wife...on my way back to the chapel...I thought I would stop by to say hello...so...hello...yes...and well...adios. Yes. Adios.

*FATHER PENA STUMBLES OUT OF THE ROOM.*

REYNALDO: Religious men should not be so concerned with the wives of industrial men.

CONNIE: His tenderness frightens you.

REYNALDO: His lack of restraint concerns me...

CONNIE: You see him attempting to comfort and it confounds you...

AURORA: (offstage) Reynaldo? Connie?

*AURORA ENTERS IN A NUN'S HABIT.*

CONNIE: (weakly) Hermana...

*REYNALDO CHECKS HER OUT AND FINDS HER ATTRACTIVE.*

REYNALDO: Aurora...

AURORA: We're moving to a new convento.

REYNALDO: Sit down. Relax. This is your home.

AURORA: I have permission to visit you for twenty-four hours.

CONNIE: Stay with us, hermana.

*CONNIE EMBRACES AURORA AND KISSES HER ON THE CHEEK. REYNALDO APPROACHES AURORA AND KISSES HER ON THE CHEEK.*

AURORA: Y los niños...your familia...your joyful life in the countryside?

CONNIE: Reynaldo didn't believe in the promise...he doubted...

REYNALDO: To doubt is to be human.

CONNIE: He no longer believes in Dios.

REYNALDO: (to Connie) Can you prove his existence?

CONNIE: We live a life of silence.

REYNALDO: Connie has been tired and bored lately. She yearns for a new and different life...which I'm going to give her. I'm now a steel mill manager and we're moving to the city.

AURORA: And abandon the house our Papi built with his hands?

REYNALDO: The boards on the side of the house are caving in. The steps on the front porch have rotted through. But soon we'll be in the middle of all the vibration...commotion...action.

CONNIE: Café?

AURORA: Sí.

*CONNIE EXITS.*

REYNALDO: You look hermosa.

AURORA: The hermanas say such flattery is not holy. But to hear those words...a certain former smoothness in my ear...

REYNALDO: I'm only reflecting what my eyes show me. Your Dios likes truth, doesn't he?

AURORA: During my ceremony of vows, I closed my eyes when Madre Teresina placed her hands upon my head, I felt a warmth on top of my skull, descending down my neck, my arms, my chest, my legs, and then...then....I saw...<u>you</u>. You were standing on the porch, watching me, as I walked, slowly toward this house, wearing an alabaster robe and cradling...an <u>infant</u> in my arms. And a deep longing burned in my belly. Since that day, I've been feeling my fertility resurgent, hour after hour, day after week, unable to do anything but pray and cry out to Dios, my internal tide shifting and an ancient ritual resurfacing, one I never thought I'd desire.

REYNALDO: So now you desire un niño of your own flesh and blood?

AURORA: Oh sí. The hermanas did not give me permission to leave. We are not moving to a new convento. I needed to escape. And I will not return. Any hermana leaving el convento unlawfully receives excommunication.

*CONNIE ENTERS WITH A COFFEE CUP. CONNIE POURS AURORA COFFEE.*

CONNIE: I want to hear all about your ceremony...how you entered the holy of holies. You can stay the whole day and night, right?

AURORA: (looking at Reynaldo) Sí.

CONNIE: Seeing you I am ashamed of the woman I've become.

GRISELDA: (offstage) (calling, sing-song) Reynaldo...Concepción...

*GRISELDA ENTERS.*

GRISELDA: No me digas. La monja. The nun has returned to visit.

AURORA: Hola señora.

GRISELDA: (a little leary) Muy buenas.

REYNALDO: She's moving to a new convento.

GRISELDA: (intrigued) Que bueno...is there any room for new postulants? (to Aurora) Maybe your sister could join you there. (to all) I've been talking to Father Pena about the rules for annulment...which he has been explaining to me quite happily. If the marriage consent was not an act of free will, but one of coercion or grave, external fear, then the marriage can be declared invalid. What good news!

REYNALDO: Mamá!

GRISELDA: Connie was coerced and terrified...so we can nullify the marriage...find you una nueva esposa and Connie can become una religiosa.

REYNALDO: Por favor...

GRISELDA: (to Reynaldo) And you can finally have your own niños.

REYNALDO: Basta ya!

GRISELDA: (to Reynaldo) Es la verdad!

AURORA: (to Reynaldo) How is the garden? I want to touch the remains of my former days.

REYNALDO: I've planted tomatoes and other vegetables where the tulips used to grow. The ground is still so fertile. So...I'll show you if you like.

AURORA: I would.

*AURORA AND REYNALDO START TO EXIT.*

AURORA: (looking at Reynaldo) I feel so contenta returning to the house of my youth.

*REYNALDO SMILES AT AURORA AS THEY EXIT.*

GRISELDA: Mi corazón me habla. My heart moans to me, "Beware of the nun."

CONNIE: (in her own world) Maybe she'll bring new life into this house.

GRISELDA: Mi corazón is sinking into the ground. Los ojos. His eyes. Her eyes.

CONNIE: (in her own world) Her eyes...so peaceful.

GRISELDA: I smell odors in the air. A familiar fertile scent from many months ago.

CONNIE: (in her own world) The aroma of new life.

GRISELDA: M'ijo...the one jewel I have left in this vida...Ay Reynaldo, por favor...

CONNIE: (in her own world) Fertile, fantástica vida.

GRISELDA: Mi esposo Manuel ran off with la puta, the baker's wife, and I was left alone. Beware.

## SCENE EIGHT

*LIGHTS RISE ON REYNALDO AND AURORA WALKING IN THE VEGETABLE GARDEN.*

REYNALDO: Tomatoes. Lettuce. Spinach. Collard Greens. Arugula. Watercress. So much variety. Connie wanted me to build a swing here. Just cover the ground with five or six long planks of pine, hang two pieces of sturdy rope from the papaya tree and attach a wooden seat so she could travel back and forth over this tierra. But I wanted the garden to continue to grow. I felt the need to till the soil and plant new life.

AURORA: Hard to imagine I used to sleep here...lie on the earth.

REYNALDO: The wild days of a former existence.

AURORA: Those days seem a distant memory slowly returning to me.

REYNALDO: Your skin radiates a pure light, Aurora.

AURORA: I look at the land and I cannot imagine digging my fingers into the soft soil like I used to.

REYNALDO: Almost as if your skin is translucent.

AURORA: And the crimson blossoms dropping...petals folding into chocolate earth.

REYNALDO: Holiness becomes you.

AURORA: I see the same lustre in the tomatoes you planted here. Fertility must remain in the soil. (beat) The air still smells new.

*REYNALDO TAKES A BIG WHIFF OF THE AIR. REYNALDO LOOKS AT AURORA.*

REYNALDO: Fresh and youthful.

*AURORA LOOKS AT REYNALDO. A FEW BEATS. REYNALDO EXITS. AURORA SITS IN THE VEGETABLE GARDEN. AS SHE HOLDS A TOMATO.*

AURORA: Luscious. Plump. Sí. The earthly sensations restored to me. Seeds need to be sown. Flesh needs to be born.

*AURORA TAKES OFF HER VEIL TO REVEAL A LONG CASCADE OF HAIR.*

AURORA: Unbuttoning each button of my life of sanctification. Replacing my days of purification with procreation.

*AURORA TAKES OFF HER NUN'S TUNIC AND LIES DOWN IN HER SLIP.*

AURORA: Lying here and waiting for him.

**SCENE NINE**

*LIGHTS RISE ON REYNALDO AND CONNIE SITTING UP IN BED.*

CONNIE: I feel my nerve endings reviving...something new is stirring inside me.

REYNALDO: Bueno then querida.

*REYNALDO TRIES TO KISS CONNIE LIGHTLY ON THE NECK.*
*CONNIE DOES NOT RESPOND.*

CONNIE: Sensation returning to my body for the first time in weeks.

REYNALDO: Then share this sensation with your esposo.

CONNIE: Rey, I need to feel this aliveness for myself...before I share it with you or anyone else.

*CONNIE GETS OUT OF BED.*

REYNALDO: Ay, Connie, por favor...

CONNIE: I can't climb back underneath the covers...not now...not yet...

*REYNALDO GETS OUT OF BED.*

REYNALDO: Es que no puedo. Es que no puedo más. Nothing for the past weeks...one thousand nocturnal hours in this bed. Nada. No touch. No caress. No union. Imposible. Maybe you don't realize how much I've had to dig deep inside to try to be patient with you, Connie.

CONNIE: (lost in her own reverie) I'm receiving newness.

REYNALDO: Our awaited promise from Dios vanished, and I was contento with only my wife and my casita but Connie, I do long for a life where I can find joy en la casa, en la cama and maybe find una familia too. (beat) I've been having alarming visions in my sleep. In my nocturnal mind, I find my newborn niño in la cama but he keeps getting lost...under los covers...so small...pequeñín...then I lift up a sheet and he appears again...barely breathing...naked...his umbilical cord belly...yellowish iodine rubbed all around it...his tiny frame revived...evidence...of the possibility of my own flesh and blood.

*CONNIE, IN HER OWN WORLD, BEGINS TO TWIRL AROUND IN*
*CIRCLES WITH HER ARMS OUTSTRETCHED.*

CONNIE: Slowly the new, vibrant energy releases into my bloodstream.

*REYNALDO STUMBLES TO HIS FEET.*

REYNALDO: As the air now fills...with a familiar...fertile... fantástica fragrance.

*REYNALDO SMELLS THE AIR AS HE EXITS.*

CONNIE: All my arteries are awakening. My ears opening up again. I can hear whisperings again...frequencies from the heavenlies... Gracias mi Dios. Gracias.

*CONNIE DANCES AROUND THE ROOM IN JOY.*

**SCENE TEN**

*LIGHTS RISE ON AURORA SITTING IN THE VEGETABLE GARDEN. WEARING HER SLIP. SHE BEGINS TO DIG HER HANDS INTO THE EARTH.*

AURORA: Madre de la Tierra. I have not stopped bleeding for my renewal in you.

*SHE BRINGS A MOUND OF EARTH UP TO HER NOSE AND REVELS IN THE AROMA OF THE SOIL.*

AURORA: The flavor of familiar...fertile...fantástica life...la santa vida.

*AURORA PUTS THE SOIL BACK DOWN AND KNEEDS THE EARTH WITH HER HANDS.*

AURORA: Whispering on butterfly wings...angel's breath in his ear...no more horse hair shirt...alabaster foot...all forces convene and await...soon will arrive...now is the time for...un niño de la TIEERRRAAAA.

*REYNALDO, WEARING PANTS AND NO SHIRT OR SHOES, ENTERS. AURORA CONTINUES TO INHALE THE AROMA OF THE SOIL.*

REYNALDO: In my waking dreams I see you calling me, your luscious lips forming each syllable as your tongue flips and curls around the sounds of my name.

AURORA: RRRREY-NAAAAL-DOOOO.

REYNALDO: Traveling toward you...

AURORA: Electric currents from my face to my breast to my hips.

*THEY BEGIN WALK IN A CIRCLE AROUND EACH OTHER.*

REYNALDO: Connected to la tierra...

AURORA: The power of dark and magical jungle rituals stirring within me...reversing my gift...to remain with one man...

REYNALDO: Yearning to create together with...

AURORA: To bear him as many little ones as our hearts desire...

REYNALDO: Fantásticos, powerful hijos.

*REYNALDO TOUCHES AURORA'S ARM.*

REYNALDO: Reynaldo. Rey. King. Aurora. Dawn. Queen. King and Queen. Rey y Reina.

REYNALDO AND AURORA: NIÑOS DE LA TIERRA!

*REYNALDO AND AURORA LIE DOWN TOGETHER IN THE VEGETABLE GARDEN.*

CONNIE: (offstage) AURORA:?!

*AURORA SITS UP, HER FACE SMEARED WITH SOIL. CONNIE RUNS JUBILANTLY OUT INTO THE GARDEN. SHE DISCOVERS THE TWO OF THEM. REYNALDO STUMBLES TO HIS FEET.*

CONNIE: AURORA! (beat) Reynaldo...

AURORA: No more sanctity of sisterly life...

REYNALDO: Dreaming to see my own flesh and blood...

AURORA: The earthly sensations restored to me.

REYNALDO: Her aroma caressing my nostrils...

AURORA: Reversing my gift to remain with one man...to choose to bear new life...

REYNALDO: A life with niños of my own...

CONNIE: (to Reynaldo) Your manhood so dashed at the prospect of no hijos with me?

REYNALDO: So you can return to the joy y felicidad of your former days.

CONNIE: (to Aurora) And your desires so overwhelming that even un convento cannot contain them? All along your thoughts leading to this momento when you have him? (to Reynaldo) My desires for un niño never left me during my sleeping or waking hours...not for un minuto.

AURORA: Our former paths...are returning, Connie but now they are renewed...transformed.

CONNIE: I do want my spiritual connection restored but does that mean I have to forever relinquish the earthly life?

AURORA: You are so much more contenta in la vida religiosa and I in la vida de la tierra.

CONNIE: Bueno then... (suddenly) Fuera. Fuera. Out. Gone. Go. Leave. To the city. (beat) Aurora if you must transform the world of your youth then so must I. Reynaldo, if you will truly be contento with Aurora, then go. I cannot bear one more day of desert. Tonight I did begin to feel my former life reviving but I didn't think it would mean I would have to say adios to everyone I've ever known in this vida.

AURORA: Connie, you always yearned be una santa.

REYNALDO: La Santa Concepción.

CONNIE: Go, to the city then, adios.

*REYNALDO AND AURORA HOLD HANDS AND EXIT. CONNIE KNEELS DOWN.*

CONNIE: (praying) Ay Dios, I became a woman in this world: my childish ways gone, my eyes and ears opened, my bare skin awakened by a man's caress. My heart became flesh through Reynaldo's love yet I am still forever bereft of female fertility. More barren than before: No husband, no familia, destined to live in solitude. (beat) How can I accept the path before me now and walk on the stone and soil that may mark the way? My will gone. (beat) Por favor...your will be done.

*A STRANGE LIGHT AND MUSIC FILL THE GARDEN. CONNIE RAISES HER ARMS TO THE SKY AND CLOSES HER EYES AS SHE BEGINS TO LEVITATE. SHE RISES GRADUALLY HIGHER AND HIGHER AS SHE SPEAKS PROPHETICALLY.*

CONNIE: My Espíritu Santo now sends and sanctifies sacred cells to multiply inside you. The time is at hand. Now arrives. La Santa Concepción.

**SCENE ELEVEN**

*EIGHT MONTHS LATER. LIGHTS RISE ON FATHER PENA PACING BY THE RIVER.*

FATHER PENA: (rehearsing) Set me as a <u>seal</u> upon your heart, ah no, así no, set <u>me</u> , yes, set <u>me</u> as a seal on your heart..for love is as strong as death...many waters cannot drench...drench?...no quench, yes, quench...many waters cannot quench desire...neither can floods drown it, says Solomon...to his beloved.

*CONNIE ENTERS. HER PREGNANCY SHOWS NOTICEABLY BENEATH HER DRESS.*

CONNIE: Father Pena...

FATHER PENA: Please, call me Alfonso...

CONNIE: Alfonso...

FATHER PENA: Oh Concepción, I want to witness all the miracles that emanate from your home. (beat, boldly) I want to be your husband.

CONNIE: Oh Alfonso...wedded life will pull me away from my calling.

FATHER PENA: I'll walk quietly along side of you.

CONNIE: I must continue in solitude with mi hija y mi Dios. This time Dios wants a girl child...to teach others life through her perspective.

FATHER PENA: We'll baptize your hijita in this river.

CONNIE: I trudged through the earth to know my barrenness so I could deliver this holy niñita onto the soil of la tierra.

FATHER PENA: Wonders...milagros...beyond the powers of corporeal nature.

CONNIE: I want my heart of flesh...never again a heart of sandstone in the desert...to seek los misterios together. Holy mysteries.

*CONNIE STARES OUT OVER THE HORIZON AS THE LIGHTS FADE.*
*END OF PLAY.*

**EARTHQUAKE CHICA**
For Alicia

EARTHQUAKE CHICA was originally presented Off-Broadway on July 20, 2004 at SPF-04 (Arielle Tepper, Founder) with the following cast:

Esmeralda......................................................Camillia Sanes
Sam...........................................................Paolo Andino

The Production was directed by Leah C. Gardiner. Set Design by Cameron Anderson; Costume Design by Emilio Sosa, and Lights, Lucrecia Briseño.

EARTHQUAKE CHICA received its world premiere on June 7, 2007 at Borderlands Theater, Tucson, AZ, (Barclay Goldsmith, Producing Director) with the following cast:

Esmeralda......................................................Alida Gunn
Sam...........................................................Joe Quintero

The Production was directed by Eva Zorilla Tessler. Set and Lighting Design by Russell Stagg; Costume Design, Elizabeth Blair, and Sound Design, Jim Klingenfus.

**CHARACTERS**

ESMERALDA PORTILLO, 30's, a secretary

SAM REYES, 30's, an accountant

**SETTING**

Present. Los Angeles. An office in a downtown highrise and various city locations.

**Note:** On pages 94, 123 & 143, quotes are from "Oda a las cosas" and "Oda al diccionario" from <u>Las Odas</u> by Pablo Neruda. On pages 94 & 131, quotes are from "Luna y panorama de los insectos" and "Tu infancia en Menton" from <u>Poeta en Nueva York</u> by Federico García Lorca. On page 94 is a quote from "Las ruinas circulares" from <u>Ficciones</u> by Jorge Luis Borges.

**EARTHQUAKE CHICA**

**ACT ONE**

**SCENE ONE**

*LIGHTS RISE ON ESMERALDA AND SAM AT AN EVENING LAW FIRM CHRISTMAS PARTY IN A DOWNTOWN HIGH-RISE.*

ESMERALDA: Earthquake. (with Anglo accent) Terremoto. My father called me that. I'm not an earthquake, alright? I'm a force of nature, though. Watch me move.

*SHE DOES A SEXY DANCE MOVE.*

SAM: You're not an earthquake.

ESMERALDA: Then what am I?

SAM: A force of nature?

ESMERALDA: What kind?

*SHE DOES ANOTHER SEXY DANCE MOVE. SHE BLOWS HIM A KISS.*

SAM: Windstorm?

*SHE DOES ANOTHER SEXY DANCE MOVE. SHE LICKS HER LIPS.*

SAM: Rainfall?

*SHE DOES ANOTHER SEXY DANCE MOVE. SHE SUCKS ON HER FINGER.*

SAM: A tidal wave?

*SHE STOPS DANCING.*

ESMERALDA: I'm not a tidal wave.

SAM: Not a tidal wave...I mean like you create waves...fantastic waves...like the kind that surfers ride and revel in because they're awesome surfers.

ESMERALDA: Drop it, Mr. Accountant-Numbers Boy.

SAM: Sam.

ESMERALDA: I know your name. Don't worry, little Sammy. I catch the drift. So what's up with the slick hair, huh? Got a little spiffed up for ye old (with over emphasized Anglo accent) fiesta de navidad?

SAM: You speak the language? Me too.

ESMERALDA: Nope. Before my dad died two months ago, his Latin face would erupt in anger, turn the color of bricks while he screamed at me, (with Anglo accent) "Terremoto. Terremoto."

SAM: I'm sorry. My condolences.

ESMERALDA: You think I'd speak the language after that?

SAM: I...I don't know.

ESMERALDA: Yeah. Whatever. So what do ya' do to have fun, soldier? Are ya' kinky? Huh? Huh? Oh come on, I know your type. The silent numbers cruncher. You sit in this damn office all day long and you crunch, crunch, crunch, until your little fingers go numb and then you go home and put on your leather and hit the bars.

SAM: I uh...read...novels and poetry. Do math.

ESMERALDA: I said fun, soldier.

SAM: I uh...like devour Latin American literature and work on math equations in my spare time...algebra mostly.

ESMERALDA: But you do like leather, don't you?

SAM: Depends on what kind.

ESMERALDA: Now we're talkin'.

SAM: Leather bound editions of my favorite novels, sure. But the kind of leather you're talking about...I don't think so.

ESMERALDA: Come on, you'd look so hot in some chaps, a harness...with a fine black cap on your head. Oh yeah.

*SHE MUSSES HIS HAIR.*

SAM: You have nice hands.

ESMERALDA: You have a nice ass.

SAM: I do? Okay...um...but you...whenever you place your boss' time sheets in my in-box I notice how long and slender and delicate your fingers are.

ESMERALDA: Do you always wear your hair like that? It would look so much cuter if you did it like this.

*ESMERALDA PLAYS WITH HIS HAIR.*

ESMERALDA: There. Much better. (beat) Do you get wasted on a regular basis because I don't. I can't. I joined one of those programs a few years ago but like I don't go anymore because I can't stand the people at those meetings and all their annoying lingo, but I know I can't drink. My body can't handle it.

SAM: I don't drink much. Only when I'm nervous.

ESMERALDA: What're you nervous about?

*SAM LOOKS AWAY NERVOUSLY.*

ESMERALDA: Me?...the lowly worm secretary on the totem pole here?

SAM: But see you're fantastic because you don't care. You willingly buck the dress code and you talk loudly to the secretaries and the lawyers. You don't seem to care much about what people think at all.

ESMERALDA: Okay, and you've had how much to drink?

SAM: Would you wanna...I mean...maybe we could, you know, have lunch together...sometime?

ESMERALDA: Oh please. You crunch numbers. I can barely type. It would never work.

SAM: Look, if you don't wanna get together during the week, maybe on a weekend day, we could you know, meet up for coffee or something.

ESMERALDA: You're too normal.

SAM: I could teach you some Spanish.

ESMERALDA: I tried. Didn't work. My father called me earthquake chica.

SAM: Alright then...uh...

ESMERALDA: "You are earthquake chica." He began to speak in Spanglish toward the end of his unhappy life.

SAM: Well...so...Merry Christmas. Feliz Navidad y Prospero Año Nuevo.

*SAM STARTS TO WALK AWAY.*

ESMERALDA: One time I saw this gypsy singer at this concert...she was like wailing in Spanish and I just burst into tears, spontaneously. But I just kinda don't fit in. Got it?

*SAM STOPS.*

SAM: The language is inside of you, Esmeralda.

ESMERALDA: He even knows my name. You're a persistent little fella, aren't ya? This fiesta is so done. I'm outta here.

SAM: So are you gonna avoid me now that we've talked, like this?

ESMERALDA: Oh yeah, like I'm gonna run away screaming every time I see your face because you asked me out and I rejected you.

SAM: Whatever. I mean I've crossed that line from professional to personal.

ESMERALDA: Listen, pal, lines don't exist with me. I'm not a lines kinda gal. Got it? So I won't avoid you. I will talk to you. I just won't go out with you.

## SCENE TWO

*LATER THAT NIGHT. LIGHTS RISE ON ESMERALDA AND SAM SITTING ON TOP OF HER BED, FULLY CLOTHED.*

SAM: Last night I dreamt I was walking through an abandoned house and un viejito a little old man gave me a dusty book. He had long white hair and a leather-lined face and he pointed for me to take the book outside. So I opened up a door and I left the sepia-toned interior for a technicolor field and sitting in the field was this girl-woman-señorita far off in the distance. And I had ese libro this book and I started running and screaming and yelling and this señorita had her back to me and when I approached her, out of breath, I gave her the red-leather bound volume and she turned around and she had your face but she was a different you. Diferente than what I had known. And she-you took the book and I sat down next to you-her in silence as we read and the wind picked up gently. (beat) Do you remember your dreams?

ESMERALDA: You don't get out much, do you?

SAM: I dated this girl once, Carina, who kept a bucket by her bed. I asked, "So what's with the bucket? Drip in the ceiling? You sick?" I mean, you know, it was the standard blue plastic kind. And she answers, "It's for my tears. I collect them. Don't make me collect more, alright?" I mean, try sleeping in a bed with a bucket of tears next to you.

ESMERALDA: The last guy I was with for like two weeks…Hector…he used to keep a large bone next to his bed. He called it, "My beautiful hueso"

SAM: What kind of bone?

ESMERALDA: Like a medium size arm bone. In a glass case by his bed. He said it reminded him of the essence of life. Said it was supposed to be like this ancient Aztec relic or some shit that he bought at a swap meet. Said it reminded him of where we all end up. Do you know how hard it is to sleep in a bed with a man, when there is an ancient bone staring at you? It's like the bone had eyes. I'd wake up in the middle of the night and want to break it out of the glass box and toss it out the window. It's like dead spirits were invading the bed. But I figured he'd be pissed. So I didn't.

SAM: Smart move.

ESMERALDA: So last night I'm lying in this bed and I'm thinking over the string of men in my life, you know.

SAM: A long string?

ESMERALDA: We're talking football field. And it's like there seems to be this pattern starting with nice, not-so-nice then never-nice-at-all. Some stay nicer longer. But most end up in the last category sooner or later.

SAM: You know, if it were me, I wouldn't end up in the last category. Not that category consideration is even issue for me, mind you. (beat) Do you worry about mud? In the office?

ESMERALDA: Mud in the office?

SAM: Because I won't carry it in my pocket and sling handfuls into unsuspecting secretaries' ears.

ESMERALDA: Sling mud? I think you mean dish dirt. Like gossip. God, my dad would always mess up sayings like that.

SAM: I won't.

ESMERALDA: I appreciate that. Not that I care what anyone thinks but you know, it can complicate things at work and make people all petty and strange.

SAM: Because I see things in you, Esmeralda. I see beneath the outer shell that keeps the deeper you submerged in water or blood or sugar or fog. It's the seeing you don't like. Which is fine. But let it be known that I do see.

ESMERALDA: I can't be with anyone right now. That's why there's a part of me that thinks I shouldn't even have asked you over to my place because I don't want you to think the wrong thing.

SAM: I won't think the wrong thing. I don't even like wrong things.

ESMERALDA: I mean in the past I would've brought you home and seduced you and shit but I'm not into that anymore. You know?

SAM: Right. Of course not.

ESMERALDA: Most people don't get me. On a good day, my sister might. My mother? Not really. And on a bad day. Forget it. No one. Zip. But you listen to me and see things in me like you say. And I like that.

SAM: My family doesn't seem to get me either. I mean my mom can't even accept the fact that I'm a grown man. She wants me to always stay her little Samuelito.

*ESMERALDA SIGHS.*

ESMERALDA: My mom lives upstairs. I moved back here after my dad got sick.

SAM: I'm sorry.

ESMERALDA: Lungs. He was sick for a few years but the end came quick.

SAM: I'm so sorry.

ESMERALDA: My mom does this secretary shit for a living too. Full time. She used to be a Spanish professor but then when dad got sick she lost her teaching job, couldn't find a new one so she had to go work in an office to support him.

SAM: Does she miss the teaching?

ESMERALDA: She says she doesn't but I don't know how she can't. And my sister is like this physicist who went to Berkeley or was it Stanford. I can never remember. She didn't get caught up in this exhausting crap.

SAM: She must be pretty smart.

ESMERALDA: So am I. I mean I can do more than organizing my boss' mountain of paper into a neat piles of folders, redwells and pendaflex files.

SAM: On my lunch breaks, I research poetic connections in algebra. I think equations can be very metaphorical. And I inhale literature. Numbers and language fill my brain. (beat) I'm sorry about your father...and mother. She taught around here?

ESMERALDA: UCLA. My dad was an artist. She taught. He painted. And he'd always rant to her, "You're the teacher. Why don't you teach your daughters to speak the language" And I was like, "Well, Dad, you're the one from Mexico."

SAM: Sorry for speaking in front of you.

ESMERALDA: He didn't like me or anyone else challenging him like that. One challenge and then like volcanic eruptions. So I never learned the language. I didn't wanna be any thing like him. Didn't wanna be someone who uses words like weapons.

SAM: Sometimes my Spanish words just slip out...but never as like grenades, or anything.

ESMERALDA: So I picked up the bad sayings, a few choice good ones but that's it.

SAM: That's a start.

ESMERALDA: I mean my sister is fluent. She travels to Guadalajara all the time to visit all our aunts, uncles, cousins. (beat) Hey, do you wanna hear my animal imitations? I do a mean poodle. Or do you wanna watch one of my dances? My hips...baby...my hips.

SAM: It's almost one. I better go.

ESMERALDA: I like how you can hear my thoughts, Samuel.

SAM: Cool. So...uh...do you like museums? You know....the Getty? They're having this outdoor concert thing on Saturday.

ESMERALDA: Look. It's not like I don't like hanging with you but I think you need to go out and meet a nice normal girl.

SAM: Fine. Whatever. Forget it.

**SCENE THREE**

*THE FOLLOWING SATURDAY NIGHT. DUSK. LIGHTS RISE ON ESMERALDA AND SAM STANDING AT A RAILING OVERLOOKING A CACTUS GARDEN AT THE GETTY MUSEUM.*

ESMERALDA: I wanna climb over this railing and run down that cactus runway, my feet hopping over the pointy parts and then take a flying leap and float over the city.

*SAM READS A BROCHURE.*

SAM: The South Promontory Cactus Garden recalls the city's pre-urban existence. Golden Barrel. Column cacti. Euphorbia. Agave. Opuntia. The runway to the stars.

ESMERALDA: My legs will meld into steel girders. My arms will sprout aluminum wings and I will soar over the city of angels like a kick ass futuristic aircraft.

SAM: Ten cuidado. Could you not step on that railing?

ESMERALDA: And on my flight, my brain will fill with the most delicious pure oxygen as I soar toward the setting sun.

SAM: Ay por favor. That's wonderful, now if you'd just step back down.

ESMERALDA: Depends.

SAM: On.

ESMERALDA: How fast you can race down a cactus runway to fly.

*ESMERALDA LAUGHS.*

ESMERALDA: The image of you all alone, cactus getting stuck in your shoes as you hop down that runway.

SAM: That won't be happening.

ESMERALDA: Because, see, I'm already out there soaring.

*ESMERALDA STARTS CLIMBING OVER THE RAILING.*

ESMERALDA: Come on, sucka. Race you.

SAM: Don't!

ESMERALDA: That look on your face. Panic. Stress. Utter embarrassment. What? I'm getting down. I'm not crazy. What? You think I'm crazy, don't you?

SAM: No. It's just that I...

*ESMERALDA SITS ON THE RAILING.*

ESMERALDA: You're thinking "Don't be seen with the crazy one. Quick. Leave." Well that sucks okay because I was just trying to have fun. You're so uptight. And judgmental. You shouldn't judge people the way you do, with your eyes.

SAM: No, it's I...I don't want you to fall.

*ESMERALDA GETS DOWN FROM THE RAILING.*

ESMERALDA: Concern. Huh.

SAM: Wanna walk back to the flowering maze or we could go the garden terrace cafe? The concert starts soon.

ESMERALDA: That was unexpected and noble, you know. Your concern right there.

SAM: Nobility? No. Infatuation-related? Maybe. Noble? I don't think so.

ESMERALDA: Please don't be infatuated with me and wanna get into my pants because that is so old, alright?

SAM: (lying) I'm not. I don't.

ESMERALDA: Oh what, is it that I'm not attractive enough? I'm ugly, now? Great. Thanks.

SAM: God. No. You're very attractive.

ESMERALDA: That's more like it.

SAM: God, you're the most attractive woman in the entire...office.

ESMERALDA: Thanks but most secretaries in the office are doing weight watchers and have a look of despair on their faces.

SAM: God, it's just that...okay. I like...your mind. The way it works. The ideas that spin inside your orb.

ESMERALDA: My orb? What are you a demented scientist? That term sounds obscene.

SAM: O.R.B. Orb. A sphere or globe. A heavenly body.

ESMERALDA: So you do want my body. I knew it.

SAM: I believe I was using the word to refer to cranial activity. The brain. Gray matter.

ESMERALDA: My orb. O.R.B.

SAM: Yep.

ESMERALDA: Right.

*MARIACHI MUSIC WAFTS THROUGH THE AIR.*

ESMERALDA: Mariachis?

SAM: The concert's starting.

ESMERALDA: I thought you said it was salsa?

SAM: So maybe it's both.

ESMERALDA: But that's like two different worlds. Salsa. Mariachis.

SAM: Mexico. The Caribbean. It's all one community. So?

ESMERALDA: You like my thoughts?

SAM: I do.

ESMERALDA: Haven't heard that line before. That's a first.

SAM: El primer.

ESMERALDA: Right. Whatever.

*AN AWKWARD BEAT.*

ESMERALDA: The workings of my mind.

SAM: Tus pensamientos.

ESMERALDA: Lost me there.

SAM: Thoughts.

ESMERALDA: You like them.

SAM: I do.

*AN AWKWARD BEAT.*

SAM: To the concert. Shall we walk or fly?

## SCENE FOUR

*MONDAY MORNING. LIGHTS RISE ON SAM AND ESMERALDA STANDING IN THE COMPUTER SYSTEMS ROOM.*

ESMERALDA: Crashed?

SAM: The server's down.

ESMERALDA: He crunches numbers. He repairs systems. He's a wonder techno boy.

SAM: Might not be up for a while.

ESMERALDA: So how much longer? My boss wants to know.

SAM: Hopefully not long. And don't worry. You don't have to talk to me again.

ESMERALDA: Okay. So I abandoned you. Okay. So I danced with ten men.

SAM: Fifteen...and a half.

ESMERALDA: The twelve year old boy didn't count.

SAM: You said you didn't feel like dancing.

ESMERALDA: I lied. (beat) You said you'd try.

SAM: I miscalculated.

ESMERALDA: So. So what? You like my thoughts only. I like to gaze at gorgeous mariachis and groove to salsa. So. So what?

SAM: Exactly.

ESMERALDA: Look, you took me to the Getty. We hung out. I danced. Dancing is the only release I have these days, alright? And you're gonna deny me that? Whatever.

SAM: I think the mainframe is overloaded. Everyone is gonna have to reboot. That'll help. But the system override may take time.

ESMERALDA: Okay. Look. I'm sorry I abandoned you.

SAM: Apology accepted. Whatever. It doesn't matter.

ESMERALDA: So I was thinking about this Spanish thing, you know. And like the truth of the matter is, I'm curious. You know, and you see things in me so like maybe, I thought you could teach me?

SAM: What?

ESMERALDA: Teach me the language.

SAM: As in you want to keep talking to me?

ESMERALDA: Don't get all excited. You know, I thought I could learn some.

SAM: You know, in this moment if I were balding and I had one long piece of hair on the side and a sturdy comb, I'd be wanting to make sure my comb-over was firmly in place.

ESMERALDA: What?

SAM: Literally bald. No. Metaphorically bald. Exposed.

ESMERALDA: Okay fine. When the system's back up let me know. We'll talk later.

SAM: You've exposed my insecurity and I desperately want to comb over that.

ESMERALDA: Insecurity?

SAM: Thinking you'd never talk to me again and I like...revere your free spirit, your desire and...thirst for knowledge.

ESMERALDA: Hold on there, camper. I said a few lessons. Not like some college training program for like retards.

SAM: Sorry. That new database program was running concurrently with the old one thus overloading the system and therefore the crash.

ESMERALDA: Are you gonna be a harsh teacher? Because if you are, we can forget about it.

SAM: I won't be harsh. Promise.

**SCENE FIVE**

*THE NEXT DAY. LIGHTS RISE ON ESMERALDA AND SAM STANDING IN A STORAGE SUPPLY CLOSET.*

ESMERALDA: I'm not hiding in here and having a lesson. If I were hiding in here it would be to do some fine UPS guy. Have you noticed how the delivery dudes always have completely chiseled calves and beautiful bulging biceps? But no, we're not here for that, are we?

SAM: Who says we're hiding?

ESMERALDA: We're standing in a storage supply closet with the door almost all the way closed.

SAM: We need supplies.

ESMERALDA: What...are we going on a field trip or something?

SAM: For our lessons. Now come on. Grab some.

*SAM GRABS SOME SUPPLIES OFF THE SHELF.*

ESMERALDA: I don't steal anymore. I gave that up with drinking and smoking.

SAM: Well, so I also brought you this.

*SAM HANDS ESMERALDA A BOOK.*

ESMERALDA: (with Anglo accent) Poesía y ficción.

SAM: (with Spanish accent) Poesía y ficción.

ESMERALDA: Yeah. Right. Whatever.

SAM: An anthology of writers. Neruda. Lorca. Borges. Excerpts. Bilingual edition. (beat) And this...

*SAM HANDS ESMERALDA ANOTHER BOOK.*

ESMERALDA: Algebra for society. I think you're getting a little carried away here. I didn't say I wanted to become like a math whiz or anything.

SAM: It kind of reviews the basics. I wasn't sure where you stood with regard to exponents and binomials.

*SAM HANDS ESMERALDA A CLEAR PLASTIC BAG FILLED WITH SAND.*

ESMERALDA: A bag of sand.

SAM: Serves several functions. The passing of time.

ESMERALDA: Did you take the bus down to the beach just to get this sand? That is like so out of your way.

SAM: And the longer evolutionary view. Once boulders. Now sand.

ESMERALDA: Listen. Forget about it. I think you're way too into this and making me into this project like I'm some kind of lame kid or something, like I can't think for myself. I graduated from high school. I got my certificate alright? I could've gone to college, but I didn't want to. I went to the college of life, alright? And just because you think you're gonna teach this poor little dumb ass girl who you're hot for so you'll condescend to her level, you're wrong. Where did you go to college anyway?

SAM: UCLA.

ESMERALDA: Oh great. Just forget it.

SAM: What?

ESMERALDA: In a moment of weakness, I asked you for help. But I don't need your big ass university special ed help. And standing here in this storage closet with two large books and a bag of sand is certainly not what I had in mind.

*SAM STARTS WHISTLING.*

ESMERALDA: What? Now you're gonna teach me a little tune?

SAM: When I'm nervous, I whistle.

ESMERALDA: Again I make you nervous.

SAM: Yes, when you threaten to take back your request for lessons, something I've been looking forward to for the past twenty-three hours and seventeen minutes since you first mentioned it. This connection through language and numbers, native and acquired, intrigues me and gives me a sense of motivation and purpose and that's new for me. I'm nervous about losing that. Yes.

ESMERALDA: So you're not gonna be like mean? Because I can't stand that.

SAM: I never would be.

ESMERALDA: You know that movie with Audrey what's-her-name and that old English dude and he like transforms her? That's not what we're talking about here. Not at all. Got that?

SAM: Right. Not at all. Can I read you a line or two?

ESMERALDA: Better be quick before one of the floor wardens breaks up our little love fest.

SAM: Neruda writes..."Amo las cosas loca, locamente. I have a crazy, crazy love of things. Amo todas las cosas, no solo las supremas, sino las infinitamente chicas. I love all things, not only the grandest but also the infinitely tiny."

ESMERALDA: Alright.

SAM: Lorca writes..."Mi corazon tendría la forma de un zapato sí cada aldea tuviera una sirena. My heart would be shaped like a shoe if a mermaid would live in every village."

ESMERALDA: Uh-huh.

SAM: Neruda is crazy. Lorca's heart is moved by mermaids. You're in good company.

ESMERALDA: Whatever. I'm not crazy and I saw that movie about the mermaid played by that tall blonde chick and she likes falls in love with the guy. Puh-lease.

SAM: Borges writes..."Sabia que su inmediata obligación era el sueño. He knew his immediate duty was to dream."

ESMERALDA: I better get back to my desk before Mr. Boss Man starts looking for me.

SAM: So, a binomial is an algebraic expression that is the sum or difference of two terms. An exponent is a symbol indicating what power of a factor is to be taken.

ESMERALDA: I didn't say I wanted any help in math, okay? I know how to use a calculator and that's about all the help I need.

SAM: But they say that if you're good in math, you're can be good at learning a foreign language. I thought the Algebra could be a nice complement to the Spanish.

*THE SOUNDS OF A COPY MACHINE ECHO INTO THE STORAGE ROOM.*

ESMERALDA: The copy machine means one of the other mud slingers is close by which means this little lesson is over.

*SAM REACHES INTO THIS PLASTIC BAG OF SAND.*

SAM: Have a pinch. To remind and guide you until the next lesson.

ESMERALDA: If it's my obligation to dream, maybe I dreamt this.

*SAM PUTS A PINCH OF SAND IN HER PALM.*

SAM: This sand reminds you that you are very much awake.

**SCENE SIX**

*THE FOLLOWING SATURDAY AFTERNOON. LIGHTS RISE ON ESMERALDA AND SAM STANDING INSIDE A BARE, STUDIO APARTMENT. ESMERALDA PACES.*

ESMERALDA: Solitary palm tree out the main window. One largish room. Smallish bathroom. Kitchenette. Decent closet. Fresh carpet and paint. Do I take it?

SAM: Do you want it?

ESMERALDA: I'm asking for your opinion.

SAM: You want my opinion?

ESMERALDA: Ah...yes.

SAM: Well, for a studio apartment, this room does get strong sunlight.

ESMERALDA: But does it get good moonlight or starlight...so I can entertain in my mediumish bed?

SAM: You could grow things in here. Have an indoor garden.

ESMERALDA: I like plants. Ivy. Spider plant. Maybe some cacti too. (playfully seductive) Or should I pronounce it cock-tie?

SAM: Tu jardin. La jardinera. You could be an indoor gardener. I mean...just the other day I read an article in the paper about this kind of flower called Passiflora. It's purple with lace and white egg shaped fruit inside that's supposedly tasty.

ESMERALDA: What if I put my bed here? Would that be following that Chinese thing? Fung something? Or should I put it here? Does your head have to be facing the door? Is that so you can like lie naked in bed watching some totally hot dude enter your room and you're like, "Let's get it on, sucka"?

SAM: The passiflora were discovered by the conquistadores who thought the flower's parts reminded them of the passion of their Lord. It is a very metaphysical flower. Passion on many levels.

ESMERALDA: Are you saying I need more passion in my life?

SAM: You're doing just fine.

ESMERALDA: I know this no-sex platonic thing might be grating on your very last nerve but well, sorry, tough, you know?

SAM: (lying) It's not.

THE SOUND OF A LOUD CRASH FILLS THE ROOM.

ESMERALDA: God almighty. I can't handle this.

SAM: Just garbage trucks. Dumpsters.

ESMERALDA: God, am I gonna hear traffic noises all night going up and down the alley? Because you know I can't handle that. I am very sensitive to noises. And smells. If I smell garbage and like car fumes, I'll get very sick. And then I won't be able to work and I won't be able to afford this apartment.

SAM: It's a quiet alley. The noise and smells will pass.

ESMERALDA: Really?

SAM: I think so.

*AN AWKWARD BEAT.*

ESMERALDA: Right. I mean it's not that you're not attractive really, I mean, you know, in a normal sort of way...

SAM: I said we don't have to....

ESMERALDA: It's just I don't wanna get into it with you and we have like two weeks of doing it in all these amazing positions and then you get all needy and I'm like whatever and then there's this fight and you hate me and you bail and it sucks and we never talk again and then it's the same old shit.

SAM: The way your mind works. The way your hands move when your thoughts flow. The ways your eyes dance when you tell your stories. Passion is there. You say you can't speak the language when it's in the very fabric of your existence.

ESMERALDA: Alright. Thank you, oh wise one.

SAM: Passion takes on many forms. Flower. Mind. Hands. Eyes. Thoughts. And of course, the more conventional. But I'm not a very conventional guy.

*A RADIO BLARES SALSA AS A CAR DRIVES BY AND IDLES.*

ESMERALDA: I wanna go dancing tonight.

SAM: As you know, I don't dance.

*AN AWKWARD BEAT.*

ESMERALDA: Come on. You have to at least know a few little moves or two, Sammy.

SAM: Not really.

ESMERALDA: Come on.

SAM: I'd rather not.

ESMERALDA: I may not speak the language with my lips but my hips, baby, my hips.

SAM: Sorry.

ESMERALDA: Please?

SAM: Don't make me.

*THE SALSA MUSIC FADES AS THE CAR DRIVES AWAY.*

ESMERALDA: Okay.

SAM: I mean what I say, Esmeralda.

ESMERALDA: Got it.

SAM: You're used to certain ways of connecting and I can tell these ways no longer work for you.

ESMERALDA: I can't even dance anymore?

SAM: You know what I mean.

ESMERALDA: What? Here's the thing. Even if we did get involved and you didn't get completely freaked out after two weeks of our all night fuck festivals and we actually hit it off...eventually you'd lose interest or I'd overwhelm you and then you'd bolt. And I'm very tired of that. So don't pretend like you don't care or think about it because I know you do but it's like you'd be outta here in a month and then...

SAM: Don't misrepresent me. It sounds like you're the one who's afraid of losing interest.

ESMERALDA: Okay, so maybe you're not like that but I know you have this agenda...like you wanna help me for some reason and look, if you think I'm gonna become some astrophysicist or Spanish guru after a few little lessons with you, you're wrong. I mean please, you're a lowly accountant who lives with his parents. You want to make me into this cultural intellectual mathematical wonder but it's not like that alright? It's not. And it won't be.

SAM: I should leave now. (beat) I'm not trying to make you into anything, Esmeralda.(beat) Rent this place. The sunlight will help.

**SCENE SEVEN**

*MONDAY MORNING. LIGHTS RISE ON SAM WASHING HIS HANDS AT THE SINK IN THE MEN'S ROOM. ESMERALDA ENTERS RUNNING.*

ESMERALDA: I have to leave.

SAM: Yeah you do.

ESMERALDA: I quit.

SAM: Could we talk outside, please?

ESMERALDA: No one cares if we talk in here.

SAM: People drink a lot of coffee here. This men's room tends to get busy this time of day.

ESMERALDA: So they come in, take a piss. I could care less.

SAM: Please could we just...

ESMERALDA: I don't care. I can't do this. The phone, fax, computer, Dictaphone, copy machine, in box out box, coffee, messenger, mailroom nightmare. After I had answered like twenty phone calls from raging clients saying why doesn't he return their calls, my boss gives me a stack of five transcription tapes, four faxes, ten letters, seven files to index and he asks me to get him his super mocha latte with extra sugar please. I am not a machine. My heart is shriveling inside. My brain is turning to mush. My fingers are falling off. My legs are asleep. I look at the stomachs of the other secretaries and I'm afraid. I can't turn into that.

SAM: You won't.

ESMERALDA: But what if I become a very large secretary? What if I am so unhappy that I binge on chocolate donuts every day and never ever exercise? 'Cause I have a problem with bingeing, alright? When I'm upset. I can't help myself, alright? I used to be much heavier in my teens. The me you see now is not the me I used to be. Large bellies bring back bad high school memories, alright?

SAM: Okay. Now let's just walk out the door and into the nice hallway.

ESMERALDA: So I walked into that office manager's office, Cindy, and I told her today is my last day and she looks at me like I'm this worthless, lowlife because I won't keep sitting at that fucking desk and get cancer from inhaling the wite-out fumes.

SAM: Cindy's a little controlling.

ESMERALDA: Okay, I might seem like a loser to you but you know I have ambitions. I am very creative. I can dance. I like to create stories. I can do animal imitations. Didn't I tell you I love poodles? And I'm very good with people. People like me, okay? My father was a painter. My mother was a professor. My sister went to Berkeley or Stanford or whatever. I mean, shit, I deserve better than this life where I feel the inside of my head turning into clay.

SAM: Then it's good that you go.

ESMERALDA: But the only time I feel a glimpse of hope is when I think about our lessons.

SAM: Can we talk about this in the hallway...how about outside even?

ESMERALDA: No one cares. If they come in, we'll tell them to go to the twenty-second floor.

SAM: Cigarette break is coming soon.

ESMERALDA: They can smoke and piss outside for all I care.

SAM: Look, you're having a hard day but...

ESMERALDA: I won't stand for this anymore. But I wanted you to know that I see you.

SAM: Fine. Great. I see you too. Now let's talk in hallway.

ESMERALDA: I see you and I see quality. I see someone who has depth. I see someone who is sensitive and wants to help others. And I think you should quit too.

SAM: I can't.

ESMERALDA: Do you wanna crunch numbers your entire life?

SAM: I need the steady paycheck.

ESMERALDA: Live your life, Sam.

SAM: I am.

ESMERALDA: Do you know how much is out there for you?

SAM: Like complete humiliation when I walk out these doors with you and become the floor celebrity because we were caught in here together.

ESMERALDA: It doesn't matter. Who gives a shit what they think? You don't deserve this.

SAM: I can't leave.

ESMERALDA: Well I am. I'm goin' places. I'm gonna be famous. I'm gonna travel and dance and communicate with animals even better than that old lady on the animal channel and someone is gonna to walk up to me and wanna pay me a lot of money for what I do. I read magazines and I see those celebrities and come on, so many people could do what they do. I could do what they do.

SAM: Good luck.

ESMERALDA: You say that but then what you're really thinking is loser, right? Loser girl quits steady job.

SAM: That wasn't what I was thinking at all.

ESMERALDA: Alright, then what you were thinking was poor loser girl will be unfulfilled in her new life of freedom because she is half Latin and doesn't speak the language. Well, I am. Half. White mom. Latin dad. And like I don't really fit into the Latin crowd, okay? (beat) Oh my god, I can't breathe. I think I'm having a panic attack.

SAM: Take a deep breath. Breathe in.

ESMERALDA: Whip it out.

SAM: Excuse me?

ESMERALDA: Whip out your pocket calculator and calculate how many vacation days you have so you can at least bust out of this place for a week and we can talk about Neruda and the other Latin dudes you love so much. Oh god.

SAM: Breathe.

ESMERALDA: And then we can travel together. We'll go to Mexico City and then to the coast and we'll lie on the beach and you'll teach me more things. Oh god, my breath. I can't. Will you say a prayer for me? I think I might be dying here.

SAM: You're not dying. Breathe in. Breathe out. Close your eyes.

*ESMERALDA CLOSES HER EYES.*

SAM: Esmeralda. Emerald. Deep. Green. Penetrating. Piercing. Valuable. Gem. You're a vibrant, blooming tree with healthy branches, sturdy bark, emerald green leaves and roots that dig deep into the earth

ESMERALDA: Are you gonna get wild on me? 'Cause that would really suck seeing as I can't breathe right now.

SAM: Deep breath. Let the oxygen fill your entire lungs.

ESMERALDA: Now you're the celibate monk?

SAM: I don't think connecting in that way is good idea right now.

ESMERALDA: Calculators can be a real turn on to some girls.

SAM: Keep breathing.

ESMERALDA: I've changed directions inside. There's like this compass inside my rib cage, stuck beneath like my third rib and it's pointing north, you know?

SAM: Let me pray for you. Give me your hand.

*ESMERALDA AND SAM HOLD HANDS AND CLOSE THEIR EYES.*

ESMERALDA: Water in the desert.

SAM: I won't bolt...

ESMERALDA: So soothing.

SAM: Te juro.

ESMERALDA: Translation please? Oh god, my breath.

*HE OPENS HIS EYES AND LOOKS AT HER INTENTLY.*

SAM: Keep breathing. The language is in you.

*SAM CLOSES HIS EYES AGAIN. HE SILENTLY MOUTHS A PRAYER.*

**SCENE EIGHT**

*LIGHTS RISE ON ESMERALDA LYING DOWN ON A COUCH IN A LAWYER'S OFFICE. SAM SITS NEXT TO HER, HOLDING HER HAND, TRYING TO COMFORT HER.*

ESMERALDA: I felt like wind through my face, in my ears, inside my chest. Not a calm breeze, but the kind where palm trees thrash and wind chimes go crazy.

SAM: Drink this.

*SAM HANDS HER A GLASS OF WATER. SHE SITS UP.*

ESMERALDA: Mr. Boss Man's gone for the day. The door's closed. The mudslingers don't care. The only good thing about this office is this couch and one last view through the glass windows. The Harbor freeway, the Hollywood Hills, Bunker Hill, Pershing Square.

SAM: Keep resting here. I...I should get back.

ESMERALDA: Don't. Come on, Sammy. I can't handle a law firm office prison existence. But I've already had like a thousand jobs. Coffee houses. Pizza parlors. Bed and breakfasts. Flower shops. Park rangers. Health clubs. Hair salons. Now I have this damn studio to pay for, paying top dollar to live next to a freak who smokes strange shit out his window and above some dude who plays electric bass at midnight. I guess I could move back in with my mom. Pathetic, right? Just when I was looking forward to our lessons and all. But I just can't do it. God, it's totally hopeless.

SAM: So then...marry me.

ESMERALDA: Are you on crack?

SAM: Marry me and I'll...I'll like...take care of you.

ESMERALDA: I thought I was the crazy one here.

SAM: Yeah, and I can help pay for your studio. And you won't have to move back in with your mom. And the lessons can begin. We can have lessons. Lots of lessons. Together. Cause we'll be married. Yeah.

ESMERALDA: We haven't even kissed.

SAM: So then...kiss me.

ESMERALDA: God, I knew this would happen eventually. Have you had a hard on for me this entire time? Geez. And I thought you were different.

SAM: Esmeralda...

ESMERALDA: We haven't kissed. We haven't had sex. I'm not marrying you. Shit. I was already feeling stressed out. I'm gonna have another panic attack, please.

SAM: Okay. Fine. I lied. I don't really wanna marry you.

ESMERALDA: Thank you. What the hell was that?

SAM: I wanna be with you though. I mean I've lived my life in books. And here you come along and talk to me and spend time with me and make that acquired knowledge vibrant as it comes out of me. I live with my parents. People don't seem to get me much.

ESMERALDA: What about Carina, the bucket girl?

SAM: I just lay in bed next to her most nights. I didn't wanna make her cry.

ESMERALDA: So you've never had sex?

SAM: Not in a long long time. My sole companions these days are books and numbers.

ESMERALDA: Are you sure you're not a priest?

SAM: I have different kinds of passion.

ESMERALDA: I'll still call you. God, you'd think I was moving to another planet.

SAM: But you won't.

ESMERALDA: I still wanna have our lessons.

SAM: Whatever.

ESMERALDA: I have this image of you sobbing over your adding machine and I feel sick.

SAM: You mean like this?

*SAM IMITATES A BIG SOB. HE STOPS ABRUPTLY.*

SAM: I don't sob. I hold it in.

ESMERALDA: Hold it in? You'll get cancer and die.

SAM: Then...go, Esmeralda. Go to Mexico City. Go to Bogotá. Go to San Juan. Go to Madrid. Explore. Read. Write. Dance with reclusive poets.

ESMERALDA: Sam, come on.

SAM: Sing to introverted mathematicians as they sit at sidewalk cafés devouring dog eared copies of Neruda.

ESMERALDA: Don't be like this.

SAM: The seeds are sown. Go.

ESMERALDA: You're coming with me.

SAM: I can't.

ESMERALDA: I'm not marrying you but you need to get the hell out of here.

SAM: My parents. I can't. I'm not proud of the fact that they help support me but I need to pay my share or else I'm out on the street and at this point I'm not really ready for that. I live a sheltered dependent existence but it's a decent existence really. I'm not complaining.

ESMERALDA: Do you wanna die when you're fifty after watching your fingers fall off one by one from hitting that damn adding machine every day of your sorry life?

SAM: You don't have to end on such a cruel note really. A little mercy will do.

ESMERALDA: Screw all of this. We're outta here.

SAM: It's not prudent.

ESMERALDA: Screw prudence.

SAM: It's not economically feasible.

ESMERALDA: Screw feasibility.

SAM: I can't spend money I don't have.

ESMERALDA: We'll live simply. Bread. Cheese. Water.

SAM: I'd have to give two weeks notice.

ESMERALDA: Leave. Now. With me.

SAM: It's an aberration in the equation.

ESMERALDA: You started this. Your seeing. Your knowing.

SAM: Alright.

ESMERALDA: Really?

SAM: Yes.

ESMERALDA: Adventure.

SAM: Abandon.

ESMERALDA: Craziness.

SAM: Celibate craziness.

ESMERALDA: Passion of another kind. Let the fiesta begin.

SAM: When?

ESMERALDA: Now.

**LIGHTS FADE. END OF ACT ONE.**

**ACT TWO**

**SCENE ONE**

*THE NEXT DAY. LIGHTS RISE ON ESMERALDA AND SAM SITTING AT A TABLE IN A COFFEE SHOP.*

SAM: Present. Presente. First person singular. I speak Spanish. Yo...

ESMERALDA: Hablo español.

SAM: Good. Past. Pretérito. Second person singular. You spoke English. Tu...

ESMERALDA: Hablastes inglés?

SAM: Hablaste.

ESMERALDA: Hablaste.

SAM: Right. No "s". Okay. Future. Futuro. First person plural. We will speak Spanish and English. Nosotros...

ESMERALDA: Hablemos español y inglés?

SAM: Hablaremos.

ESMERALDA: Hablaremos.

SAM: Excellent. Infinitive. Hablar. Plus the ending "emos". Hablaremos.

ESMERALDA: This is a waste.

SAM: Be patient.

ESMERALDA: I have a mental block.

SAM: Patience and perseverance.

ESMERALDA: All I can picture is my father's face the color of bricks.

SAM: It's in you.

ESMERALDA: Look at me. Even when I only speak a little Spanish around here, people look surprised. "You speak the language? But you don't look like you speak Spanish."

SAM: But the community encompasses Chicanos, Salvadoreños, Dominicanos, Puerto Riqueños, Españoles, Cubanos, Venezolanos, Mexicanos, and on and on.

ESMERALDA: Kinda like a United Nations or something. I don't see it though.

SAM: L.A., New York, Miami, Chicago, Dallas...travel and you will.

ESMERALDA: That's just it. We have to travel. Where should we go first?

SAM: I can't travel right away.

ESMERALDA: Why?

SAM: I don't know. I mean...the air fares. Last minute is pricey.

ESMERALDA: Maybe we'll go to Mexico first. Puerto Rico next. New York City. Madrid.

SAM: And we'll pay for this how?

ESMERALDA: We'll become flight attendants. Handing out cocktails and traveling the globe.

SAM: You have to go to school for that.

ESMERALDA: We'll lead excursions of screaming school children. We'll take them by the hand to tour the museums, ride the ferry boats, see the volcanoes, climb the pyramids.

SAM: You have to go to school for that.

ESMERALDA: We'll become like really famous reporters and have to research stories on like notorious criminals and so we have to track them down in distant countries.

SAM: You have to go to school for that.

ESMERALDA: Why do you have to go to school for fucking everything? People invent their own lives. Remember I am very creative.

SAM: I'm just saying, it isn't so easy.

ESMERALDA: You're very negative.

SAM: I'm pragmatic.

ESMERALDA: That's boring.

SAM: Listen, Esmeralda, I had a more modest vision in mind.

ESMERALDA: And what would that be?

SAM: Um, well, we could continue with our lessons. You know, and then find new jobs and then you know save up some money and maybe take a trip in you know, a few months.

ESMERALDA: Were your parents that mean to you?

SAM: What?

ESMERALDA: Or your sister?

SAM: Excuse me?

ESMERALDA: Because the way you talk. Sometimes it's like so small. It's like sometimes you look like someone is going to come over and smack you on the head.

SAM: What're you getting at?

ESMERALDA: Really. It's like if I just say this smart enough and quick enough then it'll go by fairly unnoticed.

SAM: My parents are fine. They're getting up in age. My sister and I don't speak much.

ESMERALDA: What? She hates you?

SAM: Hate is too strong. Disdain is a better word.

ESMERALDA: A diss from the sis.

SAM: She doesn't approve of my life, how quote...pathetic she feels it is.

ESMERALDA: What makes her so high and mighty?

SAM: She lives this swanky existence in Seattle with her six figure computer sales job and her huge house and her la-dee-da life.

ESMERALDA: She sounds pathetic.

SAM: Could we get back to the lesson please?

ESMERALDA: She's jealous of you. Of your poetic soul and mathematical genius...which she wished she had but doesn't so she hides behind her richy rich life.

SAM: You see you have seven simple tenses. Present indicative. Imperfect Indicative. Preterit. Future. Conditional. Present Subjunctive. Past Subjunctive.

ESMERALDA: Slow down there, pal.

SAM: Then there are seven compound tenses. Present perfect. Past perfect. Preterit perfect. Future perfect. Conditional perfect. Past Subjunctive. Past perfect subjunctive.

ESMERALDA: This is too much.

SAM: Then you have your verbs ending in ar, er and ir. As well as your irregular verbs. With each you have to compose the present or past participle to conjugate the compound tenses.

ESMERALDA: You're not listening.

SAM: For example, an irregular verb, to be, ser, is soy, eres, es, somos, sois, son.

ESMERALDA: Sam...

SAM: Now the ar form is simple. Amar, to love, Amo, amas, ama, amamos, amais, aman.

ESMERALDA: Stop.

SAM: Do not dig into my family.

ESMERALDA: I'm not trying to dig. I'm trying to help you realize that you're more than your family thinks you are.

SAM: Do not try to figure me out. It's a waste. We're here for you to learn. I'm here to teach you. That's it.

ESMERALDA: Don't take that tone with me. You're here because we both agreed to this but it seems like you have some major stick up your...

SAM: You asked me to be here. I just quit my job. I just took this flying leap into the unknown. Like one two three jump and I hope this damn parachute opens.

ESMERALDA: I don't appreciate how you're speaking to me. I really don't. And I don't need this. I don't.

*ESMERALDA GETS UP TO LEAVE.*

SAM: Esmeralda...

ESMERALDA: I won't sit here anymore.

SAM: Come on.

ESMERALDA: No. I'm outta here.

SAM: Let's start again.

ESMERALDA: I'm just observing things, alright. Like your Neruda dude, I'm looking at common objects, trying to have a keen eye, trying to utilize my powers of perception. But apparently that's not okay. Apparently you rather have everything in a book but if it comes out of a book onto your skin, then it's evil. Sorry, pal. That's where my degree in the college of life comes in. That's what you learn. Skin. Blood. Not paper and dictionaries. Alright?

SAM: I'm sorry.

ESMERALDA: Yeah, well I am too because I thought you could handle being with me, but I guess I was wrong. Oh well...the string of men just got longer.

*ESMERALDA STARTS TO EXIT.*

SAM: What do you want?

ESMERALDA: I want you to take me seriously and not dismiss me like everyone else in my life.

SAM: Okay, so how do I take you seriously?

ESMERALDA: I mean why do you always get to be the teacher? Is it like you have nothing to learn, you're like Mr. Perfecto? I don't think so.

SAM: Okay, fine. So you take a turn being the teacher. Where do your lessons take place?

ESMERALDA: Bedroom. Dancefloor. Department store. You pick.

## SCENE TWO

*LATER THAT EVENING. LIGHTS RISE ON ESMERALDA AND SAM ENTERING A NIGHTCLUB. SALSA MUSIC BLARES.*

SAM: I feel ill. I have no compass. No point of reference. No bearings.

ESMERALDA: Relax. Breathe.

SAM: I can't move my body like that.

ESMERALDA: Just try.

SAM: I can feel the vibration of the music inside my skull.

ESMERALDA: That's the point.

SAM: I just never learned this night club thing.

ESMERALDA: We're free, Sammy boy. Libre. Libre. Free.

*ESMERALDA STARTS SALSA DANCING.*

SAM: I'm not good at this.

ESMERALDA: Doesn't matter. Good is not a word in this dictionary. Move. Just move.

SAM: This is painful.

ESMERALDA: Doesn't have to be. Here. Come on.

*ESMERALDA DANCES CLOSE TO HIM. SHE TRIES TO PULL HIS ARMS ALONG.*

SAM: The eyes. Lots of eyes over here.

ESMERALDA: Doesn't matter.

SAM: To you, perhaps...but to me. Yes.

ESMERALDA: Come on, Sammy. Sammy chicky-chico.

SAM: I'm going home.

ESMERALDA: We won't stay long. Just a few.

SAM: Call me in the morning.

ESMERALDA: No. no. no.

*SAM TRIES TO LEAVE. ESMERALDA STOPS HIM AND BEGINS DANCING AROUND HIM. SHE TOUSLES HIS HAIR.*

ESMERALDA: No one's watching. Absolutely no one. Look.

*SAM LOOKS AROUND.*

SAM: This is ridiculous.

ESMERALDA: Just follow me. Watch. Right. Two. Three. Back. Two. Three. Left. Two. Three. Back. Two. Three. Now you try.

*SAM ATTEMPTS TO SALSA DANCE AS ESMERALDA TAKES HIS HAND TO LEAD HIM.*

ESMERALDA: Right. Two. Three. Back. Two. Three. Left. Two. Three. Back. Two. Three. Excellent. Work it, Sammy Salsa Boy. You got it. Now feel it in your hips. Don't think so much. Just feel the beat. Let your body take over.

*HE BEGINS TO MOVE MORE FREELY.*

SAM: Screw it all.

ESMERALDA: That's right.

SAM: Screw it all. Calculators. Spread sheets. Time sheets. Databases. Servers crash. Accounts Receivable. Payroll. Crunch. Crunch. Crash. Crunch. Crunch. Crash.

ESMERALDA: That's my Sammy.

SAM: The body. My body. Your body.

*SAM MOVES MORE AND MORE FREELY.*

ESMERALDA: Arms. Hips. Head. Ass. Good. Work it. Arms. Hips. Head. Ass.

SAM: The body, my body, your body.

*ESMERALDA AND SAM BEGIN TO DANCE A FURIOUS, SPONTANEOUS DANCE.*

SAM: Libre. Libre. Libre.

ESMERALDA: We're free.

**SCENE THREE**

*LATER THAT EVENING. LIGHTS RISE ON ESMERALDA'S STUDIO.*
*SHE SITS ON HER BED WEARING A T-SHIRT ONLY. HE SITS NEXT TO*
*HER FULLY CLOTHED.*

SAM: Are you sure you wanna do this?

ESMERALDA: I'm still the teacher here. Shoes first.

SAM: My feet smell.

ESMERALDA: Good.

SAM: You know the whole Latin lover thing? It's a myth. I awkwardly
stumble through these moments and...

ESMERALDA: Shoes and socks.

*SAM TAKES OFF HIS SHOES AND SOCKS.*

ESMERALDA: Pants.

SAM: See, this should be spontaneous. Having a lesson like this isn't
spontaneous.

ESMERALDA: Like I said. I'm the teacher here. Pants. Pantalones. Off.

SAM: Wow. Look what I've unleashed.

ESMERALDA: Vamanos. Now.

*ESMERALDA GESTURES AS IF CRACKING A WHIP.*

SAM: I have to warn you. I'm very out of shape. I should exercise. In my
mind I see myself exercising. But I don't. I sit a lot.

ESMERALDA: Chico, so let's get ready for a work out, okay?

*ESMERALDA GESTURES AGAIN, MAKING A WHIP NOISE. SAM TAKES OFF HIS PANTS. SAM STARTS TO WHISTLE.*

SAM: I wasn't prepared for this kind of a moment. Are you completely sure you wanna do this? Shouldn't the lights be off?

ESMERALDA: Nothing to be ashamed of. We need to clearly see what we're doing here at the moment.

*SAM GETS DOWN TO HIS BOXERS AND HESITATES.*

ESMERALDA: The boxers can stay on for this lesson if you want.

SAM: It's just that I'd feel more comfortable that way...for the moment...in the light like this.

ESMERALDA: Your body is a gift from God. Nothing to be ashamed about.

SAM: But my whole body is shaking, like at the dance club.

ESMERALDA: Shhh. Querido. Now. Shirt. La camisa.

*ESMERALDA BEGINS TO UNBUTTON HIS SHIRT.*

SAM: In this moment, if I were a small rodent, I'd bite a hole through the plastic paneling in the kitchen and slide down the hole behind the sink so I could congregate in safety with my other furry friends.

ESMERALDA: That's not the only hole you wanna slide down, now is it?

SAM: Uh...wow. Do you always talk like that...in moments like these?

ESMERALDA: Suave. Slowly. La camisa. Adios.

*ESMERALDA HELPS SAM TAKE OFF HIS SHIRT. HE WEARS A T-SHIRT UNDERNEATH. SAM WHISTLES AGAIN.*

SAM: The t-shirt stays on. Por favor.

ESMERALDA: Okay. Shhh.

*ESMERALDA STARTS TO KISS HIS FACE. SAM KEEPS WHISTLING.*

SAM: You know I wasn't angling for this. Alotta guys would. But not me. I wasn't scheming. Truly.

ESMERALDA: Silencio.

SAM: Okay. So. Maybe I was slightly, unobtrusively scheming at certain moments. But I'm so not like this. I'm normally not a casual...sleep over kinda guy. I jest. I pseudo feign bravado. But really, this has never happened to me.

ESMERALDA: Shhhh. Por favor. Close your eyes. Breathe.

*SAM STOPS WHISTLING AND CLOSES HIS EYES. ESMERALDA BEGINS TO KISS HIS NECK...ARMS.*

SAM: And it's like...wow...madre mia...it's like I've been on this iceberg-glacier thing floating in the Arctic Ocean...and now there's this...ay, ay, ay....this beam of light...so bright above me...descending...and like my down parka which I bought especially to keep the tundra-like freeze away is...is getting very...hot and heavy...um...yeah... okay...uh...and I desperately want to remove it but my feet are kinda stuck in ice and my hands are...wow...still...cold.

ESMERALDA: Bienvenido, amigo, to a warmer climate.

*THEY BEGIN TO KISS AS ESMERALDA TURNS OFF THE LIGHT.*

**SCENE FOUR**

*THE NEXT MORNING. LIGHTS RISE ON SAM AND ESMERALDA MAKING HER BED.*

SAM: This morning when I woke up, I heard these birds cooing and cawing in like this kinda duet or something and as I peered out your window I saw this crow and this mourning dove next to each other on the telephone wire. The huge crow, I mean at least the size of a overgrown squirrel, was all agitated but the brown dove was like so calm. And the dove remained cooing peacefully as the crow suddenly took off. And it felt like a sign...that it would be alright...that I should stay.

ESMERALDA: You're staying with me but we're packing. We're flying. We're saying adios to this city for now.

SAM: We can't take any trips yet.

ESMERALDA: But I sold things...the necklace my mother gave me, the ring my father left me...they'd want us to travel.

SAM: How can I travel with no job?

ESMERALDA: Your job right now is to be with me. Your lessons. My lessons. Our lessons.

SAM: About our lesson last night. Um...it's been a while and so...sorry if I...

ESMERALDA: No apologies. Please.

SAM: With more practice, I...

ESMERALDA: You were awesome.

SAM: Please don't lie to me. I don't do well with lying. With more lessons, I...

ESMERALDA: Stop. You were tender and present and honest.

SAM: And...

ESMERALDA: Awesome.

SAM: I was?

ESMERALDA: Absolutely.

SAM: Really?

ESMERALDA: Truly.

*AN AWKWARD BEAT.*

SAM: You seem kinda disappointed though. Sad even.

ESMERALDA: Not about last night.

SAM: Then...

ESMERALDA: So, we just quit our jobs and I thought the plan was to keep having adventures together.

SAM: I know...and...

ESMERALDA: When I talk about making plans, you get scared. I can see it in your eyes the way they get smaller and squinty.

SAM: Okay, sure, fine. I'm...concerned. For a couple of reasons.

ESMERALDA: What? Am I that unappealing as a travel companion?

SAM: Not at all. It's just that the ground is not stable underneath my feet right now and I'm not used to that.

ESMERALDA: Oh, so you think that if you fly somewhere with me that something bad will happen to you...like we'll end up in jail in some foreign country. Well thanks a lot for your vote of confidence.

SAM: I don't know where you get that idea.

ESMERALDA: Look, you think I like living like this? Having a million jobs and never finishing anything? You're supposed to help me finish this.

SAM: Finish what?

ESMERALDA: This leap into language and adventure.

SAM: You're doing fine on your own.

ESMERALDA: Oh, yeah, right. I'm doing terrific. When do I get my big "you're doing fantastic" award? Look, I won't touch you again if that's what you're concerned about.

SAM: Esmeralda, it's not that...

ESMERALDA: No really, because I can already tell that was a huge mistake. It's gonna be all weird and wrong and then I have to say goodbye to you forever.

SAM: Maybe, I should go back home.

ESMERALDA: See what I mean? Look, I'll even go to mass with you. We can walk into a church and light a candle and pray to whichever saint we need to get help on our journey. I've researched travel destinations. We can do this.

SAM: You can do it.

ESMERALDA: Now, you're bolting.

SAM: I'm not bolting. I won't go away from you, like the forever thing you mentioned. But I can't like jet-set with you. You know?

ESMERALDA: Fine. So why don't you go back home. Go back to the law firm. Just forget ever meeting me. Because I deserve better treatment than this.

SAM: I'll leave if that's what you want. I'll go back to my parents. Explain to them that I'm gonna take my old job back. That I got carried away. But I'm not gonna like leave leave. I wouldn't do that to you.

*AN AWKWARD BEAT.*

ESMERALDA: What was your other reason for being totally freaked out? You said you had a couple of reasons and...

SAM: I don't wanna globe-trot with you because then you'll need me to like...I dunno...like take care of you when I can barely pay for myself. I live with my parents for godsakes. But then if we keep on like this...with these lessons...in here...at night...I'm gonna start really, really...wanting to be with you but you're gonna like fly away and have adventures and I don't think I can do that so then I'm left missing you in this huge way and it's too much. Just too much. Okay? (beat) Um...can I hide now?

*SAM GRABS ONE OF HIS BOOKS WHICH HE THEN OPENS.*

SAM: (reading) Neruda writes...Diccionario, una mano de tus mil manos, una de tus mil esmeraldas, una sola gota de tus vertientes virginales, una grano de tus magnanimos graneros en el momento justo a mis labios conduce, al hilo de mi pluma, a mi tintero.

ESMERALDA: Sam...

SAM: Dictionary, lead one of your thousand hands, one of your thousand emeralds, one single drop from your wilderness waterfalls, one grain from your superb silo...to my lips, to the point of my pen, to my inkwell.

ESMERALDA: God, you think like I'm gonna travel and won't ever wanna see you again? Like I'm this heartless creature? Fine. Just like...walk away, then, okay? So neither of us will need anything from anyone ever again. Okay?

SAM: (whispering) I'm not walking away.

*SAM ATTEMPTS TO TOUCH ESMERALDA AND SHE PULLS AWAY.*

ESMERALDA: I'm not used to kindness, alright?

**SCENE FIVE**

*SUNDAY AFTERNOON. LIGHTS RISE ON SAM AND ESMERALDA SITTING IN A SCULPTURE GARDEN AT UCLA. SAM READS FROM A TEXT BOOK.*

SAM: This garden is a sacred space. A wide expanse of lawn surrounded by hallowed halls of learning. Sculptures of all shapes and sizes. The horse. A woman. A dancer. And peace.

ESMERALDA: My mom used to teach in the building over there. We would play in this sculpture garden. I always loved that driftwood horse the best. Driftwood made out of cast iron. I'll never forget the feeling of calm I used to experience here. As if the walls of the school chilled everyone out.

SAM: So I guess I chose a good place.

ESMERALDA: Shall we?

SAM: Algebra is a type of math designed to solve certain types of problems.

ESMERALDA: Are you saying Algebra can solve my problems? Hey, did you realize that the last three letters of algebra are bra...b.r.a.

SAM: Algebra functions on the idea that an equation is like a scale. Instead of keeping the scale balanced with weights, algebra uses numbers or constants.

ESMERALDA: I hate scales. Don't own one. After I binge, it's just too upsetting. I know I shouldn't binge. But I get overwhelmed and I have to. Usually it's a box of chocolate covered donuts, you know the kind with the milk chocolate all melty on top?

SAM: The next part of the equation is an unknown number or variable which is represented by the letter x.

ESMERALDA: X. Like in ex-boyfriend, ex-con, x-rated?

SAM: For example. X plus twenty-three equals seventy-six. Subtract twenty-three from each side, keeping the scale equal, and the result is...

ESMERALDA: I'm not good at subtraction in my head. I'm not good with much in my head. It gets too crowded you know, and then I get stressed and anxious and then I might have another panic attack and then I binge and then I feel sick and it sucks and...

SAM: Fifty-three. The result is fifty-three.

ESMERALDA: Can we stop now? I don't think math will help me with Spanish. There's just this block. The ghost of my angry father haunts the language learning part of my brain. He couldn't handle life in this country so he took it out on me. Raising his voice and his hand and his negative energy...because I wouldn't put up with his old world shit. He couldn't stand that.

SAM: My father came here from Mexico too and he wants his family to be like his family was as a kid. Another world. Another time. And so I also exist in between those two worlds. Old and new. Sheltered and Free.

ESMERALDA: My father haunts my mind and my choices in men. Instead of men who might be kind, I end up with the losers who have like tattoos on their backs, eat large quantities of processed food, watch hours of TV and have bad teeth because they can't afford to go to the dentist.

SAM: How're my teeth?

ESMERALDA: Fine. Nice. Even.

*AN AWKWARD BEAT.*

SAM: So there's this great story about Neruda and Lorca. One night they are in Argentina, at the home of a fabulously wealthy businessman. Pablo and Federico meet a tall, attractive, female poet over dinner. After the meal, the three go walking to admire the massive swimming pool and garden. There is a tower overlooking the pool. So they climb the steps to the top of the tower and gaze out over the perfect night. Soon Pablo kisses the woman and before long, the couple are on the floor of the tower. Neruda tells Lorca to get lost and make sure no one comes up the stairs. Lorca happily agrees but when he descends the steps, he falls down the darkened stairwell and both Neruda and the woman have to scramble half naked to help him up and Lorca hobbles around for two weeks after.

ESMERALDA: Horny poets.

SAM: Two poets of genius scrambling up and down a tower because of love.

ESMERALDA: Like I said, poetus horniculus. Do you really believe they were doing it because of love?

SAM: I do. So tomorrow more Neruda. Tuesday Borges. Wednesday Lorca. Thursday Márquez. Friday Paz. Saturday Fuentes. Sunday, a day of rest.

ESMERALDA: I don't know. I'm not ready for a crash course.

SAM: Crash is too negative. Immersion. I'll read to you. You'll read to me. We'll discuss.

ESMERALDA: Why don't you get a job teaching here?

SAM: Can't. I'm not a real teacher.

ESMERALDA: Excuse me? You're a good teacher. An awesome teacher.

SAM: Too late for that.

ESMERALDA: You're how old?

SAM: Old enough to know that I've already walked far enough down a certain path. Too old to retreat. I started out studying comparative literature but then my dad was like, "Do something practical" and so I caved and studied accounting at the management school here. And then I graduated, passed my CPA exam and bingo. Practical.

ESMERALDA: You limit your ways of thinking.

SAM: Perhaps.

ESMERALDA: You do.

SAM: Okay. Fine. I do.

ESMERALDA: What? What is up with your depressed energy? The small sound of your voice? The pained look on your face? You don't have that same excitement that is like full of possibility anymore, when your eyes light up and shit.

SAM: Your powers of perception are fully intact.

ESMERALDA: And...

SAM: So...um...I called Cindy last Friday. I start back at the firm in a week. She said I needed a break. Plus I had like twenty-five vacation days saved up from the past two years so...

ESMERALDA: Wow.

SAM: Just give me these two weeks of vacation, alright? Just give me these two weeks of freedom. Maybe that's all I can handle right now, alright? Let's just talk about these authors that give me a sense of belonging in the world. Alright?

ESMERALDA: You are bailing then.

SAM: When you talked to me about wanting like instant travel, I knew I couldn't do it. And then coming to this campus today, I thought of when I finished here, full of potential, the first person in my family to get my diploma and how much I owe to them.

ESMERALDA: Your family.

SAM: My parents. They helped put me through here. By very humble means. And they continue to help me. And I help them whenever I can. Financially. And other wise. So I can't just like take off. I can't.

ESMERALDA: Oh.

SAM: So.

ESMERALDA: So can we at least continue with our lessons?

SAM: Yours or mine?

ESMERALDA: Both.

## SCENE SIX

*LATER THAT AFTERNOON. LIGHTS RISE ON A MEN'S DRESSING ROOM BOOTH IN A DEPARTMENT STORE. ESMERALDA HOLDS A PAIR OF PANTS WHILE SAM, WEARING BOXERS AND A T-SHIRT, TRIES ON A NEW SHIRT.*

SAM: I can't wear this in public.

ESMERALDA: Uh-uh-uh. I'm the teacher here.

SAM: But this color is so...

ESMERALDA: Perfect on you.

SAM: And these sleeves...

ESMERALDA: Just the right length.

SAM: And this collar thing...

ESMERALDA: It's the hottest style. I know. I read the magazines. I see the celebrities in these outfits. I know hot.

SAM: But what am I trying to attract?

ESMERALDA: The new you.

SAM: What if I'm fine with the old me?

ESMERALDA: And you've had how many girlfriends?

SAM: Ouch.

ESMERALDA: Well?

SAM: This is considered hot?

ESMERALDA: (loudly) You look completely hot.

SAM: (sarcastic) Do you think you could say that just a little louder?

ESMERALDA: What? Oh you think that uptight sales dude is gonna come back here to check up on you and hear my voice and be like, "Uh, ma'am, no ladies allowed in the men's dressing room."

SAM: Yeah...and then you'll say, "Whatever" and he'll order us out and I'm not about to be escorted outta here wearing this.

ESMERALDA: Relax. Look, if that dude hassles us, I'll be like, "Yo he desperately needs my style expertise," and then he'll be like, "Shop on, fashionista."

SAM: You'd actually say that?

ESMERALDA: It's true.

*ESMERALDA HANDS HIM THE PANTS.*

ESMERALDA: Try these.

SAM: Whatever you say, Señorita fashionista.

*SAM TRIES ON THE PANTS.*

SAM: Too tight.

ESMERALDA: They're just right.

SAM: I feel naked.

ESMERALDA: You have a nice ass.

SAM: I won't wear these in public.

ESMERALDA: So instead you rather wear clothes that are two sizes too big and with that oh so fashionable color blind color scheme?

SAM: Thanks.

ESMERALDA: You're hiding.

SAM: What if I prefer to hide?

ESMERALDA: God gave you this body. Work it. Nothing to be ashamed about.

*SAM EXAMINES HIS "NEW" LOOK.*

SAM: Okay. Maybe I might consider wearing this but only when we're out together...that way if people hassle me I can tell them it's all your fault.

ESMERALDA: You want the cat calls and you know it.

SAM: What's the deal with this collar?

ESMERALDA: Wear it like this.

*ESMERALDA ADJUSTS HIS SHIRT.*

ESMERALDA: Then do your hair like this...

*ESMERALDA MUSSES HIS HAIR.*

ESMERALDA: Perfecto.

*SAM ADMIRES HIS NEW "LOOK".*

SAM: Wow. I actually could possibly consider being seen in public like this. (beat) You're talented.

ESMERALDA: You know language. I know fashion. Deal?

**SCENE SEVEN**

*WEDNESDAY. LATE AFTERNOON. LIGHTS RISE ON SAM AND ESMERALDA SITTING AT THE BEACH. SAM SPORTS HIS NEW "LOOK." ESMERALDA TAKES NOTES.*

SAM: Federico García Lorca. Eighteen ninety eight to nineteen thirty six.

ESMERALDA: Eighteen ninety-eight plus x equals nineteen thirty six. Subtract eighteen ninety-eight from both sides and you get...x equals thirty-eight. (beat) Um...he died when he was only thirty-eight?

SAM: August nineteenth. Nineteen thirty six. At the start of the Civil War in Spain.

ESMERALDA: He was a soldier?

SAM: Metaphorically. He fought for artistic expression.

ESMERALDA: And died...

SAM: Was killed because of his ideals.

ESMERALDA: Only thirty eight.

SAM: At thirty one, he journeyed from Madrid to New York in 1929. Studied English at Columbia. Wrote surrealist poetry, another play, a screenplay, lectured. Was incredibly lonely.

ESMERALDA: Are you lonely? Even out here with me?

SAM: While in New York City, Lorca wrote...(reading) Sí, tu niñez: ya fabula de fuentes. El tren y la mujer que llena el cielo.

ESMERALDA: (reading) Tu soledad esquiva en los hoteles y tu mascara pura de otro signo.

SAM: (reading) Yes, your childhood: now a fable of fountains. The train and the woman who fill the sky.

ESMERALDA: (reading) Your scornful solitude in hotels and your mask-like face purely for another destiny.

SAM: Your pronunciation is improving dramatically.

ESMERALDA: You think?

SAM: I do.

ESMERALDA: Good. This'll help me. 'Cause I got a new job. That's right. Check it out. So I'm gonna work in a...travel agency...like a travel sales assistant. (beat) Okay, so, what? Don't look at me that way.

SAM: Huh. Travel sales assistant. Why didn't you tell me before?

ESMERALDA: 'Cause I mean I interviewed on Monday but they didn't tell me I had it until this morning and like I could've told you or whatever or called you but you're all bailing and heading back to prison law firm land so I thought I'd save the surprise. What? I don't start until next week. God that look. What's with that look?

SAM: I dunno.

ESMERALDA: Don't scare me with that look. Don't make me feel bad with that look.

SAM: Whatever.

ESMERALDA: So don't you wanna hear what I'm gonna be doing?

SAM: Yeah. Sure. Go on.

ESMERALDA: You think I don't wanna study with you anymore, isn't that it? You think I don't wanna ever speak to you again. God, what an assumption. Where you do you get these ideas? I still want our lessons. I still wanna be with you. God.

SAM: Go on. Tell me. Your job.

ESMERALDA: Because look, I mean, I like our lessons. Come on. Before I was like hostile to the idea of learning this language and now...not so much. I mean I don't know that I'll be enrolling in any university any time soon...but you know...I'm improving, right? And I like the routine. The learning routine, with you, alright?

SAM: Yeah. Right. Tell me about being a travel sales assistant.

ESMERALDA: I can't. I can't tell you if you're gonna act like that.

SAM: Esmeralda…

ESMERALDA: That look on your face says it all.

SAM: Fine. Good. Look, I have to get back to my parents and....

ESMERALDA: What, and you're taking the bus home from Santa Monica all the way to Pasadena?

SAM: I've done it before.

ESMERALDA: Puh-lease. Sit down.

SAM: No really. I mean it's sort of peaceful. Sitting as the city goes whirring by.

ESMERALDA: It'll take you like five hours to get home. Sit.

SAM: Go on about your job.

ESMERALDA: Okay. Okay. So like it's this cool student-type agency with tons of people my age. I'm taking this travel training class. I'm taking a fuckin' class. Alright. Alright. No applause. If it works out, I get to help people choose tours and then after a while I get to go on the tours myself...like a discount thing, you know, for being like a good employee and shit...and I get to fly.

SAM: Great. Good.

ESMERALDA: And okay, so...the tours are mostly to Latin countries...like they have some to Mexico, Peru, Guatemala, Argentina, Costa Rica...to like the pyramids and the rivers and the jungles and the mountains. And so I'll be able to use my language skills when I help people choose like the best tour for them. Okay, so get this. (in her best telephone voice) Hello, sir, and which country would you like to travel to? Or...Buenos dias, señor. A que pais quiere usted viajar? (beat) That's what I'm talkin' about.

SAM: I think that's great.

ESMERALDA: You hate the idea. I can tell.

SAM: What? No. I don't hate it.

ESMERALDA: You think the idea of me being a bilingual travel sales assistant is like the same thing as a hot dog stand seller becoming like a nuclear scientist. Well, I'll tell you mister...I can sell a mean hot dog and discover nuclear science all at the same time. Huh? Huh?

SAM: No, I guess, I'll just you know...sort of miss...the lessons and stuff...you know.

ESMERALDA: I'm not going to Siberia...god would you look at that face.

SAM: Right. Good. Um, can we get going now?

ESMERALDA: I don't think so.

SAM: Okay. Soon it gets dark. It gets dark and the edges of society find their way down to the beach and then it's unpleasant. What once was a refuge for us becomes a refuge for them and while that's fine and well, I rather be on my way.

ESMERALDA: You're so paranoid. Relax.

SAM: I am not paranoid. Would you stop it with your pronouncements? God.

ESMERALDA: Fine. You're neurotic. Not paranoid.

SAM: Esmeralda. You really don't know. You go through your existence with this attitude that there is plenty, that when this experience is over there is another one waiting right there. Another life to fall into. I marvel at your capacity for change. That is your gift. To morph, transform from one existence to the next. Earthquake chica. But see, like the terremoto that your dear old dad named you, this force you have shifts things in its wake...shifts and rattles and dare I say destructs things in its path.

ESMERALDA: I am not destructive. I am not an earthquake.

SAM: Since we first talked at that party, I've like been googling on earthquakes okay and like a terremoto is a vibration of the earth's surface that is followed by a release of energy in the earth's crust. The crust dislocates, bends, breaks and snaps to a new position.

ESMERALDA: You know, I don't need this shit.

SAM: And earthquakes tend to occur along faults which exhibit zones of weakness of the earth's crust. And they can generate tidal waves, landslides and disintegrating the ground into liquid.

ESMERALDA: And you are like a little mole who doesn't wanna give up his hole in the ground...even though he pokes his head out and might go a few tiny steps...he always has to run back and burrow into his tunnel deep inside the earth. And he doesn't like sex because he's like practically married to his mother and it's all twisted and strange and sick.

SAM: I'm outta here.

ESMERALDA: Am I right?

SAM: Okay. So Carina was my only girlfriend alright. The bucket girl. And we actually slept together like only eight times. She was my college girlfriend, whatever, I thought it was because she was religious but then she told me she only slept with me eight times because she didn't like how I did it, couldn't practically bare it, as it turns out, but she was too scared to find someone else and that's when I just said, fine...cry in your bucket 'cause I'm outta here. Done. The end. Don't need this. Don't need anyone really. And that's it. Alright. It. And...shit. Forget it. You know, be a travel agent assistant...whatever. You know. Do it. Have fun.

ESMERALDA: Come on.

SAM: No, because you don't understand the effect you have on people. You make me feel insane inside. Sure I appear calm, but inside like tectonic plates are moving. And I don't wanna be like those tattooed wonders who used you. Alright? I don't. And if I'm not in a category then

I'm not. But now...even the opportunity to be around you is gone and that will make life harder. For me.

ESMERALDA: You want more mattress time...

SAM: Esmeralda...

ESMERALDA: But I'm not just like gonna have pity-sex with you.

SAM: It doesn't matter.

ESMERALDA: You know you want it.

SAM: Call me too whatever, no, I don't wanna head into that territory with you again because I know I'd lose the other connection quite possibly but at this point I've probably lost any connection with you which is really a large disappointment.

ESMERALDA: You picture me wearing a little pink nightie and then taking it off every night before you go to bed, don't you?

SAM: Okay, I'm taking the bus now. I like the bus. At least you don't have to talk to anyone on the bus. People can smell and stink and belch but you don't have to talk to any damn one of them.

*A FEW BEATS.*

ESMERALDA: I don't really know how to be with you, to be honest. I don't.

SAM: Really.

ESMERALDA: I fake my way through these things. Deep down I don't know how to be with you. Someone like you who doesn't run away. Someone who listens to me, stays with me, isn't freaked out by me.

SAM: And like I don't know why you want to be with me, someone like me, someone who's not like the guys you'd normally hang with, someone who if you met him in high school like you'd never ever talk to.

ESMERALDA: You know I resent the fact that you agree with my dead father. An earthquake is a horrible thing for a father to call his young daughter.

SAM: Like it or not though, it's in you. But you don't have to let it stop you like your father stopped you.

ESMERALDA: I had no choice when he's the raging head of the household and I'm a little kid trying to survive.

SAM: But now you do. He's gone, Esmeralda, but you don't have to let his ghost keep you from the true Esmeralda who wants to revel in the beauty of the world of her ancestors.

ESMERALDA: I just never wanted to be like him. I wasn't the earthquake. He was. I'm forceful, sure. But it's the destructive part. Shit.

SAM: Out in the middle of the desert, when the plates move and earthquakes occur, they do so to relieve pressure and assist the constant motion deep below the surface. In the desert, there is wide open expanse so the break in the crust becomes part of the landscape. It can be beautiful.

ESMERALDA: But you're saying that when I'm in a city I wreak havoc on buildings, homes, on unsuspecting citizens, right?

SAM: That's overstating the case but you're in the ballpark.

ESMERALDA: You have no idea, Sam. I wanna finish things. I can't. I see my sister the physicist and I feel crazy. I think of my father and I wanna run. And then my heart starts pumping. And I can't breathe. And my feet feel like lead. And my stomach fills with glass. And my chest is like a lump of charcoal. And my hair and eye lashes start to fall out. It's not enjoyable. I have to keep moving. I have to.

SAM: Your father's gone. Your sister lives her own life and so can you.

ESMERALDA: But if I stop for too long the empty lonely silence descends and I have no way out. Before booze and boys were the great escape...but I don't want that anymore...so I have to keep moving. If I don't, my mind starts to earthquake. Starts to move and shift and get destructive. So I'm earthquake chica in a way, inside my head, I guess.

SAM: Your mind can be marvelous, not destructive.

ESMERALDA: Okay maybe but now you're going back to prison law firm land and I'm going off to this awesome travel world job and yeah I'm excited but like what if I can't stand it and the office smells like toxic chemicals and the travel people are horrible and I won't have you there to talk to and oh god...my breath...and then...

SAM: Slow down. Breathe.

ESMERALDA: And then but I'll be all alone. And I hate my tiny apartment. I lie in bed and I hear my nutcase neighbor screaming at his Siamese cat or playing electric bass at midnight and I think what's the point? Why live another day? I mean why have all this craziness inside my head? Oh god...my breath.

SAM: Esmeralda, stop.

ESMERALDA: No really, what's the point? If I'm an earthquake and I'm so destructive, why keep being here on this planet? Why not just leave forever? Everyone's left me. I'm not helping anyone apparently. I'm not really good at anything. I can't finish jobs...I can't even have relationships. Really, why be here? Why not just leave for good...who really cares anyway?

SAM: Take a deep breath.

ESMERALDA: You say you care but do you really? I don't think so. I mean you can't stand to be with me so much that you're going back to that horrible job in that far away land where large bellied secretaries roam. And then you're gone just like everyone else in my life. You don't care really. No one does. But that's okay. I can just leave this planet and no one will care. I mean I lie in bed and I fantasize about how I'd do it. Pills? Razor blades? Rope? And I think maybe. Why not? Who'd care really?

SAM: The earthquake must stop now. No more tremors. No more seismic waves. No more existing along fault lines. No more aftershocking scenarios. You don't deserve it and neither do I. Listen to me, Esmeralda. I'm going back there but...I'm not gonna abandon you forever.

ESMERALDA: Really?

SAM: Really.

ESMERALDA: Oh.

SAM: Truly.

ESMERALDA: But Sammy, what if...

SAM: Shhhh. Calma. Let me say a prayer for you...for us.

ESMERALDA: Do we have to get all crazy religious at the beach?

**SCENE EIGHT**

*WEDNESDAY EVENING. LIGHTS RISE ON SAM AND ESMERALDA STANDING IN FRONT OF A BANK OF VOTIVE CANDLES IN A CATHOLIC CHURCH.*

SAM: Light it.

ESMERALDA: Makes me nervous.

SAM: Light it and say something peaceful inside your head.

ESMERALDA: You light it.

SAM: You have to.

ESMERALDA: Do you put money in here?

SAM: Some people do.

ESMERALDA: I don't think you should have to pay to pray.

SAM: Light the candle.

*ESMERALDA LIGHTS THE CANDLE. THEY CLOSE THEIR EYES. A*
*BEAT. THEY OPEN THEIR EYES.*

SAM: I think we should get married.

ESMERALDA: What? I thought we already went through this.

SAM: No, I really do. But a different kind of marriage.

ESMERALDA: There's only one kind that I know of. What different kind
do you mean?

SAM: Of the minds. A marriage of the minds.

ESMERALDA: Come on. We're in a church. Please.

SAM: No, I was thinking about it and you've been right all along. The
physical thing has really gotten in the way. I mean I think of all the men
you've done.

ESMERALDA: Sam...

SAM: Waking up in strange rooms. A few nights. A few days. All the
variety of bodies you've seen.

ESMERALDA: Please...

SAM: I'm confessing to you.

ESMERALDA: Could you confess a little softer please?

SAM: Whatever. I mean I thought about that and you know, where are
they? They're off in the universe somewhere. Gone. Adios. And I don't
wanna join them in that whatever forever place, you know?

ESMERALDA: Could we talk outside. Please?

SAM: No, Because I wanna get married.

ESMERALDA: Sam...

SAM: Seriously. Here. Now. Before God.

*SAM KNEELS DOWN ON THE FLOOR, ON ONE KNEE.*

SAM: Esmeralda Portillo, will you marry me, Samuel Reyes?

ESMERALDA: This is wrong.

SAM: Will you?

ESMERALDA: Get up off the ground. People are looking.

SAM: Who cares? Will you marry my mind? Our minds will live happily ever after together. Our minds will take care of each other in our old age.

ESMERALDA: I think we should step outside.

SAM: You haven't answered my question.

ESMERALDA: Okay...so what if I want more than just your mind?

SAM: (mock surprise) Please. We're in a church.

ESMERALDA: I'm confessing.

SAM: Fine then.

ESMERALDA: What if I marry your mind but later I want more than just your mind. What then?

SAM: Well, you see, this marriage of the minds is flexible. It's an open sort of thing. It starts up here (pointing to his head) and then it will allow other body parts to participate if the participation won't detract from the primary function of the marriage...

ESMERALDA: Which is....

SAM: To nourish and heal the mind of the other.

ESMERALDA: And who performs this ceremony?

SAM: We do.

ESMERALDA: Doesn't sound like an official marriage then, really.

SAM: It is.

ESMERALDA: And where does this ceremony take place?

SAM: Well, I believe that's right here.

ESMERALDA: But people are starting to stare at us.

SAM: So? You still haven't answered my question.

ESMERALDA: What kind of fringe benefits does it include? Daily lessons? Shacking up together? Mattress time? What?

SAM: That's to be negotiated.

ESMERALDA: Alright.

SAM: You're drivin' me crazy here. What's your answer?

ESMERALDA: I think it's a pretty strange request seeing as we haven't read together yet.

SAM: Yes we have.

ESMERALDA: Not completely together.

SAM: You mean simultaneously, breathing in and out at the same commas, semi-colons and exclamation points. Pronouncing every syllable together.

ESMERALDA: Shall we?

*SAM TAKES OUT HIS DOG-EARED BOOK.*

SAM: Inside here, now?

ESMERALDA: It's holy.

SAM: Which one do we pick?

ESMERALDA: The Neruda dude. The one he wrote about the dictionary.

SAM: Oda al diccionario.

ESMERALDA: His holy book.

SAM: Hallowed language

*ESMERALDA POINTS TO A PASSAGE.*

ESMERALDA: (reading) De tu espesa y sonora...(stopping) come on.

ESMERALDA AND SAM: (reading) De tu espesa y sonora profundidad de selva...From your dense and musical jungle depths

ESMERALDA: Give me, when I need it, one solitary trill,

SAM: a bee's abundance, a fallen fragment from your ancient wood

ESMERALDA: infused with an eternity of jasmine,

SAM: one syllable, one earthquake,

ESMERALDA: one sound, one seed:

SAM: I am of the earth

ESMERALDA: And with words I sing

ESMERALDA AND SAM: de tierra soy y con palabras canto.

ESMERALDA: I accept.

SAM: You do?

ESMERALDA: You heard me, now let's get to it, chicky-chico.

SAM: Therefore, I, Samuel, take you, Esmeralda, to be my spiritually minded partner. To have and to hold, through mental atrophy and cerebral stimulation, till death do us part.

ESMERALDA: And I, Esmeralda, take you, Samuel, to be my spiritually minded partner, to have and to hold, through mental atrophy and cerebral stimulation, till death do us part.

SAM: The book please?

*THEY BOTH HOLD THE BOOK.*

SAM: By the powers of Neruda, Lorca and Borges, I now pronounce us mindfully married.

ESMERALDA: What do we do now?

SAM: Well, we could strip naked and start spontaneously spouting poetry at the top of our lungs. Or...

ESMERALDA: We could...

*SAM AND ESMERALDA KISS.*

SAM: There. It's done.

ESMERALDA: Es todo.

**SCENE NINE**

*ONE MONTH LATER. MONDAY EVENING. LIGHTS RISE ON ESMERALDA AND SAM STANDING BY A STAIRCASE AT LAX INTERNATIONAL AIRPORT.*

SAM: Passport?

ESMERALDA: Check.

SAM: Snacks?

ESMERALDA: Mini-donuts. Check.

SAM: Reading material?

ESMERALDA: Gossip magazines. Check. How was law firm land today?

SAM: Inmates were restless. Wardens patrolled on the hour. Quite a few lifers still around. No electric chair victims yet this week.

ESMERALDA: So when Eduardo, my new manager, told me about the tour...when he said that he was so psyched with my sales assistance that I get to spend ten days on the ancient civilizations tour...I was like almost jumping up and down and not just because of what he said but because I could picture my former law slave existence and I felt free.

SAM: (deflated) Great.

ESMERALDA: You don't think I'm coming back, do you? You think I'm gonna take this tour to Mexico and Peru and Guatemala and meet some fine hombre and like abandon you forever. Don't you? I'm not gonna abandon you.

SAM: You should. You're the brave one, really.

ESMERALDA: Don't turn into such a lump of clay. Geez.

SAM: Esmeralda, offices are like way stations on the river of life. For whatever reason, you get off here. I get off here. We meet. We talk. We connect. You learn. You change. You grow. You quit. You depart. And the river takes you downstream. And you don't look back. You don't. And you don't need to really. Because you're going on to brighter things really. I knew that from the first night at the party. You were here maybe to get strong or stable or sturdy or something to move onward. It's okay though. You should go, you know.

ESMERALDA: So more lessons soon?

SAM: Yeah. Sure. Lessons. Not a problem.

ESMERALDA: You know, I'm not into infidelity. I mean I know tons of people are. But not me.

SAM: We're not married. Do what you want.

ESMERALDA: Excuse me. I believe we are, señor.

SAM: Esmeralda. Really.

ESMERALDA: I'm gonna call you.

SAM: You do that.

ESMERALDA: Check it out. I had this dream last night. And in the dream, we're both standing in the middle of this desert. And there is this huge fault line in the earth and it's filled with all kinds of vegetation and plant life and we're like leaping in and out of the rift, you and me and the sun is blinding almost, but it doesn't seem to bother us. And I wake up with the phrase earthquake chica on my tongue. And a feeling of contentment inside my body. (Spanish pronunciation) Samuel Reyes.

SAM: My mother named me after the prophet Samuel. I told her, "If you like religious names, why not pick Emmanuel? Something a bit more famous, musical perhaps."

ESMERALDA: Prophet Kings. Royalty. Seeing the future. You see. That is your gift.

*SAM PULLS HIS DOG EARED BOOK FROM HIS BRIEFCASE AND HANDS IT TO ESMERALDA.*

ESMERALDA: (with Spanish pronunciation) Poesía y ficción.

SAM: Keep it. More reading material.

ESMERALDA: But...

SAM: On the inside cover, I wrote this thing for you. It's not very good compared to...I mean...but...yeah. Um. Read it? Later?

*AN AWKWARD BEAT.*

ESMERALDA: Gracias, Samuel.

*ANOTHER AWKWARD BEAT.*

SAM: Speak tons of Spanish.

ESMERALDA: Sí, chico loco.

SAM: As you take flight.

ESMERALDA: No cactus runway.

SAM: Just asphalt, thank God in heaven above.

ESMERALDA: Are you gonna get religiously freaky on me?

SAM: (pointing to his head) In here. Silently I'll pray.

ESMERALDA: As I fly over la tierra toward the horizon.

SAM: Bye. Adios.

*SAM EXITS. ESMERALDA OPENS THE BOOK AND READS THE*
*INSCRIPTION WITH A FINE SPANISH PRONUNCIATION.*

ESMERALDA:
Una esmeralda
ahora queda adentro
y nunca termina su brillo.

Ya no está cerrado
Sino abierto.

Un portillo de esmeralda
Hacia mi corazón.

An emerald
Now lodges inside
whose beauty never fades.

A gate's
no longer closed
but open.

An emerald gate
Into my heart.

*ESMERALDA ASCENDS THE STAIRCASE AS THE LIGHTS FADE.*
*BLACKOUT. END OF PLAY.*

**MARY PEABODY IN CUBA**
For Barbara

MARY PEABODY IN CUBA has been developed at INTAR and
New Dramatists in New York City.

**CHARACTERS**

Present

AMY DIAZ, 28, Cuban-American, Ph.D. student in U.S. history
ALICE DIAZ, 21, Cuban-American, her sister
SARAH DIAZ, 55, Anglo, her mother
ROBERTO "BETO" ALVAREZ, 30, American journalist
MIGUEL CAMPOS, 40, Cuban journalist and librarian
HENRY JOHNSON, 50, professor, chair, U.S. history department

1833

MARY PEABODY, 28, English tutor
SOPHIA PEABODY, 25, her sister
JUAN VELASCO, 40, Spanish tutor
JAMES REDMOND, 50, their employer, sugar plantation owner
AMELIA REDMOND, 14, pupil, daughter of James Redmond
MRS. BATSON, 55, housekeeper to James Redmond
FRANCISCO, 30, butler to James Redmond

THE CAST SHOULD TOTAL SEVEN.

ALL ROLES SHOULD BE DOUBLED AS FOLLOWS:

AMY/MARY, ALICE/SOPHIA, SARAH/BATSON, AMELIA

BETO/FRANCISCO, MIGUEL/JUAN, HENRY/REDMOND

**SETTING**

Present. New York City and Havana, Cuba.
1833, Cuba. A sugar plantation on the outskirts of Havana.

**Note:** This unproduced play is included in this collection for it artistically completes this trio of plays. This version, though, will undoubtedly shift during a future production process.

## MARY PEABODY IN CUBA

## SCENE ONE

*SPOTLIGHT ON AMY.*

AMY: My fingers felt the traces of her nineteenth century ink. In 1833, she dipped her quill into an inkwell and created tiny letters to form cherished words which grew into elegant sentences. I get ahead of myself though. Before I touch the delicate pages, before I'm buzzed into the Special Collections room, before I climb the stone steps to the New York Public Library, before I exit the Times Square subway station and scurry up Forty-Third street, I want nothing to do with her or her destination.

*LIGHTS SHIFT. NEW YORK CITY. PRESENT. LIGHTS RISE ON AMY, SARAH AND ALICE AT DINNER IN SARAH'S APARTMENT.*

AMY: So I'm heading down Seventh Avenue...

ALICE: On a kick-ass date?

SARAH: Started writing your first chapter yet, Amy?

ALICE: A semi-kick-ass date?

SARAH: Do you know the percentage of students who never finish their doctorate?

ALICE: Meet a fellow doctor. Doctor love, that's what I'm talkin' about.

SARAH: Momentum, Amy. Maintain forward momentum.

AMY: And this anxiety thing...

ALICE: Stressed, Ames? Try yoga. Tree pose. Very calming.

SARAH: Your exams are over.

ALICE: Or do meditation...visualize...chant.

AMY: I felt kind of...

SARAH: Now onto the first chapter...

ALICE: Or hook up...with inappropriate people.

SARAH: Of your dissertation...

ALICE: Or all of the above, really...

SARAH: if you plan to finish your degree.

AMY: So...I ended up in the emergency room this afternoon...

SARAH: Jesus. Why didn't you say something?

ALICE: What's up with that?

AMY: Yeah and if you'd let me get a word in, I mean...

SARAH: Where did you...

ALICE: Amy, spill it.

AMY: St. Vincent's. Shortness of breath. Numbness of the tongue.

ALICE: This is what I'm talking about.

AMY: Got an EKG. Normal. Then this doctor with kind blue eyes and rather hairy arms told me to breathe into a paper bag. Reabsorbs the carbon dioxide.

SARAH: God.

AMY: Called it a stress related condition. Sees it all the time in grad students. (beat) So I'm thinking...I wanna quit.

SARAH: And end up stuck behind a desk, pushing paper in some menial office job on the fortieth floor of a downtown highrise for the rest of your life? Don't be disgusting.

AMY: I thought I might rent a car...

ALICE: A Maserati.

AMY: (getting caught up in a reverie) Escape the Upper East Side, drive down FDR drive, across the Triborough bridge, up Grand Central parkway to LaGuardia...

ALICE: I'm down with that. Can I come with?

AMY: And then, hop on a plane...

ALICE: A private Lear jet.

AMY: To the South Pacific. Fiji maybe.

ALICE: I can help you feel liberated and not so disgusting.

SARAH: Oh please...

ALICE: What...I could.

AMY: Would it be so disgusting to be a secretary on the island of Fiji?

SARAH: After three years in a Ph.D. program with nothing to show for it? Yes. Forty to fifty percent drop out, Amy. Forty to fifty.

AMY: Okay, so...as I'm lecturing on Horace Mann today and I'm saying...in 1837 blah blah blah Horace Mann posits a new model for the U.S. educational reform quote...Education must be universal. Every addition to true knowledge is an addition to human power...I look out at my students and they're either comatose or hungover or asleep...and I feel this tingling on the left side of my face and I'm having a hard time catching my breath and then it stops....and I think I'm done...outta here...and then I'm walking down Seventh Avenue and the numbness starts and I duck into St. Vincent's.

SARAH: Thank god you're okay. (beat) But you're not quitting. Alice, pass your sister some meatloaf.

*AWKWARD SILENCE.*

AMY: I wonder what this moment would be like if Papi were sitting at this table.

ALICE: He wouldn't be sitting with us. He'd be parked on the living room couch, with his dinner on a tray, watching the nightly news with the volume turned up really loud to drown out this conversation. We'd be hearing about robberies and murders at this point.

SARAH: Oh and your father would say, "Fine just quit."

AMY: He clearly got me on a deeper level.

SARAH: And what level is that?

AMY: He certainly wouldn't endlessly nag me when he could plainly see that I'm exhausted.

*AWKWARD BEAT.*

ALICE: I wonder how Mother ever fell in love with a Cuban.

SARAH: Can we not discuss your father while we're eating?

ALICE: Sarah Peabody hooks up with Fernando Diaz.

SARAH: Alice...

ALICE: Oh come on...why won't you tell us about your hot Cuban sex life?

SARAH: Stop it.

ALICE: "Stop it." Would you listen to her?

AMY: Al, forget it. She'll never answer.

ALICE: Why not?

SARAH: Some things are better left unsaid.

AMY: Why're they better left unsaid?

ALICE: Okay, so when I was eleven and we're at Papi's memorial service and I'm hearing you talk about like your enduring love for him and then after, at the reception, I'm pestering you like..."What's enduring love?" and you're all, "Later, later." Okay, at that moment, unsaid was a decent choice. But now? I don't think so.

AMY: She has a point.

SARAH: Amy, you're going to start the first chapter of your dissertation on Horace Mann.

AMY: Why won't she ever even talk about Papi?

SARAH: And you must include a chapter on Horace's wife, Mary Peabody.

AMY: Why will she only ever discuss the office, the university, the movies, the weather but any deeper level and it's like hitting a wall of granite or like Plymouth Rock for godsakes.

ALICE: Because, apparently, some things are better left unsaid.

SARAH: My mother's family lineage connects directly to Horace's wife, Mary Peabody Mann. It's unforgivable if you don't include her.

AMY: Fine. Great. Got it.

SARAH: Mary worked with Horace tirelessly. She even translated his work into Spanish. I mean Mary Peabody traveled to Cuba for godssakes.

AMY: Is she even listening to me?

ALICE: Ah...that would be a no.

SARAH: Grandmother kept saying that's why I married your father. That it's in the blood. This connection to that island.

AMY: (to Sarah) In the blood...huh.

**SCENE TWO**

*SPOTLIGHT ON AMY.*

AMY: At that time, on the left side of my face, there was this tightness which sometimes traveled down my left arm. And on certain days I felt a constriction beneath my ribcage, like a hand trying to compress my insides. And beneath this is a feeling that another part of me lay submerged. Dormant. Unknown. Hard to grasp. Almost caged. And the key? This Mary Peabody. 1806 to 1887. Mother's ancestor. My ancestor. Married Horace Mann in 1843. Her sister, Sophia Peabody married Nathaniel Hawthorne that same year. Yet a decade earlier, the unmarried sisters traveled to Cuba. I didn't seem to care but beneath the resistance I did. Something propelled me forward, to dig, to search for a small opening inside.

**SCENE THREE**

*LIGHTS RISE ON AMY AND HENRY IN HENRY'S UNIVERSITY OFFICE.*

HENRY: Horace Mann's wife should be cited in a footnote and then move on.

AMY: But come on, Henry, a section or even a chapter on her could support my argument for diverse influences on his educational model and...

HENRY: (interrupting) While I appreciate your initiative, you need to focus on passing your written exams.

AMY: But you yourself suggested I investigate new lines of inquiry.

HENRY: I can appreciate the impulse. And of course, this moment is...well...challenging but this is a time to refocus, regroup and not rethink your entire project.

AMY: I thought that rethinking the project could help.

HENRY: Your committee is looking for you to retake your exams at the end of next semester...not embark on some new line of inquiry regarding a sojourn in Havana. You're not a Carribeanist.

AMY: I'm well aware of that.

HENRY: Amy Diaz, Ph.D. student, U.S. History. Nineteenth century Americanist. At this juncture, that's your path.

AMY: What if that path is like made of tiny gray jagged rocks and I'm barefoot and...

HENRY: You're not the first person to fail her exams in this department.

AMY: I'm suffering from some serious sleep deprivation.

HENRY: Have you tried ambien?

AMY: I can barely drag myself to class.

HENRY: You'll get through this.

AMY: So I'm lying in bed at 3:34 A.M. and I think...maybe this new angle will impress my committee that I have a renewed commitment to my topic and...

HENRY: I'm afraid not.

AMY: Huh.

HENRY: This isn't just about you, Amy.

AMY: I realize that but...

HENRY: You take this diversion, you go off on this tangent and you jeopardize finishing your degree. If you don't finish your degree then this impacts this department's standing in this university, not to mention the field at large, and as chair, I have to mitigate these possibilities.

AMY: So if I fail again, you look bad.

HENRY: It's not about looking bad, it's about funding, it's about reputation, it's about career livelihood, for both of us, frankly.

AMY: But the thing of it is, Henry, I need this new angle. I studied my ass off. I failed. If I fail again, then I drop out. If I drop out, I'm saddled with student loan payments with no income. I get some sorry ass job and try not to become suicidal. So before I reach that juncture, I've decided that I'll be researching and writing about this Mary Peabody so maybe just maybe she'll reignite my passion which apparently is being suffocated and extinguished by this department.

**SCENE FOUR**

*LIGHTS RISE ON BETO AND AMY IN A CAFE.*

BETO: I cover current day Caribbean issues. I'm not a nineteenth centuryist.

AMY: Yeah, I realize that, but Professor Olaria in Latin American studies told me about your article on the Cuban writers...

BETO: My piece on the independent journalists...

AMY: Right...and he recommended I contact you...

BETO: Carlos.

AMY: Carlos said you might have some suggestions for my research and so...

BETO: Look, I'm on deadline right now. If you need someone to help you bridge the historic U.S.- Cuban divide, I'm not your guy.

AMY: Excuse me?

BETO: U.S. Anglo culture's obsession with revolutionary Cuba.

AMY: But I'm researching pre-revolutionary colonial Cuba.

BETO: Forget it. For most people in the U.S., Cuban history starts in 1959.

AMY: So why even meet me?

BETO: Carlos is an old friend. Former professor, actually. Thought I'd set one of his students straight.

AMY: He's not my professor. We work in the same department. And does he know you're always this rude to his quote students unquote?

BETO: I'm not being rude. You academics often don't wanna hear the truth...

AMY: Is this the part where you set me straight?

BETO: ...about your often misguided research.

AMY: Misguided.

BETO: Don't waste your time when most U.S. citizens could care less about what happens down there at this point.

AMY: Well then doesn't that make your job obsolete?

BETO: I freelance for foreign press agencies mostly.

AMY: I aim to write for academic journals mostly.

BETO: And you're accusing me of being obsolete?

AMY: You know, I gotta go. Good luck with that deadline.

*AMY STARTS TO LEAVE.*

BETO: Look...check out the New York Public Library Special Collections department. I used it once for an article. You might find something unobsolete there. Maybe.

## SCENE FIVE

*SPOTLIGHT ON AMY.*

AMY: I take the two train uptown. I get off at Times Square. I walk up past Bryant Park to Fifth Avenue. I climb the stone steps past the regal lions. I take the elevator to the third floor. I am buzzed into the wood paneled room. I am handed a delicate tome filled with handwritten letters. Cuba Journal. Brown ink on faded white paper. Right slanting cursive with the curling y's and beautiful f's. One hundred and three pages. Twenty-four lines on a page. Twelve words per line. Her words.

*LIGHTS SHIFT. 1833. SPOTLIGHT ON MARY.*

MARY: My dearest Mother and Father, here we are just one month after setting sail from our beloved Boston which at present seems but a distant memory. I will allow that you were right in your expectations that Sophia would be cured by this same trip to Cuba. In accordance with Doctor Nimmock's orders, I have no doubt that the tropical air will have a positive effect on her headaches. Please tell Elizabeth that I regret my initial reluctance whereupon she informed me that as our sister's guardian, I would be gone for a year, possibly two. And please tell Mr. Horace Mann that this particular Peabody sister shall miss the opportunity to engage in intellectual debate for quite some time. Oh how I wish you could see this remarkable landscape which surrounds us now. I dare say the Italian coast would pale in comparison.

## SCENE SIX

*PRESENT. THE NEXT DAY. LIGHTS RISE ON AMY AND BETO IN A CAFE. AMY HANDS BETO A TYPEWRITTEN PAGE.*

AMY: I only transcribed four. The handwriting's so condensed and the cursive's hard to read at times. I'll go back to the library tomorrow. There's this one part where Mary quotes a letter entirely in Spanish from a Juan someone. Could you translate?

*AMY POINTS TO A SECTION ON THE PAGE.*

BETO: Querida María. Dear Mary. I...he mentions something about a poem and her teaching Emerson on the hacienda. Signed Juan. Maybe she had a Cuban lover.

AMY: But she returns to Boston and marries Horace, and together they promote his common school philosophy which creates the foundation for the U.S. public education system and...

BETO: But maybe Mary had a pre-Horace, nineteenth century Cuban fling.

*BETO LOOKS OVER THE REST OF THE LETTER.*

AMY: She mentions in here something about a Mr. Velasco, I think.

BETO: Velasco. Juan Velasco?

*AMY LOOKS THROUGH HER TRANSCRIBED LETTERS.*

AMY: Uh...here she writes, "One of the company today was Mr. Velasco, a charming and well educated Cuban gentleman." She doesn't say Juan, who was...

BETO: Come on...Velasco? Nineteenth century revolutionary poet? And you're getting your Ph.D. in history?

AMY: U.S. history. Sorry...

BETO: And your father was Cuban?

AMY: Okay...what?

BETO: Velasco helped create Los Soles Y Los Rayos de Bolivar...the suns and rays of Bolivar...one of the earliest efforts in the fight for Cuban independence from Spain. It's like saying you've never heard of Benjamin Franklin...or Patrick Henry...or...

AMY: Okay. Fine. I get it. (beat) So then why would he write to her?

BETO: If you could prove Mrs. Mary Peabody Mann had a fling with Juan Velasco before she married Horace...now then you'd be on to something. You know what you have to do don't you?

AMY: Spend the next year of my life in the special collections department. And completely change my dissertation title from Nineteenth Century Education Reform in Antebellum New England to include Cuba or the Caribbean or something.

BETO: Visit the island.

AMY: Well, that's not happening.

BETO: Research there.

AMY: I don't think so.

BETO: Talk to some of my contacts.

AMY: Thanks for the offer but...

BETO: Do field work of your own.

AMY: Not happening.

BETO: I'm flying there in a few weeks. Researching another story about the independent journalists. You could be my quote - research assistant - unquote.

AMY: Even while he was still conscious, lying on his hospital bed, hours before his death, his breathing labored, his spirit departing, my father swore he'd never return. I just won't do it.

BETO: Amy, he's not around anymore. Do whatever you want.

AMY: Don't you feel at all conflicted about traveling there?

BETO: I'm only reporting...off the record. I arrive. I report. I leave.

AMY: My father left the island at age seven. He would never ever talk about his childhood there and a kind of sadness and resentment always hovered over him his entire life.

BETO: Any relatives still there?

AMY: Passed away. My father was an only child. His parents were immigrants from Spain...Asturias, I think.

BETO: And you have no interest in ever...ever traveling there?

AMY: Interest isn't the issue. Principle.

BETO: You're an educator. Education. Raising awareness. You just found this link between influential nineteenth century figures and you'd just rather not go. I'd say it's fear, not principle stopping you.

AMY: I'm late for lecture.

*AMY GETS UP TO LEAVE. BETO GRABS HER HAND AND LOOKS AT HER INTENTLY.*

BETO: Consider my offer. Don't be afraid. Experience the island for yourself.

**SCENE SEVEN**

*A WEEK LATER. LIGHTS RISE ON AMY AND HENRY IN HENRY'S UNIVERSITY OFFICE.*

AMY: Henry, I need this break. I'll keep studying for my exams on the plane. I'll study while I'm there. I just feel this could develop my topic further, looking at the influences on Mann's educational model...

HENRY: If you need a break, then spend a week in the Hamptons. However, Americanist takes Cubanist research detour? I won't be party to that misstep.

AMY: Henry, come on. Ten days.

HENRY: It's more than just ten days. The rest of your committee, not to mention this department, learns of your Caribbeanist activities and doubts your seriousness as an Americanist scholar when you divert your energies from your research topic at a crucial moment in your academic career.

AMY: So I spend ten days on the island and there goes my exams, my research, my degree, my job search, my hope for a tenure-track position?

HENRY: You won't be able to go through this university. NYU won't approve it without my signature. I'm sorry.

AMY: So you can't just sign this form, as a favor?

HENRY: I owe you favors?

AMY: As one human being to the next?

HENRY: So I'm inhuman if I don't sign this?

AMY: What if you had the opportunity to travel to the land of your father's birth, a land you'd always heard of but never been able to visit, and all of a sudden, the universe gives you this opening and you feel that maybe, just maybe this visit may help you, may very well be a key to unlocking things inside of you.

HENRY: I sign this form and I'm liable. The department's liable. The university's liable. How do I know what you're doing on this trip?

AMY: So now I'm a liability?

HENRY: Yes. Your trip has a tenuous connection to your research topic. Now is not the time to be traveling anywhere except to the library, actually.

AMY: What if you lived in some distant country and your daughter wanted to visit New York City, this exotic land where her father lived and worked, and her advisor wouldn't let her, wouldn't allow her to try to access this part of herself.

HENRY: On a personal level, I sympathize with your position. But this is strictly a professional situation and I resent the fact that you're trying to present it as otherwise.

AMY: See, here's the thing. The personal and professional are not separate entities, Henry. You sign this form, I get the student visa, my mother sees I am taking this approved research trip and then she, the ever staunch English professor, supports me and actually takes pride in my efforts and then I go, research, come back, reinvigorated, pass my exams, and go onto a glorious academic career.

HENRY: I realize the challenges in telling your mother about your exams may seem insurmountable but taking this trip as a diversion will only compound the matter.

AMY: (lying) She knows. This isn't about not telling her. This is about me. And my process.

HENRY: She does. She knows?

AMY: (lying) Of course.

HENRY: And so all this is about your committing yourself to studying nineteenth century U.S. history by traveling to a controversial and conflicted twenty-first century Caribbean island?

AMY: Is this what I have to look forward to? Cold-hearted academics who live by rules and regulations?

HENRY: We're done here, Amy. Go home. Get some rest. Study.

AMY: In your seminar, you expounded upon the theories of Horace Mann and his desire to create access to universal education for all. You inspired me to delve further into his theories. And now there is some sort of dividing line where this exploration can no longer take place?

HENRY: I'm sorry, Amy.

AMY: Unconvincing, Henry.

HENRY: Tell your mother about your exams. She'll understand. (beat) And if you do go, you'll have to find yourself another advisor.

*AMY EXITS HIS OFFICE.*

**SCENE EIGHT**

*A WEEK LATER. LIGHT RISE ON AMY AND SARAH IN SARAH'S BEDROOM.*

SARAH: You just met this man a week ago.

AMY: Two weeks ago and Beto travels there all the time. He has a lot of contacts on the island.

SARAH: The embargo is on for a reason.

AMY: Come on...

SARAH: I'm serious.

AMY: Are you afraid history is going repeat itself? That I'm going to fall in love with some Cuban guy and end up supporting him because he's gets sick and can't work and then he ends up dying and I'm up a creek working in some shitty job with no life? Look, I know Papi would never go back, but it's not like you ultimately cared about what he thought anyhow. I mean, how could you share this bed with Papi for all those years and not care at all about his world?

SARAH: I don't appreciate your tone. I cared about what he thought. There were many happy years spent in this apartment. You constantly focus on those final years...strained, difficult, unbearable at times...and you seem to forget the many days full of laughter.

AMY: But I still dream about him when he looked sick. Somehow my brain doesn't want to remember those other times.

SARAH: Nor do you seem to remember that I chose this path...to support my husband and children.

AMY: And I don't appreciate the fact that you won't even support me right now.

SARAH: This has nothing to do with support and everything to do with avoidance.

AMY: Oh...and I'm avoiding...

SARAH: Your academic responsibilities at a crucial moment.

AMY: You know what's crucial? The fact that ten years have passed and I've forgotten what Papi's voice sounded like. He had a Cuban accent but I just cannot remember it. And if I travel there, and hear those tones, those sounds, maybe my insides won't feel so vacant...and the side of my face won't go numb because I can barely breathe anymore.

SARAH: You're...you're doing this to sabotage...your academic commitments...your career...and I won't support your destructive behavior.

AMY: Do you even hear what I'm saying?

SARAH: Quite clearly.

AMY: I'll repay you in cash...over the summer.

SARAH: This isn't about the money.

AMY: I'm not trying to sabotage anything...I want to go there to research your ancestor.

SARAH: Ah yes...and now you care so much about your ancestors.

AMY: What if I do?

SARAH: Please.

AMY: You've never been comfortable with Papi's culture. You never kept us in touch with any of it.

SARAH: Don't blame this on me. Don't criticize me for not taking you to Spanish lessons or cultural events or what have you. Your father wasn't comfortable with his own culture. He never talked about it. Almost like he wanted to erase it from his memory. I would have exposed you to his world but I didn't want to upset him by dwelling on it when it was the last thing he wanted to talk about. When you marry a man and you sense the sorrow beneath his skin, you make choices not to engage that grief for the betterment of your family. Perhaps it wasn't the most well informed choice but at the time, I did the best I could, a fact you don't seem to appreciate at all.

AMY: The other night, in my dream, I'm walking down this beach and its nighttime and there are these palm trees and like no one else is on the beach and I walk for miles and miles and for some reason I don't get tired but then I fall through this hole in the sand and I end up in a jail cell and I start yelling for help and its dark and musty and I can hear water dripping somewhere and then in the distance I see this key, like those old fashioned brass kind on a hook and its illuminated and I can't reach it.

SARAH: I have no intention of financially supporting this diversion. I'm sorry. When you finish your degree, you'll get your full time teaching job. You'll save. You'll take this trip eventually. Not now.

AMY: I don't know. I don't think so.

SARAH: If you want to. You will.

AMY: Actually, I probably won't.

SARAH: You just finished your exams. You'll write your thesis. And onward.

AMY: Uh-huh.

SARAH: You know...your father would be very proud of you.

AMY: Yeah. Right. Proud of the fact that I failed my exams.

*AWKWARD SILENCE.*

AMY: Yeah. I doubt it. And you're thinking, "Why didn't she tell me?" I thought I could figure something out. Some other plan. And then this opportunity to travel there presented itself...a way to a new beginning. A fresh approach. Reinvigorate my research. Help me piece something together inside. And...

SARAH: (interrupting) It's late. I have to lecture in the morning. And you have to teach. And study. And forget about this trip.

AMY: I'm not forgetting about this trip.

SARAH: Do what you want then.

AMY: Has it ever occurred to you that maybe I'm just not cut out for academia like you are?

SARAH: I have to go to sleep.

AMY: Okay. I get it.

SARAH: I don't understand you, Amy.

AMY: Clearly.

**SCENE NINE**

*LIGHTS RISE ON AMY AND ALICE IN A CLOTHING BOUTIQUE.*

ALICE: And when do you see the smokin' Cuban journalist again?

AMY: He's Dominican.

ALICE: When do you two hook up?

AMY: My meeting with Beto Alvarez wasn't a date. God. Why is everything always about sex with you? (beat) We're meeting on Sunday and we're not hooking up.

ALICE: You are so in denial.

*AMY HOLDS UP A CONSERVATIVE DRESS. ALICE SHAKES HER HEAD.*

ALICE: Too asexual. Next?

AMY: Mom won't lend me any cash.

ALICE: And this surprises you?

*ALICE HOLDS UP A SLINKY DRESS. AMY SHAKES HER HEAD.*

AMY: Too...I don't think so.

ALICE: Come on...

AMY: Not me.

ALICE: Okay, moving on.

*ALICE HOLDS UP A SEMI-SLINKY DRESS.*

AMY: I am not riding the subway in that.

ALICE: So you like wear a trash bag over yourself and take it off once you get to the restaurant.

AMY: Do you remember when you were like in third grade and I made you that stained glass mirror in like industrial arts and you were obsessing about it every two minutes, and like asking how did I make it and how long did it take. Al...it's like I'm this kid obsessing over this Mary Juan connection and I have a million questions and...

ALICE: And...that's not all your obsessing about.

AMY: I wonder if Beto can help me research some other way.

ALICE: I bet you want Beto to help you in many ways.

AMY: Come on...

ALICE: What...you think I don't get the importance of your research, blah blah blah...that just because I didn't go to college and I work here at the moment...that I'm a dumb ass fashionista?

AMY: Uh...what?

ALICE: Look, maybe I'll go back to school one day and like study fashion design or whatever but right now, this is where I am and I see things on people's bodies, like their energy, their emotions and your situation is so not about researching books or whatever, Amy. You wanna research other...um...areas, alright?

AMY: God. Enough. I'm so not into him. Okay?

ALICE: Interesting how you feel you have to continue to lie to me about this.

*ALICE HANDS AMY THE SLINKY DRESS.*

ALICE: Wear this tonight. Call me in the morning. I want all the nasty details.

**SCENE TEN**

*LIGHTS RISE ON AMY AND BETO FINISHING A MEAL IN A RESTAURANT. AMY WEARS A BULKY JACKET OVER HER SLINKY DRESS.*

AMY: So, I...um...think I need to take a rain check on your offer.

BETO: You think you do?

AMY: I do. Yeah. I do.

BETO: So, you've actually considered the possibility...

AMY: It's just that...

BETO: You decided to go against principle...to be courageous. And you really wanna go but...your boyfriend says no because he's the jealous type.

AMY: Um. Wow. No, actually, I'm not with anyone...in any relationship at the moment but...

BETO: Your father's and grandparents' spirits are floating high above the island of Manhattan looking down on you and whispering in your ear that if you go you'll be a dishonorable daughter.

AMY: You're right about that but actually...

BETO: You're a starving graduate student and who can travel on a teaching assistant's salary anyway?

AMY: Without a student visa.

BETO: Okay. Look. Got loads of frequent flier miles. A good deal at a hotel. Let me cover it. We'll go through Canada. You'll pay me back at some point in the not too distant future.

AMY: I mean...okay...that's um...generous...but I barely know you...and...

BETO: You're a friend of Carlos therefore a friend of mine.

AMY: I don't really know Carlos....I saw him at a department meeting and told him I needed some resources for researching Cuba in the nineteenth century, he gives me your e-mail. Not exactly close pals.

BETO: I don't normally do this but I want to invest in you. In this project.

AMY: I'm a project now?

BETO: A Pulitzer-prize winning article about a young Cuban-American scholar following Mary Peabody to Cuba. New World. Old World. Historical cross cultural connection. Very timely and sexy, trust me.

AMY: So what happened to no one cares what's happening down there...blah...blah...blah?

BETO: I'm not allowed to change my mind, professor?

AMY: And what's with sexy?

BETO: I'm serious. About the offer.

**SCENE ELEVEN**

*LIGHTS RISE ON AMY AND ALICE IN AN AISLE AT THE GROCERY
STORE.*

AMY: And then he offers to fly me there...put me up in a hotel...write an
article about me....and then he gives me this intense stare and....and...I
freaked. I'm like, "I'll be right back" and I walked toward the ladies room
and right out of the restaurant, back to my place where I lay in bed with a
quart of double mint chocolate chip.

ALICE: Okay. You have to call him up and be like, "Dude, I was wrong
but hey, wanna hook up?"

AMY: I'm not calling him. Maybe an e-mail. Or I-M.

*ALICE MAKES A BUZZER SOUND.*

ALICE: Wrong answer.

AMY: I mean, Al, I seriously don't know this guy.

*ALICE MAKES ANOTHER BUZZER SOUND.*

ALICE: Wrong answer again. You'll accept his offer. You'll fly together
while pretending to watch in-flight movies when his ass is so right next to
you. Then, you'll arrive, check in, you'll get separate but adjoining rooms
so you can finally have that midnight hook up you know you're craving but
yet still have your space.

AMY: How can I borrow all that money when I already have a pile of
student loans racking up interest which I have to start paying back in like, I
don't know six months and...

ALICE: You wanted to borrow that money from mom...

AMY: I wouldn't feel nearly as guilty as...

ALICE: Borrowing from a totally hot stranger.

AMY: And the truth of it is, I don't know how I'd pay it back...

ALICE: When you get that kick-ass teaching gig...

AMY: Not happening.

ALICE: What's up with the negativity?

AMY: Well for one, I actually failed my exams. Yup.

ALICE: Shit.

AMY: Exactly.

ALICE: Does mom know?

AMY: She does now.

ALICE: Double shit.

AMY: So I drop out, get some lame ass job and I'm swimming in debt and forget it...I don't want to add some stranger to my list of IOUs.

*ALICE MAKES YET ANOTHER BUZZER SOUND.*

ALICE: Your time's up. Survey says stop living in fear and take a walk on the wild side for once in your life.

**SCENE TWELVE**

*LIGHTS RISE ON AMY MAKING A PHONE CALL TO BETO. BETO'S CELL PHONE RINGS. LIGHTS RISE ON BETO.*

BETO: Hey.

AMY: Uh...Beto...

BETO: Yeah.

AMY: Look...I...

BETO: What?

AMY: I'm not sure.

BETO: Clearly.

AMY: But, so...I...

BETO: The offer.

AMY: Right and...

BETO: Which you blew off. Ditch your date. Nice.

AMY: Date?

BETO: Whatever. Meeting.

AMY: Um...okay.

BETO: Look, do you wanna go or not?

AMY: I...um...

BETO: Fine. Whatever. You have my information if you change...

AMY: (non-stop, nervous) Okay. So. I really really wanna retrace Mary's footsteps and research Mary and Juan's connection and walk where she walked and breathe the ocean air she breathed and step into that historical time warp...did she read his poetry...did he teach her Spanish...did Horace ever find out... and I don't know...if I don't go, it's like I'll drift farther and farther away from this thing inside of me and...

BETO: Fear...

AMY: Yeah...but...

BETO: Is normal.

AMY: I mean, you want to write an article about me?

BETO: Maybe.

AMY: So you don't?

BETO: Look, I'll book our rooms on separate floors of the hotel if you're uncomfortable with...

AMY: Huh?

BETO: Right.

AMY: I'm not nervous about that...

BETO: Okay.

AMY: I mean what if I get caught...going there...like this.

BETO: Do you know how many U.S. tourists do this? Many. Besides, you'll look like you fit in there.

AMY: Huh?

BETO: Uh...yeah.

AMY: Okay...I usually don't get that.

BETO: Not everyone knows the faces down there. Most people operate with a limited knowledge. Not me.

AMY: I would fit in there?

BETO: Until you speak.

AMY: I'm working on my Spanish.

BETO: Good.

AMY: But I don't want to jeopardize your work, I mean...

BETO: Look, my parents grew up in Santo Domingo. Left the Dominican Republic when I was eight. I fly back and visit my aunts and uncles and cousins there once a year. Twice if I want to. Then I meet someone like yourself who says she can never visit the land of her father's and it makes me kinda crazy, you know? I'm in a position to help and so you know, it's the least I can do. Good samaritan and shit.

AMY: Are you religious?

BETO: That would be no. I'm not on a mission here. I'm just trying to help.

AMY: Um...really. So...okay...

BETO: Then...

AMY: To your offer.

BETO: Good. Done. Let's meet for a drink. Oyster Bar. Grand Central?

AMY: Okay. But I don't drink.

BETO: You should.

**SCENE THIRTEEN**

*1833. SPOTLIGHT ON MARY.*

MARY: After debarking from our vessel, we saw sights in Havana as we have never seen before. It is equally impossible to describe the roads from Havana to here. We rode from half past six in the morning till sunset, occasionally to rest, and get orange water and very nice cake. The roads were filled with the flowering myrtle, convolvulus of every kind and many flowers of brilliant hues, which I never saw or heard of before. As we approached the plantation, the beauty of the scenery increased.

**SCENE FOURTEEN**

*CUBA. PRESENT. LIGHTS RISE ON AMY AND BETO IN THE
TERMINAL AT THE JOSE MARTI INTERNATIONAL AIRPORT IN
HAVANA AS MIGUEL ENTERS.*

MIGUEL: Bienvenidos. [Welcome.]

*MIGUEL AND BETO GREET EACH OTHER WITH A BEAR HUG. AMY
PUTS OUT HER HAND TO SHAKE AND MIGUEL BYPASSES HER
HAND AND KISSES HER ON BOTH CHEEKS, SOMEWHAT STARTLING
AMY.*

MIGUEL: Bienvenida, señorita.

BETO: Amy Diaz. Miguel Campos.

MIGUEL: Friend. Fellow journalist. And occasional tour guide.

BETO: A donde vamos, Miguelin? [Where to?]

MIGUEL: A tomar un taxi primero. [To take a taxi first.]

BETO: Y despues? [And after?]

MIGUEL: A comer, no? [To eat.]

BETO: Bueno y que me cuentas? [Well, and what's new?]

MIGUEL: Nada mucho. No es fácil. [No much. Not easy.}

BETO: No es fácil.

*MIGUEL LOOKS AT AMY.*

MIGUEL: Such horrible manners we have, Betito, ignoring our
compañera.

AMY: No, no, please, go on.

BETO: Look, it's just that I haven't seen Miguel in a year and...

AMY: Would you please keep on?

MIGUEL: (to Amy) Pero tu hablas? [But you speak?]

BETO: She's learning.

MIGUEL: (to Amy) Is he teaching you?

AMY: No. I'm studying on my own.

MIGUEL: Señorita, but if you'll allow me, I will teach you....

AMY: (to Beto, half in jest) Is he always this forward?

BETO: Always.

AMY: Good. I like that in a teacher. Hablaremos español. [We will speak Spanish.]

MIGUEL: Bueno, claro que sí. [Well, then of course.] Oye, Beto, where did you find this woman who is so extraordinary?

BETO: She found me.

AMY: I needed his help to get me here.

MIGUEL: (jovial) Ah, but now that you're here, I will be the one to assist you.

BETO: I'm sure you will.

AMY: Is it always this humid?

MIGUEL: Every day. You like it?

AMY: Sure. I just hope I don't pass out.

MIGUEL: Pass out?

BETO: Desmayar. [To faint.]

MIGUEL: (to Amy) Tranquila. Tranquila. Don't worry. You will not faint. Perhaps Beto. But you? No.

BETO: If I pass out, it'll be from one too many mojitos, not the heat.

MIGUEL: Where are you taking her first, Betito?

BETO: Artemisa...mañana.

MIGUEL: Ah...to the outskirts of the city. Exuberant vegetation. Sugar plantations. Muy interesante.

AMY: For my historical research.

MIGUEL: So then tomorrow, you'll need an expert tour guide on your hunt for history. I know Artemisa well.

BETO: Very intimately, I'm sure.

MIGUEL: Don't be jealous, compañero. I, a humble tour guide, am here to help. You are still the macho dominicano journalist.

**SCENE FIFTEEN**

*CUBA. 1833. LIGHTS RISE ON THE HACIENDA PARLOR. MR. REDMOND, MARY, SOPHIA AND JUAN STAND WITH CHAMPAGNE GLASSES RAISED IN THE AIR. AMELIA SITS AT THE PIANO. FRANCISCO AND MRS. BATSON STAND OFF TO THE SIDE.*

REDMOND: And now...we at La Recompensa...raise our glass to the education of my dear daughter Amelia...Miss Mary Peabody in English and Señor Juan Velasco in Spanish. My wife, Florence, whose life was defined by a staunch commitment to education, may she rest in everlasting peace, would be oh so proud.

JUAN: Here here.

*THEY ALL TOAST AND DRINK. AMELIA BEGINS TO PLAY THE PIANO.*

JUAN: (to Mary) La Americana sails such a long distance to teach.

MARY: Where else can one appreciate such landscape?

JUAN: For this I do not have the answer. (to Sophia) And I hope you will be healed by the climate of our island, Señorita Peabody...or may I call you Sofía?

SOPHIA: Why yes, but my name is pronounced Sophia...long i...as in island.

JUAN: Ah, I should know better than to translate your name too quickly.

*ALL APPLAUD AS AMELIA FINISHES PLAYING HER PIECE. AMELIA CURTSIES AND THEN RUNS TO KISS HER FATHER ON THE CHEEK.*

REDMOND: (to Amelia) Excellent, my darling, now time to run along.

AMELIA: But can't I stay here with you and our new Boston guests?

REDMOND: You will spend many an hour with them...as such you must get your rest...after Mrs. Batson makes certain you receive a special serving of mango tart in the kitchen.

*AMELIA KISSES HER FATHER ON THE CHEEK.*

AMELIA: In that case, very well...good night all.

MRS. BATSON: Yes, good evening. And again, welcome to our home.

*SHE DASHES OUT AS MRS. BATSON FOLLOWS HER.*

REDMOND: (to Mary, smiling) She has a certain fondness for confections...an insatiable taste for the vocation of her father...endless hours concerned with creating sweetness.

MARY: Yes. Naturally.

REDMOND: We Northerners must learn a new way of life here. The natives of this island do not always respect those foreign to their shores. Much less their servants. The emancipados seem to be respectful enough, however.

MARY: Emancipados?

REDMOND: Free men. In servitude no longer. Pay them a wage and they quiet down. We are doing them a service by putting so many to useful work.

MARY: My sister Elizabeth assured me you were doing the same.

REDMOND: It is my duty to protect you in this at times savage territory.

JUAN: Savage, señor?

REDMOND: Unchartered is perhaps a better description.

JUAN: Indeed.

REDMOND: Women of your class do not travel outside the environs of the hacienda unescorted.

MARY: While my sister and I are accustomed to freedom of movement, we will heed your advice...

SOPHIA: Indeed we will...

MARY: as we become acquainted with this new landscape.

REDMOND CATCHES JUAN STARING AT MARY. JUAN THEN LOOKS AT REDMOND, RAISES HIS GLASS AND TAKES ANOTHER DRINK.

REDMOND: (re: Juan) And I daresay this new landscape longs to become acquainted with you.

MARY: Your hospitality is most appreciated.

REDMOND: Your presence is quite welcome in a hacienda needing more feminine attentions.

MARY: My condolences for your loss.

REDMOND: This island claimed my wife, Florence, but it will not claim me. I am too strong for these fevers and skirmishes. But thank you for your sentiment.

SOPHIA: As our sister Elizabeth arranged our stay on your hacienda, she spoke very highly of Mrs. Redmond.

REDMOND: Enough wallowing. Well, if you care to see the city of San Marcos, please allow me to escort you and your sister into the center tomorrow. I have not taken our volanta carriage out in months.

MARY: The journey from Havana to La Recompensa exhausted my sister. We may not be ready for such an excursion quite yet.

SOPHIA: Mary, please. Mr. Redmond, I should be delighted to survey the city in your volanta carriage.

REDMOND: Florence used to find great pleasure in the trips down the avenues, viewing all the hustle and bustle from the safe remove of her seat. It is the only accepted way for a woman to see the sights here. It would be my honor to escort you.

MARY: We will give you our measured response in the morning. Thank you.

REDMOND: Well then. Your classes will commence promptly at nine.

MARY: Certainly.

REDMOND: And Señor Velasco at ten.

JUAN: Yes, sir.

REDMOND: Very well then. We best conserve our energies for the morrow, shall we not?

*JUAN TAKES SOPHIA'S HAND AND KISSES IT.*

JUAN: Señorita Sophia Peabody...until tomorrow...or as I prefer to say, hasta mañana.

SOPHIA: Ha...sta...ma...nya...na?

JUAN: Muy bien, until then.

*JUAN TRIES TO TAKE MARY'S HAND BUT SHE DOESN'T ALLOW IT.*

JUAN: Hasta mañana.

MARY: Very well, Señor Velasco. Until tomorrow.

JUAN: Mr. Redmond?

REDMOND: Good evening, Juan. Francisco, see that Mr. Velasco's horse is brought up from the stable.

FRANCISCO: Sí, señor Redmond.

*FRANCISCO EXITS AS JUAN FOLLOWS.*

REDMOND: Spirited and dashing professor from the neighboring hacienda. On sabbatical from the University of Havana. Our good fortune. A gifted teacher and raconteur. Quite the bon vivant and Amelia's language skills improve daily as well.

*AWKWARD PAUSE.*

REDMOND: Very well, then. I will bid adieu until tomorrow, mademoiselles.

MARY: Oui monsieur.

REDMOND: Parlez-vous français?

MARY: Un peu.

REDMOND: Très bien. At last, an international hacienda. (beat) Buenas noches. Bonne nuit. Good night.

*MR. REDMOND EXITS.*

**SCENE SIXTEEN.**

*LATER THAT EVENING. LIGHTS RISE ON MARY AND SOPHIA IN THEIR BEDROOM.*

SOPHIA: Oh Mary, he is quite charming.

MARY: Charming is not an adjective I would use for our host. Stately, perhaps. But charming?

SOPHIA: Oh Mary. I refer to Señor Juan Velasco.

MARY: Charming is not the correct adjective for him either.

SOPHIA: Did you see how his teeth glimmered when he bade me farewell?

MARY: Supercilious.

SOPHIA: And how his lips lightly touched the white lacework on my glove?

MARY: Ill-mannered.

SOPHIA: And his eyes...they seemed to widen ever so slightly as he stared at me and said my name. Se...nyor..ita... Peeee...body.

MARY: Laden with chicanery.

SOPHIA: I wonder what he thinks of us.

MARY: Sophia, I must warn you now not to humor him.

SOPHIA: (embarrassed) Mary please.

MARY: You are an attractive young woman and you will not have some Cuban lothario improperly wooing your hand. This is not why we have come here.

SOPHIA: Honestly, he was simply being courteous. I will not have you hovering about me so.

MARY: I promised Mother that I would take care of you and so that makes me your guardian. We are here for your convalescence to seek a cure for your incessant and debilitating headaches. Would you rather be spending this month huddled next to the fireplace in Boston, the cold compounding your condition, or here, reclining on a chaise in the afternoon heat?

SOPHIA: (indignant) Please.

MARY: Now not another word about Señor Velasco.

*A FEW BEATS.*

SOPHIA: He is a poet you know.

MARY: Most likely a phrase he employs with all the young ladies.

SOPHIA: He said I could attend the lesson in the morning and learn about the language surrounding us now.

MARY: And?

SOPHIA: I accepted.

MARY: You will not do so unaccompanied.

SOPHIA: Of course not.

MARY: We both do have need of improving our Spanish.

SOPHIA: Then...ma...nya...na...the Señoritas Peabody will learn a thing or two from the teacher and poet, Señor Juan Velasco.

MARY: Not another word.

**SCENE SEVENTEEN**

*PRESENT. LIGHTS RISE ON AMY, BETO AND MIGUEL STANDING IN AN OLD ABANDONED HACIENDA NEAR ARTEMISA. BETO AND MIGUEL WALK AROUND SLOWLY WHILE AMY MOVES ENERGETICALLY AROUND THE HACIENDA FRAME. AMY HOLDS A MAP.*

AMY: The orange, banana, majagua, guacima and cedar trees that lined the hacienda could have been over here.

MIGUEL: And the roses...

AMY: There. The front hacienda gallery could have been back here. And the back gallery here.

MIGUEL: And Mary's bedroom?

*AMY MOVES TO THE SIDE OF THE HACIENDA FRAME.*

AMY: Right here. This really might have been La Recompensa.

MIGUEL: And what would Mary be doing right now?

AMY: Reading...in the parlor...

*AMY MOVES TO THE CENTER OF THE HACIENDA FRAME.*

AMY: Because she's unable to sleep during the siesta.

MIGUEL: Is she alone?

*MIGUEL WALKS UP TO HER.*

AMY: Until Juan Velasco enters the room.

*BETO WALKS AROUND THE FRAME, EYEING MIGUEL.*

MIGUEL: So did Mary like Juan?

AMY: Yes. But she pined for Horace back home.

MIGUEL: Perhaps Juan was more passionate.

BETO: (sarcastic) Ah, so then she was secretly attracted to Juan.

MIGUEL: Attracted to his mind.

AMY: Definitely.

BETO: (sarcastic) Right...until he pries off her corset and they have mad passionate sex on the parlor floor in the noonday heat while everyone else takes their siesta. Juan was quite the bodice ripper.

*AWKWARD BEAT AS AMY IGNORES BETO'S REMARK.*

MIGUEL: And what did they discuss, Mary and Juan?

AMY: Poetry...the English romantics...Byron, perhaps?

MIGUEL: And his Spanish counterpart...Espronceda.

AMY: And as they discuss poetry, her soul roams free.

MIGUEL: Exactamente. [Exactly.]

BETO: What's the point of this exercise? Who even knows if La Recompensa was here. Our expert tour guide may have led us astray, as they say.

MIGUEL: Heat bothering you, Betito?

BETO: No, just your overindulgent romanticized tour.

MIGUEL: And now nostalgia is a crime?

BETO: Not even. It's your largest export and I'm over it. I flew here to interview you and we're standing in this field in the middle of this insane heat talking about...

AMY: I really don't want to leave here yet...

MIGUEL: We're not going to leave. Ay Betito...so many years on the continent have twisted your perception. Don't you understand that if I bring you out into the middle of this field we can speak more freely and I can tell you things...

BETO:  Like...

MIGUEL: Two days ago, an independent journalist...twenty-one years old...was detained and arrested because he posted an article on the internet about a friend, another journalist, who was sentenced to twenty-six years in jail for undermining national independence and territorial integrity.

BETO: Where was he arrested?

MIGUEL: Old Havana.

BETO: And...

MIGUEL: They took away his laptop. And later, an angry crowd burned the roof of his house. They have him in a prison which is a known torture center. This I can tell you in the middle of this field.

BETO: Any trial?

MIGUEL: No. Not yet.

AMY: Twenty-six years?

MIGUEL: So, Betito, are there anymore objections if I prefer to spend a few hours in the world of historical conjecture? (beat) Bueno...

**SCENE EIGHTEEN**

*1833. LIGHTS RISE ON MARY AND AMELIA DURING THEIR LESSON. MARY DICTATES AS AMELIA WRITES. JUAN STANDS OFF TO THE SIDE, UNNOTICED.*

MARY: Ever the Poet from the land
Steers his bark and trims his sail;
Right out to sea his courses stand,
New worlds to find in pinnacle frail.

*AMELIA FINISHES WRITING.*

MARY: Mr. Ralph Waldo Emerson's quatrain.

AMELIA: What are the men like in Boston?

MARY: Proper. Intelligent. Kind.

AMELIA: Have you a beau in Boston, Miss Peabody?

MARY: We must refrain from personal discussion during our lesson.

AMELIA: Oh, Miss Peabody, do you like me?

MARY: Of course I like you.

AMELIA: Please forgive me for continuing the personal discussion. I do get so lonely for feminine companionship here.

MARY: I understand.

AMELIA: I want to live a life like you and Miss Sophia in Boston when I grow up.

MARY: But you have a lovely life here at La Recompensa.

AMELIA: Not really. Father is so concerned with his beloved sugar cane that there isn't much for me to do at home except to study. And I do miss Mother.

MARY: My condolences for your loss.

AMELIA: These last months I haven't wanted to study. But Father insists I continue, for her sake.

MARY: I'm sure she would be quite proud.

AMELIA: You truly think so? I should like to live in Boston when I am a lady and be attended to by all the fancy young men from the universities there.

MARY: Well, if you do not study then you will never attain such a goal. A woman must be valued for her mind as well as her comportment. Now...a quatrain is....

AMELIA: Um...a quatrain is...oh...

*JUAN APPROACHES THEM.*

JUAN: A stanza consisting of four lines or as we say, un cuarteto.

*MARY LOOKS UP, STARTLED. JUAN APPROACHES.*

JUAN: I believe my lesson begins in ten minutes time and Señorita Amelia here will need a small repose.

MARY: Señor Velasco...yes...well...Amelia you are dismissed for today...I shall expect you to have read the first chapter of Miss Austen's Pride and Prejudice by tomorrow.

AMELIA: Thank you, Miss Peabody.

*AMELIA EXITS RUNNING.*

JUAN: Perhaps you and your sister will attend my lesson today?

MARY: Perhaps.

**SCENE NINETEEN**

*PRESENT. LIGHTS RISE ON MIGUEL AND BETO SITTING IN MIGUEL'S HUMBLE DINING ROOM.*

MIGUEL: Café?

BETO: No, no, no.

MIGUEL: Bueno...

BETO: Bueno y hay más sobre...[Well, and is there more about...]

MIGUEL: En inglés, por favor. [English, please.]

BETO: Y eso? [Huh?]

MIGUEL: Because not everyone I meet can speak your second language.

BETO: Right. And...then we can discuss certain things.

MIGUEL: Certain things, yes. Are you sure, no café?

BETO: Serve it to someone more important.

MIGUEL: Ay Betito. And you are not important?

BETO: Any word about your compañero?

MIGUEL: He is still being detained without a hearing. But the other who is serving his twenty six year sentence...his wife went for a conjugal visit. Said he was being kept in subhuman conditions...lack of sanitation... disgusting food...little medical attention...poor ventilation in sweltering heat with foul odors. Like animals.

BETO: And if he complains...

MIGUEL: Last time he complained they put him in solitary confinement.

BETO: How many journalists are serving time?

MIGUEL: Eighteen that I know of. No es fácil.

*A FEW BEATS.*

BETO: And your most recent piece is...

MIGUEL: At the moment...nothing.

BETO: Nothing.

MIGUEL: Yes.

BETO: Blocked?

MIGUEL: You could say.

BETO: Meaning.

MIGUEL: What you refer to is unintentional. What I refer to is intentional.

BETO: So you're censoring yourself.

MIGUEL: There's a difference between intentional inactivity and censorship.

BETO: You have to continue.

MIGUEL: Your Yankee optimism is touching.

BETO: Miguel. Look, if you need me to help you, I could bring something back with me and...

MIGUEL: So then I put you in jeopardy too?

BETO: You wouldn't. I would be putting myself in jeopardy.

MIGUEL: No, compañero. My talking to you is enough.

BETO: So you're not writing anymore?

MIGUEL: Is it a crime if I just want to sit in my dining room and enjoy the sunlight and ocean air filling my apartment?

BETO: For an afternoon no? For days, months, years? Yes.

*A FEW BEATS.*

MIGUEL: So tell me more about this Amy.

BETO: What do you want to know?

MIGUEL: You want to sleep with her?

BETO: And you don't?

MIGUEL: She doesn't seem like your type.

BETO: Meaning...

MIGUEL: Too smart for you.

BETO: And you don't think I value intelligence?

MIGUEL: There's intelligence and then there's intelligence.

BETO: And you?

MIGUEL: What?

BETO: And you don't?

MIGUEL: Are you sure I can't offer you café?

BETO: She's not your type.

MIGUEL: I have a type?

BETO: She's not revolutionary enough.

MIGUEL: What is that game you play where one insults the other?

BETO: Are we playing that game right now?

MIGUEL: We could, seeing as you've already begun.

BETO: Then is it your turn?

MIGUEL: If you say so.

BETO: Bueno...

MIGUEL: How do you say...uh...Arrogant prick.

BETO: Cowardly hack.

MIGUEL: Machista pig.

BETO: Spineless fraud.

MIGUEL: Ignorant ass.

BETO: Failed revolutionary.

MIGUEL: You like this game, don't you?

BETO: Only as much as you do.

MIGUEL: I like this game because one can speak freely with no repercussion...the words have no real meaning. But with you...I think you enjoy this game because you get to say words you mean. There's a difference.

BETO: And you don't mean the words you say?

MIGUEL: Not in the same way you do.

BETO: You're giving up.

MIGUEL: No entiendes. [You don't understand.]

BETO: I understand. You're a journalist who's given up. But, like you say, no es fácil.

MIGUEL: Adios, Betito.

BETO: Now you want to get rid of me because I'm speaking truthfully? Bueno...then...

*BETO EXITS.*

**SCENE TWENTY**

*1833. LIGHTS RISE ON JUAN GIVING AMELIA HER SPANISH LESSON. MARY AND SOPHIA SIT OFF TO ONE SIDE, OBSERVING.*

JUAN: We will continue with the first person, past perfect subjunctive of amar.

AMELIA: I might have loved. Yo hubiera amado.

JUAN: Muy bien. Third person singular, conditional perfect.

AMELIA: He would have loved. El habría amado.

JUAN: Muy bien, Señorita Redmond. Aprendes bien. Now, to end our lesson...tenemos...we have...las oraciónes?

AMELIA: The sentences.

JUAN: Gracias, señorita. (beat) Me alegro que el poeta haya escrito muchos poemas de amor.

*AMELIA WRITES FURIOUSLY.*

JUAN: Señorita?

AMELIA: I am happy that the poet has written many poems of love.

JUAN: Excelente. Ahora. [Excellent. Now]
El corazón anda dondequiera

Entre las palmas majestuosas
Através de la isla magnífica
Siempre busca su pareja
Haciendo lo que desea
Para encontrar otra alma bella

*AMELIA WRITES FURIOUSLY THEN STOPS.*

AMELIA: That was a rather long one, Señor Velasco. I only could capture the first part.

JUAN: Bueno, tell us what you have.

AMELIA: The heart walks where it wants amidst the majestic palms.

JUAN: Bueno, entonces, that was the more significant line anyway.

*MARY AND SOPHIA APPROACH.*

SOPHIA: What did the rest of that poem mean? It truly sounded so lovely. And the author?

*JUAN INDICATES HIMSELF.*

SOPHIA: One of your own?

JUAN: Yes, but it is nothing really. Just a mere...how do you say...trifle?

MARY: Trifle...yes.

SOPHIA: I should hope that you would tell us the translation or perhaps we should learn your language to decipher it in the future.

JUAN: Let us hope for the latter, señorita.

**SCENE TWENTY ONE**

*PRESENT. LIGHTS RISE ON BETO AND AMY SITTING IN HIS HOTEL ROOM, AFTER A COUPLE OF DRINKS.*

AMY: Ask me again. Wait. We're off the record now?

BETO: We went off the record after the second mojito.

AMY: Then ask me again.

BETO: So, you've never been married?

*AMY SHAKES HER HEAD.*

BETO: I could tell. Your energy.

AMY: Would that be the "single forever" energy?

BETO: Not forever. A while perhaps.

AMY: Couple years. My ex...grad student in econ. From the Midwest. Got a job in DC. Moved.

BETO: Didn't want to move with him?

AMY: In the end, we were strangers really. Connection here.

*SHE POINTS TO HER HEAD.*

AMY: But not here.

*SHE MOTIONS TO HER HEART.*

AMY: You?

BETO: My ex and I split up eight years ago.

AMY: Painful.

BETO: Yeah but..."Mejor solo que mal acompañado."

AMY: Better alone than bad...

BETO: company. (beat) My daughter lives with her in Baltimore. I see her twice a month.

AMY: How old?

BETO: Twelve.

AMY: Her name?

BETO: Maricela.

*THE LIGHTS SUDDENLY CUT OUT.*

AMY: What the...?

BETO: Happens all the time...every tourist hotel has its own generator.

AMY: All the time?

BETO: There's a candle over here somewhere.

*BETO RUMMAGES TO FIND A CANDLE.*

AMY: God...

BETO: There.

*BETO FINDS A CANDLE WHICH HE LIGHTS QUICKLY. AWKWARD BEAT.*

AMY: What next...do we have like a séance or something?

BETO: Yeah right and what spirits should we call upon?

AMY: The spirit of Mary.

BETO: (jokingly) Then we call upon Mary. (beat) Hmmm. Mary tells me that Miguel clearly has a little thing for you.

AMY: She thinks so?

BETO: Uh-huh.

AMY: (teasing) And does she think Beto has little thing for me too?

BETO: (teasing yet sincere) And what if he does?

*BETO MOVES IN CLOSE AND HOLDS AMY AROUND HER WAIST.*

BETO: Would that surprise you?

AMY: Not really.

BETO: And she thinks you might have a little thing for me too.

AMY: She does, does she?

BETO: Yes.

AMY: And does she think that you've been waiting for this opportune moment to...

*BETO KISSES AMY.*

AMY: Okay.

BETO: Yeah?

AMY: Yeah.

BETO: Good.

AMY: Really?

BETO: Uh. Yeah.

*THEY KISS AGAIN AS THE LIGHTS COME BACK ON.*

AMY: Okay.

BETO: Lights off again?

AMY: Yeah.

*BETO TURNS THE LIGHTS OFF.*

**SCENE TWENTY TWO**

*1833. LIGHTS RISE ON SOPHIA LOUNGING ON A SETTEE AS SHE SKETCHES IN A BOOK. FRANCISCO PASSES THROUGH THE ROOM AND STOPS, UNBEKNOWNST TO SOPHIA, AS HE TRIES TO CATCH A GLIMPSE OF HER DRAWING.*

FRANCISCO: La artista.

*SOPHIA, STARTLED, TURNS AROUND.*

SOPHIA: Francisco...you gave me quite a start.

*FRANCISCO POINTS TO HER SKETCH BOOK.*

FRANCISCO: La artista.

SOPHIA: I like to draw. Draw?

*SHE POINTS TO HER PENCIL AND MAKES DRAWING MOTIONS.*

FRANCISCO: Dibujar.  [To draw.]

SOPHIA: Sí. Sí. Dibu...

FRANCISCO: Dibujar.

SOPHIA: Dibujar.

*SOPHIA BECKONS HIM OVER TO HER SETTEE. HE APPROACHES HER AND GLANCES OVER HER SHOULDER.*

SOPHIA: Dibujar...las...palm trees.

FRANCISCO: Las palmeras. [Palm trees]

SOPHIA: Palmeras y las flowers.

FRANCISCO: Las florecitas. [the little flowers.] Usted tiene mucho talento. [You have a lot of talent.]

SOPHIA: Soon I draw you?

*FRANCISCO POINTS TO HIMSELF QUESTIONINGLY AS SOPHIA NODS. MRS. BATSON ENTERS. FRANCISCO SEES HER AND EXITS QUICKLY.*

MRS. BATSON: Miss Sophia, our meal will be ready in an hour's time.

SOPHIA: Mrs. Batson, why did Francisco scurry off?

MRS. BATSON: Mr. Redmond prefers that the house servants not fraternize with the guests.

SOPHIA: Is that why he says so little or does he not speak English?

MRS. BATSON: He understands quite well and he is learning to speak our language...but his quiet demeanor speaks of his obedience more so than his linguistic aptitude.

SOPHIA: He must be thinking of so many things yet holding his tongue.

MRS. BATSON: I wouldn't worry your head too much about him. You need to avoid any mental anxiety and focus on your recuperation.

SOPHIA: But really. No fraternization? I didn't imagine Mr. Redmond would be so...

MRS. BATSON: Backward?

SOPHIA: In that respect, yes.

MRS. BATSON: Once his wife died, his rigidity increased. A desire for control. Foolish. But he provides for us...and so.

SOPHIA: And you? Are you happy here?

MRS. BATSON: My poor health induced me to take this position and leave my family in Philadelphia. I've grown quite attached to Amelia, even more so since Mrs. Redmond's passing.

SOPHIA: Never have I experienced such landscape of ineffable beauty and palpable human injustice.

MRS. BATSON: A contradictory island which seeps into one's skin.

SOPHIA: Contradictory, indeed.

## SCENE TWENTY THREE

*PRESENT. LIGHTS RISE ON AMY AND BETO IN BED IN BETO'S HOTEL ROOM. AMY GETS OUT OF BED AND STARTS TO PUT ON HER CLOTHING.*

BETO: Outta here?

AMY: Mmm-hmm.

BETO: Because?

AMY: Because.

BETO: Right.

AMY: Yup.

BETO: You don't want to come back over this way?

AMY: Not really.

BETO: Okay. (beat) Can I ask you why?

AMY: I don't know.

BETO: You don't know if I can ask you why or you don't know why?

AMY: Yeah.

BETO: Okay.

AMY: I just rather not.

BETO: Do this?

AMY: Right.

BETO: Because...

AMY: I don't know.

BETO: Okay.

AMY: Look, I have to...

BETO: Right.

AMY: I don't know, Beto. I'm sorry.

BETO: No apologies. Alright?

AMY: This just isn't me.

BETO: This just isn't you. Right. Got it.

AMY: It's not that you were...I mean...

BETO: Okay. I got it.

AMY: I mean on one level, it was...

BETO: Please don't go into Ph.D. mode on me, okay?

AMY: What?

BETO: Dissecting everything so you can feel superior.

AMY: Wow.

BETO: Right. So. You're uncomfortable here, aren't you? Yeah. That's pretty apparent.

AMY: Look, Beto...

BETO: Somewhere deep inside, you're rattled. Being here. This trip. Your two cultures colliding. Oil and water. You say you desire your Cuban side yet you desperately cling to your New England side.

AMY: God just because I don't wanna sleep with you again, you don't have to...

BETO: That's how I experienced you. Withholding. Reserved. Cold.

AMY: Really. Yeah well, you have absolutely no idea what's deep inside of me.

BETO: And I don't think you do either.

*AMY STORMS OUT OF HIS ROOM.*

**SCENE TWENTY FOUR**

*1833. LIGHTS RISE ON THE GARDEN. MR. REDMOND, SOPHIA, MARY, JUAN AND AMELIA PLAY A GAME OF CROQUET. ALL HOLD CROQUET MALLETS WHILE MR. REDMOND READS FROM A SMALL BOOK. FRANCISCO STANDS NEXT TO A SMALL TABLE WITH A PITCHER OF LEMONADE AND GLASSES.*

REDMOND: (reading) And finally..."A correct eye, steady hands and nerves, good judgment and clear brain, are the essential qualifications for a good player, and the possession of these advantages of course, is not dependent upon the age, sex or condition of the person." Well then, many a fine eye and hand in this company.

AMELIA: We know how to play, Father

REDMOND: Well then, we shall have two teams...Miss Mary, Amelia and myself and Miss Sophia and Señor Velasco.

MARY: I should be on the team with my sister.

SOPHIA: I'd rather not play. I'll sit here and watch.

MARY: Then I shan't play either.

SOPHIA: Nonsense. You take my place with Señor Velasco.

MARY: Very well then.

*MARY JOINS JUAN AND THE GAME BEGINS. REDMOND AND AMELIA HIT THEIR CROQUET BALLS. SOPHIA SITS FRANCISCO POURS HER A GLASS OF LEMONADE. SHE SMILES APPRECIATIVELY. HE LOOKS AT HER WITH KINDNESS. LIGHTS SHIFT.*

*LIGHTS RISE ON MARY AND JUAN PLAYING CROQUET.*

JUAN: We must be winning or they have abandoned us forever.

*MARY SWINGS AND HITS THE BALL.*

JUAN: It is not every day that gentlemen are in the company of young ladies who swing their hips and raise their skirts several inches off the ground.

MARY: Are skirts your sole concern, Mr. Velasco? I would imagine your predilections to be of a higher order.

JUAN: Please, begin to call me Juan as we must not be so far apart in age.

MARY: In New England, it is not proper to address acquaintances by their Christian name nor discuss their age.

JUAN: Is it therefore only appropriate when in the company of a family member or a Bostonian suitor, perhaps?

*A FEW BEATS.*

MARY: You enjoy the game of croquet often, I presume?

JUAN: I understand. It is also not proper to discuss subjects of an amorous nature with las señoritas from Boston.

*A FEW BEATS.*

JUAN: Perhaps we could discuss the desire one has for objects inanimate such as books...although certainly the lifeblood of an author courses through paper bound in leather.

MARY: Very well.

JUAN: I prefer the Spanish Romantic poets.

MARY: I would imagine you'd prefer a poet from your own shores.

JUAN: Paradox, perhaps?

MARY: Slightly.

JUAN: I do abhor those Spaniards who hold the development of a people at bay for their own political or economic gain. However, the world of letters and the world of power are separate and often the former needs to transform the latter.

MARY: I suppose one could infer a similar relation between my countrymen's attitude toward England's world of letters versus her political precepts.

JUAN: Precisely. Well then...."La Canción del Pirata"....José de Espronceda. If I may give you a morsel?

*MARY NODS AS SHE ATTEMPTS TO HIT HER CROQUET BALL THROUGH THE LOOP AND MISSES.*

JUAN: Very well.
Que es mi barco mi tesoro
que es mi Dios la libertad.
mi ley, la fuerza y el viento
mi única patria la mar.

MARY: (momentarily taken aback) That does sound quite...lovely. All those melodious vowels...ahhs and oohhs and uuuuuus. You recite rather effectively. (beat, collecting herself) However, I cannot comprehend this morsel, as you call it.

JUAN: That my boat is my treasure,
That my God is my liberty.
My law, my strength and my wind.
My only homeland, the sea.

MARY: Perhaps your Mother tongue is better suited for poetry of this nature. The sounds are not nearly as...affecting in my language.

JUAN: I can only give you the literal translation and you must take the emotion you hear from my Spanish and unite the two to perhaps achieve a semblance of the poem in the original.

MARY: His verse sounds rather like that of Byron.

JUAN: Espronceda called himself the "Spanish" Byron. Both were libertines, exiled, and died before seeing the age of forty. His verse also exalts a love of the natural world and a desire to rebel against the established human order.

MARY: Byron was a libertine indeed but with such a gifted verse. Perhaps similarities do exist as you say between him and your fellow...Es...

JUAN: Espronceda.

MARY: Would you care for a morsel from the English counterpart?

JUAN: I will not attempt to hit this ball until I have received said morsel.

MARY: Though the ocean roar around me,
Yet it still shall bear me on;
Though a desert should surround me,
It hath springs that may be one.

"My Boat is on the Shore" as he sailed off into distant exile.

JUAN: Do you feel like one in exile?...

MARY: At times, I suppose. But nothing like that of Byron who never did return to his country...never...dreadful.

*JUAN HITS THE BALL.*

MARY: For all your bravado, you appear to be a man of letters.

JUAN: For all your reserve, you appear to be a woman of literary passion.

*JUAN TAKES A FOLDED PAPER FROM HIS JACKET POCKET AND HANDS IT TO MARY.*

JUAN: To further your education, perhaps you might like this. If you continue to attend my class, you will be able to decipher my poem in no time.

MARY: Gracias.

*LIGHTS SHIFT. LIGHTS RISE ON AMELIA AND REDMOND PLAYING CROQUET. AMELIA HITS THE BALL.*

AMELIA: Father, what a shame neither Miss Mary nor Miss Sophia could play on our team. I should like to play with Miss Mary.

REDMOND: Yes, shame indeed.

*AMELIA TRIES TO HIT THE BALL AGAIN. MISSES THE LOOP.*

AMELIA: I do so like her. Do you think she might stay with us forever?

REDMOND: My darling, please, such notions...

*AMELIA HITS THE BALL AND MAKES IT THROUGH THE LOOP.*

AMELIA: Oh I hope so, how I do hope so.

*LIGHTS SHIFT. LIGHTS RISE ON MARY, SOPHIA AND JUAN
COOLING OFF DRINKING GLASSES OF LEMONADE. JUAN LOOKS
AT MARY. SOPHIA SEES JUAN'S GAZE. FRANCISCO OFFERS TO
REFILL HER GLASS. SHE SHAKES HER HEAD. FRANCISCO
CONTINUES TO OFFER, SMILING A BIT TOO WIDELY. REDMOND
ENTERS WITH AMELIA.*

REDMOND: The wayward ball rescued from the palm.

AMELIA: I whacked it too hard.

SOPHIA: If you will excuse me, the rising heat is causing me to feel a bit
light headed.

MARY: Sister, I shall accompany you.

SOPHIA: No, you stay on and play.

*SOPHIA EXITS.*

MARY: My apologies, Mr. Redmond, but I feel I must accompany my
sister, even if it be against her wishes.

REDMOND: Very well.

MARY: Excuse me.

*MARY EXITS.*

AMELIA: Father, we cannot lose players in mid game. Is that not against
the rules?

REDMOND: Rules are created to be manipulated, my darling.

JUAN: However, you must forfeit the game if the players are disinterested
and leave.

**SCENE TWENTY FIVE**

*PRESENT. LIGHTS RISE ON AMY SITTING IN MIGUEL'S DINING ROOM AS HE SERVES HER A CUP OF COFFEE.*

AMY: Is my visiting you at home inconvenient or something? I could've called only I didn't know your number and...

MIGUEL: I'm sure the Committee for the Defense of the Revolution already knows you're here.

AMY: The committee...

MIGUEL: Informants. Every neighborhood has them.

AMY: I should leave then.

MIGUEL: Tranquila.

*MIGUEL PLACES THE TRAY WITH COFFEE IN FRONT OF AMY.*

AMY: Gracias, but you didn't have to make me...

MIGUEL: I was able to get some coffee this month. So please...

AMY: I don't want to drink your ration and...

*HE PLACES A CUP OF COFFEE INTO HER HANDS, AS THEIR HANDS TOUCH MOMENTARILY.*

AMY: Gracias.

*MIGUEL HOLDS AMY'S HAND AND LOOKS HER IN THE EYE.*

MIGUEL: Ay, poor Betito will be so jealous...

*AMY GESTICULATES EMPHATICALLY.*

AMY: I could care less what he thinks.

MIGUEL: Spoken like a true Cubana.

*AMY LOOKS AROUND MIGUEL'S DINING ROOM.*

AMY: So you might be thinking, "What is she doing in my dining room?"

MIGUEL: Bueno...so you are a mind reader?

AMY: Or you're thinking, "When will she leave?"

MIGUEL: But your power to read my mind must be refined.

AMY: Am I keeping you from your work?

MIGUEL: My work as a host to my esteemed guest? Absolutely not.

AMY: Journalistic work, I mean.

MIGUEL: In this moment? No. How do you say...I'm in between projects.

AMY: Because they detained your friend?

MIGUEL: That doesn't stop me. On the contrary. I'm awaiting a visitation from the muse...

AMY: The mysteries of the muse.

MIGUEL: I'd like her to give me inspiration and the necessary linguistic power to achieve perfection.

AMY: I'd like to read your work.

MIGUEL: Bueno. Maybe later on.

*AWKWARD BEAT.*

AMY: I mean...the power of the pen is so palpable here.

MIGUEL: Or the liability...depending how one uses it...but always there exists the potential to transform. Like Velasco.

AMY: How did Velasco's verse transform the island?

MIGUEL: His verse transports one to another level where it is as if one sits on a cloud formation and observes all the natural beauty of the island and at the same time sees the strength of her population and in this way his verse galvanized generations of cubanos with pride and power as to what is possible.

AMY: And this galvanized the struggle for independence from Spain?

MIGUEL: His verse inspired first his students and then dissidents and later almost any person who read his poems.

AMY: How did he die so young?

MIGUEL: Velasco became a visible figure for the resistance. During a lecture at the university, he was shot and killed.

AMY: How old?

MIGUEL: Fifty. Had a wife and two young sons.

AMY: Tragic.

MIGUEL: No es fácil. Not easy.

AMY: I desperately want a collection of his poems. Where could I find one?

MIGUEL: My library. Mi biblioteca ilegal.

## SCENE TWENTY SIX

*LIGHTS RISE ON AMY AND MIGUEL IN HIS LIBRARY HOUSED IN A WALK-IN CLOSET. BOOKSHELVES OVERFLOW. STACKS OF BOOKS ON THE FLOOR. AN INNER SANCTUM OF SORTS.*

AMY: An illegal library?

MIGUEL: The closet itself? No. What's inside this closet? Yes.

AMY: Such peaceful solitude.

MIGUEL: Here peace with a price.

*MIGUEL DIGS THROUGH A PILE AND FINDS A SLIM VOLUME AND HANDS IT TO HER.*

AMY: Ralph Waldo Emerson...illegal?

MIGUEL: In this place? No. Outside of this place? Yes.

AMY: What happens to you if the authorities discover this?

*SHE HANDS THE BOOK BACK TO HIM AS HE BEGINS TO READ.*

MIGUEL: Ever the Poet from the land
Steers his bark and trims his sail;
Right out to sea his courses stand,
New worlds to find in pinnacle frail.

*MIGUEL CONTINUES SEARCHING. HE PULLS OUT ANOTHER SLIM VOLUME.*

MIGUEL: This one? Legal.

*MIGUEL SHOWS HER THE VOLUME.*

AMY: Poemas. Velasco.

*MIGUEL OPENS THE BOOK AND READS.*

MIGUEL: El corazón anda dondequiera
Entre las palmas majestuosas
Através de la isla magnífica
Siempre busca su pareja
Haciendo lo que desea
Para encontrar otra alma bella.

AMY: The heart walks...

MIGUEL: Where it wants.

AMY: Majestic palms. Magnificent island.

MIGUEL: His verse carries me to a space where only I exist, united with the virtues of nature, the ocean, the sky and without one drop of failure nor any memory of conquest.

AMY: I wonder if Mary ever wrestled with his verse...attempting to translate?

MIGUEL: Why do you pursue this Mary?

AMY: I feel as if she's pursued me...and drawn me here.

MIGUEL: And why does she pursue you?

AMY: She knows I exist hovering...not part of either world entirely...and so...

MIGUEL: So you journey across the ocean to find her?

AMY: To try to find her.

MIGUEL: And you haven't found her yet, no?

AMY: Not really no.

*AMY LOOKS AT MIGUEL AS HE SMILES AND NODS.*

AMY: What?

*MIGUEL KEEPS SMILING.*

AMY: Oh, right. (attempting to read his mind) So you're probably thinking, "Then let me help Amy find this...Mary."

MIGUEL: Very soon, I won't have to say anything at all.

## SCENE TWENTY SEVEN

*1833. LIGHTS RISE ON MARY'S BEDROOM. MARY SITS WRITING AT A TABLE WITH DICTIONARIES, A THESAURUS AND A PILE OF PAPER.*

MARY: Siempre busca su pareja
Haciendo lo que desea
Para encontrar otra alma bella

Always searching its pair
Doing what it wants
To find another soul of....
bella...bella...bella

*MARY PICKS UP A SPANISH DICTIONARY.*

MARY: Bella. Beautiful. Lovely. (beat) To find another soul of beauty.
(beat)  Pair...pair...

*MARY PICKS UP THE THESAURUS.*

MARY: Pair...twain...couple...yoke...twain...twain...yes
Always searching its twain
As doing would be fain
For another beauteous soul the gain

Yes...yes...yes

The heart meanders all the while
Twixt the majestic palm
O'er the magnificent isle.
Always searching its twain
As doing would be fain
For another beauteous soul the gain

O...sí...sí...SÍ!

*MARY CLUTCHES THE PAPERS TO HER CHEST AND RUNS AROUND THE ROOM AS SOPHIA ENTERS.*

SOPHIA: Sister. (beat) What afflicts you?

MARY: Oh...language, hermana...to cross the bridge between two worlds...balancing my toes on tomes containing thousands of words...words...and more words...to unlock the passions of my heart...for all to enjoy.

SOPHIA: I have never seen you so demonstrative.

MARY: Oh Sophia, to translate a Spanish poem is to unlock its beauty...to bring this tender fluid creature into the harsh sounds of our Germanic tongue quietly... carefully...to watch it take flight and fly...fly...directly into the center of my chest.

*MARY FALLS ONTO HER BED CLUTCHING HER PAPERS.*

MARY: Oh Sophia...you must not tell a soul...not one peep.

*SOPHIA PICKS UP A PAPER FROM THE DESK.*

SOPHIA: Velasco. (beat) Señor Velasco gave you his verse?

*MARY RUNS AROUND THE ROOM.*

MARY: Sí...sí...sí!

SOPHIA: Could this be the same sister who forewarned me concerning a certain lack of restraint on this island?

MARY: When I am with Señor Velasco, I am able to discuss subjects such as we would with our dearest friends at home. Discussion on a meaningful level, not the usual commonplace pleasantries bandied about on the hacienda.

SOPHIA: How daring of you.

MARY: And he gave me his poems to read...and I have just...translated one. Oh. (beat) I wanted to unlock the meaning. And so I did it. Oh, sister. Reserve no longer seems a proper response when the world cries out by turns in agony and exhilaration. (beat) A bridge can be built...I speak in metaphor...a bridge can be constructed and the force of this culture that nourishes me can return with us sister... in our minds, in our souls, in the future work of my hands.

*MARY HOLDS UP A DICTIONARY.*

MARY: Our community is in desperate need of this infusion, Sophia. And we will be the harbingers of la vida pasionada to our New England. Sí, Sofía?

SOPHIA: Sí, María.

**SCENE TWENTY EIGHT**

*LIGHTS RISE ON SOPHIA ON THE SETTEE, SKETCHING AS FRANCISCO SITS IN A CHAIR IN FRONT OF HER POSING FOR HIS PORTRAIT.*

FRANCISCO: Rápido.

SOPHIA: Rápido no. One must never rush a portrait.

*SOPHIA GESTURES FOR FRANCISCO TO MOVE TO THE LEFT.*

SOPHIA: Could you move to the left and tilt your head to the side?

*FRANCISCO LOOKS AT HER, NOT COMPREHENDING HER INSTRUCTION. SOPHIA WALKS OVER TO FRANCISCO AND ARRANGES HIS HANDS ON HIS LAP, MOVES HIS HEAD TO ONE SIDE, PUSHES HIS LEFT SHOULDER BACK TO IMPROVE HIS POSE. HE IS STARTLED BY HER BOLDNESS. SHE CONTINUES TO SKETCH HIM AS REDMOND, WHO HAS SEEN HER TOUCH HIM, PPROACHES THEM. REDMOND GIVES FRANCISCO A STERN LOOK AS FRANCISCO, CAUGHT UNAWARE, SCRAMBLES TO HIS FEET AND LEAVES, STARTLING SOPHIA. REDMOND APPROACHES SOPHIA.*

REDMOND: You are not to consort with the servants in this way. Understood?

SOPHIA: But Mr. Redmond, I was not consorting. I was simply sketching and...

*MARY ENTERS.*

REDMOND: You must monitor your sister's behavior with the servants. Impropriety with the emancipados is unacceptable.

MARY: I'm certain Sophia did not nothing improper. She has the best of intentions.

REDMOND: Intentions and actions are two distinct realities.

SOPHIA: I shall go rest now so as not to be improper.

*SOPHIA GATHERS HER THINGS AND EXITS. MARY STARTS TO FOLLOW HER.*

REDMOND: Otherwise, your sister's health improves I presume.

MARY: The headaches only visit her once daily, if that.

REDMOND: A rapid recovery does benefit her but does not bode well for me.

*REDMOND WALKS TOWARD HER NERVOUSLY.*

REDMOND: This will appear inappropriate. I should most likely approach this differently but seeing as I am of the moment, I would like to ask you to stay on longer should your sister recover quite rapidly.

MARY: Amelia's reading and writing skills are improving but I'm certain that you will be able to find another tutor quite easily who can continue with her when I depart and...

REDMOND: To replace you would be quite difficult...

MARY: I'm pleased my work has been satisfactory but...

REDMOND: I speak not only of your work.

*MARY LOOKS AT HIM QUESTIONINGLY.*

REDMOND: You bring me and my daughter comfort and I would hope we do the same.

MARY: You are a generous host.

REDMOND: My generosity is offered willingly when in the presence of such a generous guest.

MARY: I'm only fulfilling my duties as tutor and...

REDMOND: I don't imagine you've lost a loved on yet, at your age. One can never be prepared for such a shock. In the wilds of this plantation life, Florence brought great warmth to this home creating an oasis of culture and civilization, a needed antidote to the rigors of the fields. I blame myself for her loss daily. Not since before my wife's illness, have I so enjoyed a feminine presence in my home.

MARY: I'm pleased that my sister and I are able to provide comfort to you and your daughter during this difficult time.

REDMOND: Florence named our hacienda. La Recompensa. The Recompense. The Reward. She felt living surrounded by such beauty was a reward for all the years of toil to attain this position. Tragically, this very reward was the cause of her demise. Since we buried her a year ago, I never thought I could receive another reward in this lifetime.

MARY: May you receive many such rewards.

REDMOND: I suppose there is no other way than to speak more plainly. I would like you to stay at length so that I may properly court you.

MARY: Mr. Redmond, I am taking care of my sister...aside from my duties as English tutor, Sophia is my chief responsibility. She is ill. When she recovers, I will act upon that which is in her best interests...that chiefly being to return to our home in Boston.

REDMOND: Of course, but...well...perhaps you could reconsider this position and...

*AWKWARD PAUSE.*

MARY: Good evening.

*MARY EXITS.*

**SCENE TWENTY NINE**

*LIGHTS RISE ON MARY, SOPHIA AND MRS. BATSON IN MARY AND SOPHIA'S ROOM. SOPHIA LIES DOWN AS MRS. BATSON PRESSES A COLD COMPRESS TO HER HEAD.*

SOPHIA: I loathe him.

MARY: He is our host.

SOPHIA: How do you tolerate him?

MARY: I do my best.

MRS. BATSON: Soon you will heal and return to the North and a land without these sharp divisions which cause such upsetting attitudes.

MARY: How do you reconcile his behavior?

MRS. BATSON: At my age, in this era, I'm fortunate to have this position. I try to educate Amelia in the ways of tolerance. And I hope for future generations of women who won't be in such a position as I.

MARY: This position of the disenfranchised.

SOPHIA: Unbearable.

MRS. BATSON: You young ladies have the benefit of your education, which will most likely provide numerous opportunities for you.

SOPHIA: You speak as if you have no future opportunities of your own.

MRS. BATSON: I value the opportunity to be this close to verdant nature and the ocean air which seem to heal my body and soul.

SOPHIA: But doesn't what you see burden your soul?

MARY: Sophia, don't pester her.

MRS. BATSON: An inquisitive mind is a gift. I don't take offense. You women are young yet and full of ideals which will no doubt lead you onward to positions of influence.

MARY: One can only hope.

SOPHIA: For men who will not subjugate as he does.

MRS. BATSON: Hope indeed.

SOPHIA: I was sketching a leaf yesterday and I was surprised by the myriad veins under its emerald skin and by the divine order of her symmetry and I thought if only such symmetry and order were reflected in humanity here.

MRS. BATSON: An artist and philosopher.

MARY: You could return with us to New England.

MRS. BATSON: While I appreciate your kindness, I must say that this is my home now. While I do miss my parents, I take certain pride in residing on this island and respecting her power and doing my best to teach those around me to do the same, however limited my sphere of influence.

MARY: Wouldn't Mrs. Batson like to meet Mr. Thoreau and Mr. Emerson in Boston? Such thoughts would be welcomed there.

SOPHIA: Indeed.

MRS. BATSON: A kind suggestion but if I leave here, I risk my ill health returning. A prefer a life on this island, albeit with certain challenges, but where I can move about each day, rather than spending months out of the year bed ridden when the cold season descends in the North.

MARY: Is this compress helping?

SOPHIA: The pounding in my temples has subsided. The blinding paroxysms rarely afflict me anymore. I can appreciate your position, Mrs. Batson.

MRS. BATSON: And for this reason, you must continue to rest, Miss Sophia, for you do not want to reach my age, having spent the majority of your life in ill health and foregoing any possibility of a vibrant future.

## SCENE THIRTY

*PRESENT. SPOTLIGHT ON AMY.*

AMY: Calle Obispo. Plaza de la Catedral. La Bodeguita del Medio. Miguel and I cross cobblestone streets lined with Baroque buildings and teeming with the locals as vintage 1950's U.S. automobiles and tiny Russian cars sputter by. As vendors hawk their homemade wares, musicians create infectious rhythms while sitting on the crumbling steps of aged buildings. Beauty juxtaposed against decay. Make-shift horse drawn carriages. Kids on bicycles. Vendors at the side of the road selling an assortment of papayas, guayabas and plátanos. Billboards bearing revolutionary slogans.

## SCENE THIRTY ONE

*1833. LIGHTS RISE ON AMELIA, WEARING AN ELEGANT DRESS ENTERING THE ROOM WITH EXCITEMENT, INTERRUPTING REDMOND WHO SITS WRITING IN A LEDGER.*

AMELIA: Father, am I a young lady now?

*REDMOND LOOKS UP FROM HIS LEDGER.*

REDMOND: Your mother would be most proud.

AMELIA: Father, won't you join us this evening at the Velascos?

REDMOND: Much to attend to.

AMELIA: But Father, then you could dance with Miss Mary and hold her hand and gaze into her eyes. Won't you come, please?

*MARY ENTERS THE ROOM ALSO WEARING A TASTEFULLY FANCY DRESS. AMELIA RUSHES UP TO HER.*

AMELIA: Three princesas attending the ball.

MARY: I'm afraid it's only you and I. Sophia is resting.

AMELIA: Just like the ball at Meryton in Miss Austen's book. I've never been to a ball before. What will it be like?

MARY: Parties in Boston, I know. A Cuban ball? We shall have to wait and see.

REDMOND: Yes you will. Behave yourself, Amelia. Good evening.

*REDMOND EXITS.*

AMELIA: Will Señor Velasco be wearing a coat with tails? I wonder? Will he be dancing with all the ladies from Havana? He is so dashing. Oh I do hope I remember all the proper Spanish words. Buenos noches, Señor Velasco. Buenos? Buenas? Buenas noches. Too bad Father couldn't come with us.

**SCENE THIRTY TWO**

*LIGHTS RISE ON AMELIA AND MARY APPROACHING JUAN AT THE BALL.*

JUAN: Bienvenidas, señoritas.

AMELIA: Gracias.

JUAN: (to Mary) Would you give me the pleasure of a dance?

MARY: No thank you. Dance with Amelia.

AMELIA: Sí, sí por favor.

*LIGHTS SHIFT. PRESENT. SPOTLIGHT ON AMY.*

AMY: Miguel and I walk down a pristine beach. Endless sapphire sky. Spotless ivory white sand. Sparkling turquoise tranquil water. A sanctuary seemingly untouched by humankind. And then in the evening...

*LIGHTS SHIFT. LIGHTS RISE ON AMY AND MIGUEL AT A DANCE CLUB. HE HOLDS HER HAND TO LEAD HER ONTO THE DANCEFLOOR AS SHE SHAKES HER HEAD.*

MIGUEL: Try.

AMY: I'd rather watch.

MIGUEL: One dance...

AMY: You're probably quite good. As for me, I didn't inherit the salsa gene from my father's side of the family.

MIGUEL: Not possible. Come on.

AMY: I'd rather not.

*LIGHTS SHIFT. 1833. LIGHTS RISE ON JUAN AND MARY.*

JUAN: The Bostonian ladies enjoy dancing the waltz.

MARY: Sí. [Yes.]

JUAN: And do they know or like to dance the contradanza?

MARY: They don't know.

JUAN: Well, then, they need a teacher.

*LIGHTS SHIFT. PRESENT. LIGHTS RISE ON AMY AND MIGUEL AS THEY DANCE.*

AMY: Sorry.

MIGUEL: No excuses.

AMY: I'm slowing you down.

MIGUEL: Don't think so much.

AMY: But...

MIGUEL: Permit your body to feel the rhythm and breathe.

*AMY BEGINS TO TRUST MIGUEL'S LEAD AND AS SHE RELAXES INTO THE STEADY SALSA BEAT. LIGHTS SHIFT.*

*1833. LIGHTS RISE ON JUAN AND MARY DOING THE CONTRADANCE AS THEY PROMENADE DOWN A CENTER AISLE.*

JUAN: I believe you do know la contradanza.

MARY: It is similar to contradancing in Boston.

JUAN: Do the intellectuals in Boston dance?

MARY: When in the appropriate setting.

JUAN: Our island is appropriate then?

MARY: Indeed.

*THE DANCE ENDS AS AMELIA ENTERS.*

AMELIA: Señor Velasco, several of the ladies are asking for you in the dining room.

JUAN: If you'll excuse me.

*JUAN EXITS AS MARY WATCHES HIM.*

AMELIA: Miss Mary. Please, we have to leave now. Father will be upset if I'm not in bed soon. And all those ladies are clamoring to dance with Señor Velasco. One young lady with beautiful brown hair and a very pretty nose told me that Señor Velasco was in love with her. And that she was in love with him too. He has so many admirers.

MARY: Yes, then, we should depart.

AMELIA: But shouldn't we bid farewell to our host?

MARY: He is most otherwise engaged.

**SCENE THIRTY THREE**

*LIGHTS RISE ON SOPHIA SKETCHING AS FRANCISCO APPROACHES HER. SHE MOTIONS FOR HIM TO SIT NEXT TO HER BUT HE SHAKES HIS HEAD.*

SOPHIA: And why not? Por favor?

FRANCISCO: Señor Redmond dice que es prohibido. [Mr. Redmond says it's prohibited.]

SOPHIA: Prohibited?

FRANCISCO: No podemos hablar así. [We cannot talk like this.]

SOPHIA: We can't speak? Nonsense. But we are as friends.

*FRANCISCO SHAKES HIS HEAD.*

SOPHIA: But you are an emancipado. We are the same. Free. Libres?

FRANCISCO: No.

*FRANCISCO STARTS TO LEAVE.*

SOPHIA: Francisco, please. Wait.

*FRANCISCO STOPS.*

SOPHIA: We are as equals. Igual.

FRANCISCO: Aqui? No. [Here? No.]

SOPHIA: But I want to complete your portrait.

FRANCISCO: Lo siento. [I'm sorry.]

*FRANCISCO RUNS OFF.*

SOPHIA: Francisco, please. Wait.

*SOPHIA RUNS OFF AFTER FRANCISCO.*

**SCENE THIRTY FOUR**

*PRESENT. LIGHTS RISE ON AMY AND MIGUEL STANDING OUTSIDE HER HOTEL.*

AMY: Drinks. Inside?

MIGUEL: Only for tourists.

AMY: So I can't invite you as my guest?

MIGUEL: Here? No.

AMY: That's ridiculous.

MIGUEL: No es fácil.

AMY: It's just...um...for most of my life, I've had a diminishing connection to this island.

*MIGUEL TAKES HER HAND IN HIS.*

AMY: But...today, you guided me to...connect and...like...see this island through Mary's eyes and...

MIGUEL: Tranquila...tranquila. (beat) Because you are la Americana y la Cubana.

*AMY NODS. MIGUEL TAKES HER HAND AND KISSES IT. AMY DRAWS IN CLOSER AND IMPULSIVELY KISSES MIGUEL THEN PULLS AWAY SUDDENLY.*

AMY: (flustered) I'm sorry I...shouldn't have and I...

MIGUEL: Now that was an American kiss. A Cuban kiss would've lasted much longer.

AMY: I didn't mean to and I'm sorry that I...I don't want that with you. I'm not like that. I'm really quite professional. I can assure you. It's that...I just felt...

MIGUEL: Tranquila, mi amor. You don't need to feel anything for me. But you do need to continue to feel.

AMY: How? I leave here tomorrow afternoon. Back to a land where I don't seem to have access to this deeper place within me. And yet here...and with you...

MIGUEL: You could read Velasco's poetry.

AMY: Unfortunately, my language skills are still too elementary at this point to read the original.

MIGUEL: Stay with the original text. Read it out loud. Let the music fall on your ear and your heart. Breathe in the sounds of the poetic language.

AMY: Which poems?

MIGUEL: I have a collection I can give you.

AMY: But I leave...

MIGUEL: Come to my place tomorrow morning.

AMY: And will you read the poems to me so I can bury the sound of your voice in my mind?

MIGUEL: I could.

AMY: Somehow if I could just tape record your voice and listen to you read Velasco...

MIGUEL: Unfortunately, I don't have the equipment for that.

AMY: You don't realize how much you miss a place or a person until you hear the absent sounds. How could I miss this island when I'd never been here? How can I miss you when we've barely met?

MIGUEL: Somehow we find ways to remember. Maintain the memory in sound, word, image...so we won't forget. For some, this island lives in its music for those who cannot return. For others, the words transported are a means to memory.

AMY: Mañana then?

MIGUEL: So that you can continue to feel.

**SCENE THIRTY FIVE**

*1833. LIGHTS RISE ON MARY WALKING ALONE ON A ROAD BY THE HACIENDA ILLUMINED ONLY BY MOONLIGHT. JUAN WALKS UP BEHIND HER STARTLING HER.*

JUAN: It is unwise to walk unaccompanied at such an hour, María.

MARY: Did you call me, María?

JUAN: I am sorry. Señorita Mary.

MARY: I will allow María...like this...in private.

JUAN: Very well, María. You may call me Juan.

MARY: Juan.

JUAN: You left before I could properly bid farewell to my Bostonian guest and so...

MARY: Amelia was tiring and had to return home.

*THEY WALK IN SILENCE FOR A FEW BEATS.*

JUAN: Did you decipher the poem I gave you?

MARY: I did my best to, yes.

JUAN: And you found some enjoyment?

MARY: Yes. I did. Sí.

JUAN: Very well. Perhaps you would like another.

*HE DIGS INTO THIS VEST POCKET AND PULLS OUT ANOTHER POEM.*

MARY: Gracias.

*JUAN STOPS WALKING AND RECITES THE POEM TO MARY. THEY DRAW CLOSER TO EACH OTHER AS THE INTENSITY OF THE WORDS INCREASE.*

JUAN: En tus ojos, la esperanza.
En tus manos, la libertad.
En tu boca, el espíritu
De nuestra humanidad.

MARY: In your...

JUAN: eyes...

MARY: the

JUAN: hope.

MARY: In your

JUAN: hands...

MARY: the liberty? In your

JUAN: mouth...

MARY: the spirit of our...

JUAN AND MARY: humanity.

MARY: Oh my. Quite lovely. And its title?

JUAN: Oda a María.

*JUAN TAKES HER HAND IN HIS.*

MARY: But I...really...

*JUAN KISSES HER HAND.*

MARY: Oh...Juan...please...por favor...I cannot.

JUAN: Your cheek, so tender, longs for this, no?

MARY: I am terribly sorry. You are ever so kind...and I...well...

JUAN: Accept the affection of la isla.

MARY: I...I just cannot.

JUAN: You cannot or you will not. There is a distinct difference between these two verb tenses, no?

MARY: I suppose there is.

JUAN: Which do you prefer?

MARY: The latter without the negation.

JUAN: Which means you will accept the affection of the island.

*JUAN KISSES MARY, SLOWLY, TENDERLY ON EACH CHEEK WHICH IS MORE THAN SHE CAN BEAR.*

MARY: My sister is waiting for me.

JUAN: She can wait a little longer, can she not?

MARY: I do not know how to respond.

*JUAN AND MARY FALL INTO A TENDER YET PASSIONATE KISS. HE THEN BRINGS HIS HAND TO HER CHEEK. SHE PUTS HER HEAD DOWN, EMBARRASSED. HE GENTLY RAISES HER HEAD SO THAT THEY CAN LOOK AT EACH OTHER EYE TO EYE.*

JUAN: You are different, María. Many North Americans come here fueled by their greed and corrupt ways. But you desire to know and be immersed in my culture and to return to your Boston with the island influence.

MARY: Hasta mañana, Juan.

JUAN: Hasta mañana, María.

*JUAN TAKES HER HAND PROTECTIVELY AS THEY HEAR SOMEONE APPROACHING. REDMOND APPEARS HOLDING A LANTERN.*

REDMOND: Miss Mary, please return to the hacienda immediately.

JUAN: I have been escorting her.

REDMOND: More than that, I'm afraid.

*MARY TURNS HER HEAD AWAY, EMBARRASSED.*

REDMOND: Velasco. Leave my property this instant.

JUAN: Señor Redmond, I can assure you I...

REDMOND: I no longer have any need for your services.

JUAN: Buenas noches, María. [Good night, María.]

*JUAN WALKS AWAY IN ANGER.*

REDMOND: Miss Mary, come immediately, Miss Sophia is in need of you.

**SCENE THIRTY SIX**

*PRESENT. LIGHTS RISE ON AMY OUTSIDE HER HOTEL ROOM DOOR AS BETO APPROACHES HER. HE'S BEEN DRINKING.*

BETO: And where did Miguel take you today?

*AMY GOES BACK TO FINDING HER ROOM KEY. SHE STOPS.*

AMY: Does it matter?

BETO: Yeah it matters.

AMY: I can take care of myself.

BETO: Really.

AMY: Uh-huh.

BETO: You owe me...

AMY: (interrupting) Look, I realize I owe you a shitload of money, alright?

BETO: Owe me the courtesy of letting me know if you're okay.

AMY: Fine. I'm okay. I'm great. No worries.

BETO: Oh, I'm not worried.

AMY: Good.

BETO: I'm onto what you're up to.

AMY: Up to?

BETO: You think you want to experience the authentic island with an authentic journalist. But you really want some affair to satisfy a kind of oedipal need you have inside to like reclaim the fatherland. I never pegged you for a sexual tourist at first but then, I'm not always the best judge of character.

AMY: Incredible. You sure you're not really a fiction writer...do you always invent new angles for your journalistic pieces?

BETO: I have no designs on any story about you at this point.

AMY: Good.

BETO: Nor Miguel, my interview subject who you've coopted or been coopted by. Maybe Miguel is writing about you now.

AMY: He's not.

BETO: You sure now?

AMY: But you know he should because Miguel gets me and you clearly don't.

BETO: Really? Oh now he gets you now?

AMY: Whatever.

BETO: Yeah. Yeah, he gets that his exotic Cuban charm works wonders on a gullible, insecure American woman.

AMY: What do you want, Beto?

BETO: Common courtesy.

AMY: And you would call this courteous behavior? I feel sorry for your ex-wife.

BETO: There is no ex-wife.

AMY: You're still married? Jesus.

BETO: Never married.

AMY: No kid?

BETO: Nope.

AMY: Wow. So do you use that line often?

BETO: When the mood strikes.

AMY: Fascinating.

BETO: Yeah. Wow. Oh boy. He lied.

AMY: So he could hook up with the gullible American.

BETO: No one forced you to come here.

AMY: I wanted to come here.

BETO: And here you are.

AMY: But things didn't go according to your plan.

BETO: Not really. No.

AMY: But see I'm not a gullible American. On a certain level, I knew. But I needed to be here. Not proud of how I got here but there you have it.

BETO: So you knew, huh? About me.

AMY: My inner Cubana knew.

BETO: Please.

AMY: And my inner Cubana is telling me that this conversation is so over and when we get off that plane tomorrow and step back onto the island of Manhattan, I will never have to talk to you ever again.

*AMY OPENS THE DOOR TO HER ROOM AND EXITS.*

**SCENE THIRTY SEVEN**

*1833. LIGHTS RISE ON MARY DABBING A COLD COMPRESS ON SOPHIA, WHO LIES IN BED.*

SOPHIA: And I ran outside to follow Francisco...

MARY: Shhhh....

SOPHIA: And I saw him enter the servants' quarters. And I knocked on the door and an elderly man with a hollow smile let me in and I just stood there as they stared at me, their sunworn faces bearing signs of utter exhaustion and I could feel my blood run cold as I sensed their suffering...and I scurried back to the hacienda, straight into my bed.

MARY: It's over now.

SOPHIA: These people are called emancipados but the misery...I can't stay here...any longer.

MARY: And your...

SOPHIA: My headaches have lessened so. But then I was waiting and waiting for you and I fell asleep and had this horrid dream...I dreamt I walked across the sand at night as the full moon shone and the ground suddenly turned to snow and my feet were bare and raw and I ran up to the edge of the water where I saw two caskets raised on a small platform and I looked inside them and there lay mother and father with faces of ashen white. And I suddenly jumped into the tropical blue water but I could not swim and I started sinking, my chest as if made of lead.

MARY: Your temples must be pounding.

SOPHIA: And I awoke with such a fright, yelling and Mr. Redmond passed by in the hallway, assuring me he would find you.

MARY: And here I am.

SOPHIA: Such sadness overcomes me. I fear I will never return to live my life with those I love.

MARY: Upon our return you will live a satisfying life. You will paint portraits and landscapes and be surrounded by loved ones.

SOPHIA: I do wish I were strong enough to return tomorrow so I could prove my current sentiments wrong in the company of my own kind.

MARY: We will return with the knowledge of the luxuriance and ills of this island...and we will share this knowledge with our community in need of such awareness. I dare say this island has provided healing for more than just one sister.

SOPHIA: But what has ailed you?

MARY: At times an impenetrable reserve which lacks an exposure to the depths of passionate expression. This exposure gained in large part by the literary cultivation on this island will ultimately strengthen our private as well as public education.

SOPHIA: Horace will enjoy hearing you speak so. Mother's letters mention his continual inquiries as to your well being.

MARY: Yes, we will speak with him of this knowledge received during our travels, as we will with Mother, Father, Elizabeth and even our neighbor, Nathaniel. I dare say neither Mr. Hawthorne nor Mr. Mann can boast of such adventures.

## SCENE THIRTY EIGHT

*NEW YORK CITY. PRESENT. TWO WEEKS LATER. LIGHTS RISE ON AMY, SARAH AND ALICE FINISHING A MEAL IN SARAH'S APARTMENT.*

AMY: I know it'll take me another several years but I have to.

SARAH: You don't have to. You choose to.

ALICE: Mother, stop. So now she's like this Latin American studies Ph.D. student or whatever. So what?

SARAH: So what? She's entirely abandoned her U.S. history degree, wasted several years of her life not to mention the debt that's mounting.

AMY: But Mary Peabody...

SARAH: You don't care one iota about Mary Peabody...

ALICE: Ah...yes, she does.

AMY: (to Sarah) You don't get it. Your ancestor helped me connect my two cultures, mother.

SARAH: Something I've never wanted.

ALICE: Jesus.

AMY: That explains it.

ALICE: What is up with that?

AMY: No exposure to Papi's world. He dies and his culture dies with him. Fascinating.

ALICE: You seriously never wanted us to be like...Cubana (pronounced kew-bana)? (to Amy) Is that how you say it?

AMY: Cubana. (pronounced koo-bana)

ALICE: Right. That.

SARAH: Your Cuban father was a proud man, but deeply proud to the point of being broken, broken by living in exile, broken by this country not being his own. His exile was not kind to him or our family. He never spoke of his life there. He never spoke of exactly how they left but the anger...the rage he carried for what happened to his island ate at his insides. It ruined our marriage and it ultimately killed him.

AMY: Yeah...but it didn't kill me. Or her. Or you.

ALICE: Hello.

AMY: We're still standing here. Breathing. Or trying to.

SARAH: The bitterness almost did me in. I wanted to spare you all of that.

AMY: I can't be spared any longer. I don't want to be spared. I don't want to live this internal exile any more. Cut off from...this part of me...deeply submerged. A way of connecting that is born of passion...deep inside...which exists at the pit of my stomach...and I cannot be denied access to this world any longer. And so this need propels me onward. To live and breathe a different atmosphere. Not to deny your world but to enrich, enliven, broaden and fulfill the destiny of your ancestors, of our ancestors. To honor Mary...Mary Peabody in Cuba.

**SCENE THIRTY NINE**

*SPOTLIGHT ON AMY.*

AMY: Five months later, after my return to Manhattan, I received a call from Beto. As I heard his voice, my entire being froze when...he told me of Miguel's arrest for subversive behavior. And as we both sat on the phone in silence, time seemed to stop. And when he said that all of Miguel's one thousand books had been confiscated and burned and that Miguel was languishing in solitary confinement miles away from his home, I could barely breathe. I feared for him and worried that my being with him or my actions in some way might have caused his arrest and...

I immediately began organizing an international letter writing campaign to protest Miguel's imprisonment when I came across Horace Mann's 1841 lecture. Quote: My friends, I look upon this as one of the grandest moral enterprises of our age....Public libraries will scatter, free and abundant, the seeds of wisdom and virtue, in the desert places of the land. Public libraries will prove as powerful an agent in the world of the mind as the use of steam has done in the world of matter.

And I tried to recall how the air in Miguel's library was stale yet carried the weight of possibilities too great to ignore. Words. Guarded. Secret. Yet waiting for yearning minds.

## SCENE FORTY

*CUBA. SIX MONTHS EARLIER. LIGHTS RISE ON AMY AND MIGUEL IN MIGUEL'S LIBRARY. AMY RIFLES THROUGH THE BOOKSHELVES.*

AMY: Why won't you let me mail you boxes of books? I mean, no Dickenson? My river runs to thee. And what about Thoreau? On Walden Pond. And then there's Whitman. Leaves of Grass. I mean...how can a library be complete without Dickenson?

MIGUEL: We survive with what we have.

AMY: And you continue to lend books when you know you might...

MIGUEL: No es fácil.

*AMY CONTINUES TO EXAMINE HIS BOOKSHELVES.*

AMY: What if you travel to New York City? I could get my university to sponsor you and then...

MIGUEL: Traveling's not permitted. So I stay here. To work for change here. Like Velasco.

AMY: I don't want to fly away from this island...or...you. I mean, I want to help you...the power of the pen, right?

MIGUEL: But now you have this bridge. This conscious bridge constructed by the blood of your ancestors connecting your two cultures, your two countries, your two selves.

AMY: I don't know that I really found Mary Peabody though.

MIGUEL: Didn't she lead you here...to my library?

AMY: Miguel, but I...

MIGUEL: (interrupting) Campos is my father's name.

AMY: Okay...

MIGUEL: My entire name is Miguel Campos Velasco.

AMY: Velasco?

MIGUEL: Mother's name. Juan...her ancestor. My ancestor. Blood memory. Synchronicity. You listened to that need inside of you. To relive history.

AMY: And you weren't even going to tell me?

MIGUEL: At the appropriate moment.

AMY: Which is now? The morning before I fly on a plane to return to a land where I will have virtually no contact with you?

MIGUEL: We try to journey on these paths but many times the forces of history distract us. But these paths continue.

AMY: I don't deserve this.

MIGUEL: No es fácil.

AMY: I'm sick of that saying. Not easy. Not easy. Is anything ever easy? Living this life between two worlds? Never looking the part but deep inside a fire smoulders beneath this cool exterior. And I come here and I meet you and we're connected and now I have to live away from this and you? And you tell me this at the very last moment?

*AMY STARTS TO BOLT OUT OF THE LIBRARY.*

MIGUEL: Tranquila. Por favor. Wait.

*AMY STOPS. MIGUEL QUICKLY GRABS A THICK VOLUME WHICH HE HANDS TO AMY.*

MIGUEL: Velasco. Complete works. For you.

*AMY OPENS THE BOOK AND FINDS A FOLDED PAPER WHICH SHE TAKES OUT AND UNFOLDS.*

MIGUEL: And that too...

*AMY BEGINS TO LOOK AT THE PAPER.*

MIGUEL: The first day you visited my library, I was not waiting for the muse. I was abandoning the muse. I just wanted stay in the apartment forever because at that moment, any other effort appeared futile. But so, your constantly seeking this Mary made me consider that time works differently in the ancestral realm and that as you called upon Mary, I could call upon Juan. And centuries could vanish in an instant. As bridges between our worlds, once destroyed, could be reconstructed again, word by word.

AMY: A new article of yours?

MIGUEL: A return of the muse.

AMY: About...

MIGUEL: Mis compañeros. My journalist friends. Still detained.

AMY: For me?

MIGUEL: Yes but with a favor.

AMY: And that is...

MIGUEL: If you could transport my article in this volume of Velasco...

AMY: As I leave...

MIGUEL: And when you return home, send it to the address at the top of the article...one of my press contacts in Spain.

AMY: Um...

MIGUEL: And perhaps you could even educate your students about the plight of our movement and our desire for a free exchange of ideas. The voices of international intellectuals supporting our right to peaceful change would be a courageous contribution in this difficult hour.

*AWKARD PAUSE.*

AMY: I'll do it then...transport your words.

MIGUEL: Bueno...Muchissimas gracias.

*AWKWARD PAUSE. AMY PLACES THE FOLDED ARTICLE WITHIN THE PAGES OF THE VOLUME AND THEN BEGINS TO LOOKS THROUGH THE BOOK.*

AMY: But...I'll never be able to translate this entire volume.

MIGUEL: Why not start now?

AMY: Miguel, I...

MIGUEL: Only a few lines.

*AMY HOLDS THE BOOK AS MIGUEL TURNS TO A PAGE AND BEGINS TO READ.*

MIGUEL: En tus ojos, la esperanza.

AMY: In your eyes, the...

AMY AND MIGUEL: hope.

MIGUEL: En tus manos, la libertad.

AMY: In your hands, the liberty,

MIGUEL: En tu boca, el espíritu,

AMY: In your mouth, the spirit,

MIGUEL: de nuestra humanidad.

AMY: of our humanity.

*LIGHTS FADE. END OF PLAY.*

Afterward: This play is inspired by the true journey of Bostonian sisters, Mary and Sophia Peabody to the island of Cuba in 1833. Later in life, Mary married educator Horace Mann and Sophia married renowned author Nathaniel Hawthorne. On pages 160 and 177, Mary's monologues to her parents are based on actual letters written by Mary Peabody from Cuba Journals 1833-5, an original manuscript housed in the Berg Collection at the New York Public Library.

# Contributors

<u>Juliette Carrillo:</u> As a member of Cornerstone Theater's ensemble, Juliette has directed three critically acclaimed community collaborations: *Los Faustinos* by Bernardo Solano, *As Vishnu Dreams* by Shishir Kurup and *Lethe* by Octavio Solis. Juliette was an Artistic Associate at South Coast Repertory Theatre for seven years. She directed regularly in their season and ran the Hispanic Playwright's Project, collaborating with established and emerging Latino writers across the country. A graduate of the Yale School of Drama, she currently directs as a freelance artist throughout the US. Some of her favorite productions have been the West Coast premiere of the 2003 Pulitzer Prize winner, *Anna in the Tropics* by Nilo Cruz at South Coast Repertory, the World Premiere of *References to Salvador Dali Make Me Hot* by José Rivera, also at South Coast Repertory, and the West Coast premiere of Sam Shepard's *Eyes For Consuela* at the Magic Theatre in San Francisco. She is a recipient of several awards, including the prestigious NEA/TCG Directing Fellowship.

<u>Anne García-Romero:</u> Other plays include *Desert Longing, Juanita's Statue* and *Pandorado*. Her plays have been developed and produced most notably at the New York Shakespeare Festival/Public Theater, Arielle Tepper Productions' Summer Play Festival (Off-Broadway), The Mark Taper Forum, Hartford Stage, Borderlands Theater and South Coast Repertory. She has received commissions from the Public Theater, The Mark Taper Forum, and South Coast Repertory. She has also written for Peninsula Films, Elysian Films and Disney Creative Entertainment. She's been a Jerome Fellow at the Playwrights Center of Minneapolis as well as a MacDowell Colony fellow. She's taught at Cal Arts, UC Santa Barbara, UC Riverside, Wesleyan University and Macalester College. She holds an MFA in Playwriting from the Yale School of Drama and is an alumna of New Dramatists.